To

Carly

WALLED

I know
where you
live!

IN

DAVID OWAIN HUGHES

Copyright © 2013 David Owain Hughes

This Edition Published 2014 by Crowded
Quarantine Publications
The moral right of the author has been asserted

*All characters in this publication are fictitious
and any resemblance to real persons, living or dead,
is purely coincidental.*

All rights reserved.
No part of this publication may be reproduced,
stored in a retrieval system, or transmitted, in any
form or by any means without the prior
permission in writing of the publisher, nor be
otherwise circulated in any form of binding or
cover other than that in which it is published
and without a similar condition including this
condition being imposed on the subsequent purchase.

A CIP catalogue record for this book
is available from the British Library

ISBN 978-0-9576480-8-1

Crowded Quarantine Publications
34 Cheviot Road
Wolverhampton
West Midlands
WV2 2HD

For Gethin David Hughes

"Welcome to my nightmare."
- Alice Cooper

Chapter 1

The cottage stood alone in a slightly overgrown field, its door closed. The bottom windows were covered in grime, and web-like cracks could be found in the panes. A few crows had gathered on the old slate roof. They were settling down for the night. All around smoke rose to the skies from fires burning in surrounding fields and towns, leaving behind a thick blanket of smog in the night air. Out of the smoke came a family of four, heading for the cottage.

Bryn turned the doorknob slowly, but the door didn't budge. He had to force it open on its rusted hinges, before easing it open with the pickaxe handle he had found; he'd used it to club a few of them to death. Their blood clung to the front of his shirt and gelled his hair. He peered around the sliver of open doorway and scanned the big, front room. Nothing. Then his eyes fell on the fireplace. It was out, but there was enough wood stacked by its side to get the thing going. The place seemed safe enough for a few nights. He pushed the door fully open then called his for family.

"Come on, mun. It's going to be nice and safe here."

Bryn moved into the living room and headed for the fireplace. He found some papers scattered on the floor and threw them into the grate along with some wood. He pulled a lighter from his pocket and began starting a fire.

"Daddy, do you think it *is* going to be safe here?" Amy, Bryn's youngest daughter, said.

"Yes, bach. I'll get this fire going now, then we can settle down for the night. Where's Mam, then? I thought you were with her?"

"She's just outside, Dad."

Bryn turned around to face the door, and saw Rosie standing there; his eldest daughter.

"Mam says she is too scared to come in, and that we should have stayed put in that barn over there."

"Well, Mam is wrong. Come on in, Cariad," he shouted. "It's not safe to be standing out there on your own, mun. You too, Rosie. Get in here."

"But is it though, Bryn?" he heard Cariad call from outside. "There could be someone in there. Like upstairs, for instance."

"It's fine, beaut, honestly. Now come on in." There was a slight annoyance in his voice.

Amy watched her mother come through the door, and clutched Rosie's hand. "We'll be okay, Mammy,"

Amy said. "Daddy found this cool fireplace that he is going to light." Cariad smiled at her daughter. "But I think you should close the door, Mam, just in case there are more of them out there."

"Good idea, Amy, bach," Bryn said.

"Shall we see if we can find something to barricade it with, Dad?" Rosie said.

Bryn nodded. "I think just closing it for now will be good enough, gal," he said then pulled back from the fireplace as the kindling and paper caught. A fire began to crackle and spit. Bryn put his hands up in front of the heat, and let his skin absorb it. The rest of his family huddled about him. "I don't think we will have much trouble tonight."

"How can you tell, Bryn?"

"There weren't many of them out there, and I killed the ones that were."

"There could be more though, love."

"Let's wait and see a minute?" he said.

She gulped hard, and bit back tears. Dawn was a few more hours away and anything could hit them before sunrise.

"Try not to worry, Mam," Rosie said. "I think Dad is right; it's quiet out there."

Cariad nodded. When had Rosie become such a grown up? All brave and shock resistant. She was almost a woman now. Cariad could still remember the nights when she used to tuck the older girl into bed and tell her fairytales. But that seemed like a forgotten time and land, for they were living in a new world now.

"Such a brave young woman, aren't you, beaut?" she said, stroking Rosie's cheek.

"What about me then, Mam? Remember how I poked one of Mrs Caradog's eyes out when she was attacking you?"

Cariad looked down at her youngest daughter, and smiled. "Yes love, you're very brave too."
This brought a smile to the child's face. A warm glow that made Cariad think of their little house in Cwmparc, the place they had fled from in the middle of the night. Then she thought about the army, and the way in which they had marched through the small coal mining village with their guns and tanks; and how they had mowed down every living human in their sight. They'd burnt the bodies down on the old coal tip. The cindered remains of the dead had resembled that of a slag heap. Her father had worked that mine in Cwmparc, man and boy.

"If it had not been for me, Mam," the young girl continued, "then Mrs Caradog might have really hurt you."

"Yes, beaut, I know."

"I hope Gwen is okay, Mam. Do you think Gwen and her mam and dad made it to safety?

Cariad didn't know what to tell her daughter about Gwen, Amy's friend. She didn't know what to say anymore, about *anything*. She opened her mouth to speak, but Rosie got there first.

"Everyone is died, like. Think, stupid," Rosie said, whilst poking the side of her head with her finger. The younger girl looked startled, and then poked her tongue out at her sister whilst making a 'raspberry' sound.

"They might have made it. You don't know everything, Rosie."

"You saw what the soldiers done, mun. They killed everyone in Eglwys Street."

"Yeah, and? We escaped it."

"Don't be such a silly bitch, Monster."

"*Rosie!*" Cariad snapped. "Where'd you hear language like that then? Damned Angela Gibbons, I bet, is it?"

"Sorry, Mam. I just…"

"Ha-ha! You had a row," Amy ribbed.

"Iesu, God alive! Will you two knock it off over there. You're acting like a pair of bloody babies, the two of you," Bryn yelled, making Cariad flinch.

"Shh, Bryn, love," Cariad said, holding onto his arm. "Don't shout at them, mun."

9

He looked at her; the shadow of the fire danced across his face, and she could see tears forming in his eyes. "Sorry, bach, I don't know what came over me. I...It's...just I'm trying to do my best here. Sorry." He smiled at their worried faces.

"It's okay, Dad," Amy said. "We know how you're feeling." She smiled at him. Her plucky attitude picked him up slightly.

"Thanks," he said.

"Maybe we should think about blocking that door then. What do you think, Cariad, gal?"

"Yes, love. I'd feel much better if we did."

"Okay then."

"There is no way of locking it, see Bryn. They could just walk straight in here."

"Yes, I see. Take the girls and search the kitchen then. There may be a table out there or something."

"Will you search out there first?"

"I think they would have come in here by now if there was someone out there, gal."

"*Please*, Bryn."

Bryn took a deep breath, and sighed.

"Please."

"Duw-duw, okay."

He picked up the axe handle and headed for the kitchen. He looked through the narrow entrance but couldn't see much due to the darkness. Anything could be lurking in the shadows, he thought. He carefully walked onwards, the shaft of wood held out in front of him. He bent at an angle, trying to see around the frame, but he was not very successful.

His heart smashed at his ribs as he neared the kitchen entrance. He kept waiting for someone, or something, to lunge at him. But nothing did. His heartbeat slowed as he stood in the doorway, scanning the almost empty room. One dishevelled table adorned the centre. Bryn's shoulders slumped, and he let out a nervous breath. He turned to his family, all of whom also seemed to take a deep sigh of relief.

"Told you," he said. "Nothing out here, mun," he said, walking back to his family. "There is a table out there though, Cariad."

"Shall I give you a hand to move it then?"

"Yes. Best we get that front door covered soon," he said.

Cariad stepped from behind the two girls to go to Bryn, but then the front door burst open, and slammed shut. Amy and Rosie both screamed as Bryn rushed from the kitchen doorway over to the large man standing at the entrance, breathing erratically. His face appeared scarred. Bryn was about to bring the axe handle down onto the man's head when the man spoke. He wasn't one of them.

"Stop, wait. I'm not messed up. I'm fine, honest. Please, just don't hit me with that thing." He threw his arms up over his face and head for protection. He backed off, and cowed down by the door. Bryn could hear him blubbering like a child.

Bryn stepped back, giving the man some breathing space. "Dear God."

The man looked up at Bryn with wet eyes; the horrid marks on his face were unsettling. "You won't hurt me, will you?"

"No, I won't hurt you."

"I never thought I'd find…well…"

"It's okay. You're safe here with us," Bryn cooed. "Why not come and have a warm, then?" Bryn offered his hand to the man. "Come on, take it."

The man clasped Bryn's hand and was pulled to his feet. He scanned the rest of the people in the room. "This is your family, is it?" Bryn nodded in reply. "And are you local?" he asked.

"Rhondda valleys – we were making our way down from there to try to make Cardiff, see," Bryn said.

"Why?"

"We—"

"We heard on the radio that there were safe houses set up there," Cariad butted in.

"Duw," the man said. "You won't find much in Cardiff. The place fell only hours ago. Overrun it is."

"You came from there, then?" Cariad said.

"Aye, had to fight my way through it all, and on foot too. Couldn't find a bloody car. Nothing but burning wrecks about the place. Do you have a vehicle?" he said. The nervousness had totally gone from the man now.

"No," Bryn said, cutting his wife off this time. "We lost our car out on the main road there."

"Oh, how is that then?"

"Ambushed, we were. There must have been a dozen or more of them out there on the road."

The man looked at the end of the wood Bryn was holding. It was mottled red. *Blood* red.

"Had to fight them off. Bloody bastards went for my girls," Bryn said.

Amy walked over to her father, and put her arm around his waist.

"And what's your name then, beaut?" the man asked.

"Amy, sir."

"Ha! *Sir*, is it?"

"My Daddy always taught me to be proper polite to grown-ups."

"Well then, nothing wrong with that, is there?"

"What's your name then?" Rosie asked.

"Eddie," he said, looking over at the other girl.

Eddie walked over to the fireplace and put his hands in front of the roaring warmth. He let out a deep sigh. "Lovely this heat is. Not been inside a house for days."

"How come?" Cariad wanted to know.

"Duw, let the man have a bit of warmth and relaxation first, mun, before you go interrogating him."

"I was only asking, mun, Bryn." She glared up at him.

"It's okay, she can ask. Bryn, is it?"

"Yes," Bryn said. "And this is my wife, Cariad. And our two girls, Amy and Rosie."

"Nice to meet you all," he said, nodding.

Bryn thought Eddie was tame enough. He was just like them: a survivor looking for a place to be safe. He leant the axe handle against the wall by the side of the door, thinking he wouldn't need it. And now that there was another man with them, Bryn and his family had a better chance of fending them off, if more of them showed up tonight, Bryn thought.

"So how come you have not been in a house for days then?" Cariad pushed. She could feel Bryn's eyes burning a hole in her skull.

"I had to leave my house, see. It became overrun. Not safe to stay in one place for too long. They linger, wait for you to make mistakes then take their

14

chances. They like to hide in the shadows close to your home and wait. They can smell blood and fear. I caught many of them licking the glass of my house. They knew I was in there hiding from them. They were all over my home, like bees to a hive as they say."

"They got in?" Cariad asked.

"Eventually."

"Didn't you try to stop them?" asked Bryn.

"Duw aye, I did. But there were too many in the end. They're strong, much stronger than I first thought. They managed to rip the planks of wood off the windows I had put across them for protection, and broke the glass."

Cariad looked at the man for long moments at a time. Something didn't add up. He seemed unafraid, unlike when he'd first walked in. He fidgeted when he spoke as though he was not comfy by what he was telling them, and his eyes darted around the room. Beads of sweat had also appeared on his brow. What was this man, this *Eddie*, hiding from them, she wondered?

"So what made you head this way, Eddie?" Cariad asked.

"Well…I…I just thought that maybe heading out into the open would be better. Their numbers would be few like, you know?"

"Hmm, yeah." She eyed him with distrust.

Eddie walked from the fireplace over to where Bryn and Amy stood.

"Well I guess that was a smart thing to do then," Bryn said. "It appears to be bloody dead around here now."

"Aye," Eddie said. "Thanks to you and your axe handle."

Bryn felt a swell of pride rise in him. "I guess it was nothing really, mun, you know? Looking out for my family, I was." Bryn turned to his wife. "Isn't that right, Cariad?"

"Daddy, watch out," he heard Rosie scream, just before feeling a harsh whack at the base of his skull. The sound was hollow and empty. Bryn crashed to the floor and his face slammed the wood, loosening a few of his teeth.

Eddie pulled a straight-razor out of his trousers pocket and grabbed Amy by her hair, yanking her backwards into his flabby body. He put the gleaming razor edge to her throat. "Get over here then, bitches, and tie him up. If you don't, I'll slice this young whore open," he said, digging the blade into the girl's flesh until beads of blood began popping up across Amy's neckline. "I suggest you move it, like," he said. A smirk ripped across his face.

16

"Please, don't hurt her, she is only young," Cariad protested.

"Best hurry then, love."

"But there is nothing here we can use to tie him up with, Eddie. Please, just let us go. We don't have a car or money. Please…"

Amy squealed as she felt the blade dig a little deeper. "Look in the cellar, over there." He flicked his head to the left, to indicate a door. Cariad guessed it led to the cellar. "Get a fucking move on."

Rosie made a move to go with her mother, but was told to stay put. "You stay where the hell you are, good girl."

Cariad came back upstairs with a length of rope, which Eddie cut into sections. He then ordered her to tie her husband up with it, then her daughters. She begged and pleaded with him as she did so, only to be slapped and cursed at. After she'd tied her family up, Eddie beat her to a state of near unconsciousness as her daughters watched and cried. He wanted to make sure she could not go anywhere whilst he took care of a few things.

Firstly, he went outside and found the spare key to the house under a rock. Then he scanned the surrounding area for his brother. Must be held up, he thought. Eddie locked the door.

Secondly, he dragged Bryn to the top of the cellar stairs and shoved him down them. Two of Bryn's ribs cracked in the fall. Then it was Cariad's turn. Once both parents were in the cellar, Eddie went down and tied them to opposite sides of the room. He bound Cariad to an old stove, and Bryn to some pipes. Bryn hadn't moved since he'd clubbed him. Maybe that blow had done him in?

He looked at Cariad. At her legs. They were slender. He wanted her, but then he remembered the two girls upstairs and started back up towards them, his excitement almost irrepressible.

Chapter 2

Eddie sat in the corner of the room facing the two girls. Rosie was dead. He'd cut her throat open with his straight-razor about an hour ago. He was just biding his time, waiting for the body to go cold. Amy was weeping silently under her gag. Eddie liked the fact that she was crying; it excited him. He kept an eye on her. On her young, undeveloped breasts. Every so often they would jiggle under her torn, Mickey Mouse t-shirt whenever the young girl had a spasm created by her soft crying. He just wished his brother was here to see it.

He rose from the old wicker chair and looked out through the window. There were quite a few of *them* gathered around the back of the house, but nothing his brother and he couldn't handle if forced to. They were just standing there, looking up at him, waiting for their chance to take a chunk out of him. Not going to happen, fuckers, he thought, and turned from the window. "Where in the hell are you, brother, mun?" Eddie sat back in the chair, lowering himself softly in case it gave way under his weight. Next to him, on top of a decrepit table, was a cassette player. Eddie leaned over, and got the thing going. The *Sex Pistols* filled the room.

"Ah, this takes me back to my youth."

He cast his eye back over to the younger sister – there were tears rolling down the side of her pretty innocent face. God, how she had screamed when he had taken his razor to her sister's throat.

Eddie had both the girls tied spread-eagle on two old twin beds; they had been his and his brother's beds when they were kids. This was the room they used to sleep in when they stayed with their grandparents. That was before Eddie's brother killed them both, that is. Eddie could still recall the day his younger brother smashed their grandfather's skull in with the old man's mining helmet; repeatedly he'd belted the man as he lay dying in his own bed. Then he had proceeded to strangle their grandmother with his bare hands.

The dead girl was naked. He'd left the younger one for last, that way he could have more fun once his need had been dampened slightly by the older girl. Eddie just sat there, stroking the scarred side of his face. His ear was melted, his hair patchy, his mouth had a slight sag. The results of a prison attack. Eddie caught the girl looking at him while he smoothed his scar.

"This is what happens to people like me on the inside, gal. We get boiling hot sugar thrown in our faces. They use sugar because it sticks to the skin better, see. I was lucky they never caught me full on, or I'd have been blinded. Tell you one thing though, beaut. The fucking prick that did this to me never saw another night through in the great hotel called Broadmoor. Twenty-seven years I have served there with my brother in total." A smile began to spread across his face. "And in those twenty-seven years, I managed to kill seven jailbirds and two screws." He reached over to the wonky table, and plucked his Superkings off it. He drew one from the box, and lit it. When he spoke again, smoke escaped his mouth in copious amounts. "Shouldn't be long now, beaut – your sister's been dead a good hour. And after I have finished with her, we can have our fun." This brought fresh tears streaming down her face, and a wave of contractions which put an electric-like shockwave of pleasure down Eddie's back.

Once the fag was down to its hilt, he stamped it out on the carpet. He then lifted himself gently from the seat as "God Save The Queen" pumped out of the player, and ambled over to the lifeless body with the chair in tow. The carcass had a smooth chill to it.

"Just right," Eddie said.

He'd already prepped a bowl of water, a bar of soap and lather brush before he had even killed the girl; the soap and brush had come from the bathroom. The water from a pump outside. Eddie had whispered into her ear what he was planning on doing to her once she was dead. This had made her flay like a wild animal. It had also made the younger sister excitable. Eddie had let them go on like this for a few moments, before ripping the elder's gullet apart with a fierce stroke. As her windpipe gargled and spat tiny droplets of blood, Eddie had spoken calmly into her face.

It had taken the girl little time to die from such a wound, but it had taken the younger sibling a good forty-minutes to calm down. The slap he had issued to her face had helped matters.

Amy watched as he began to soap her sister's 'private place', then shave the area clean with his knife. He whistled, *Whistle While You Work,* as he did so. A tune her father used to sing to her.

She watched as he took his time, being careful. Why? What was he doing to Rosie? She wanted her mother.

"Got to watch I don't break her skin, see," he said. "Don't want blood in my mouth."

Once he was pleased with his work, he stripped. He folded all his clothes neatly over the back of the

22

chair. Amy turned to face the wall. He smiled. Amy began to slowly and silently wriggle her wrists free from the rope he had used to lash her hands to the bed. His knotting had not been the best, and now, whilst he was busy with Rosie, she took her chance. She closed her eyes tight, not wanting to know what he was doing. His harsh gasping made her feel sick, and she could taste bile in her throat. She had to stay strong. Amy held in her mind a memory of a holiday her family had taken to Porthcawl one summer. She had only been ten that year. Her father had taken her for a donkey ride out on the sands every day that fortnight spent in the seaside town. The weather had been glorious. The hottest summer for years, so Mam had said.

She could feel the ropes loosen at her hands. She felt hope rise inside at this, and also at the fact he had not noticed. She could hear him moaning and grunting, and she caught a glimpse of his buttocks pumping in and out. She *knew* what he was doing. The older boys at school often spoke about it. They were just trying to be cool in front of the girls.

Amy stopped trying to free her hands for a moment. She thought of her sister. *Rosie has been so good to me when we were growing up together, we never argued*, she thought. She regained composure by telling herself that Rosie had gone to a better place; that whatever he did to her now could not harm Rosie anymore, and so she continued to try and unbind herself from the bed. Then, all of a sudden, the jousting from her side stopped with an almighty screech which chilled her to the centre. The thundering noise of the springs squealing out in pain ceased. Her heart raced. She turned to see him get off Rosie.

"Don't know what it is about dead girls," he said, panting. "But it doesn't half get me hot and bothered, you know what I mean?"

He let out a guttural laugh, and winked at Amy. He wiped the sweat from his brow. His whole, flabby body was peppered with beads of water. He staggered about the room for a bit, clamping his eyes on his razor, then on Amy. He gave her a silly grin, then knocked the radio off before advancing on her.

"I'm going to cut you up into tiny little pieces, just like I did your mammy and daddy."

She thrashed on the bed, trying to free her hands to give herself some sort of fighting chance, but nothing. He knocked bowl over and onto the floor as he made for her. Then, a noise from downstairs brought him to a stop. He stood in the middle of the room, listening with pricked ears. Amy wriggled and wriggled in his distraction, determined to be loose.

When the loud, rushing footfalls came up the stairs, he dashed for the door, his razor up in the air. Amy just hoped the infected had not got in; she'd rather take her chances with Eddie.

*

Ollie was a big guy. Six-foot-six and eighteen stone, and nothing scared him; until the epidemic. That scared the shit out of him. Plus, shooting your own pals dead does nothing for your sanity, he thought.

He was part of a biker group called "The Boas." Ollie never knew why in the hell they called themselves "The Boas," but that's just the way it was. They were your typical biker gang: leather and denim jackets that featured their logo on the back: a great embroidered snake. Bandanas, holey jeans and bad attitudes; they lived their lives on the road.

They'd hit the road when the virus had started to get serious. Cities were not safe to stay in. The roads had proved just as big a nightmare as the boroughs; they had lost six gang members within the space of hours, including Dutch – the leader of "The Boas". Ollie, being Dutch's right-hand-man, had taken over what was left of the gang (which was three) and had now led them to a minuscule village somewhere in South Wales. The place was in the middle of nowhere.

Ollie was observing a small cottage standing on its own from some nearby bushes. The infected had it vaguely surrounded. He spied two of them fumbling by the door, trying to do *something*, but he couldn't quite make out what they were up to. For all he knew there could be people holed up in there and they were trying to get in to butcher them.

The place was dark. No lights on upstairs or down. Ollie knew he and the two with him needed to move swiftly, to take out the problem by the door, and get inside fast. It was foolish to be outside and not on the move or in hiding until daylight came.

The other two, Ollie's girl Roxie and Axle, were hiding out in a well-enclosed area of vegetation and shrubbery, guarding the bikes. Both the men were skilled enough to take care of themselves and those around them. Roxie, who was also skilled, was not as confident. Ollie went back to them and told them what he had found.

"Look, I say I go take them out. There are only two of them and I reckon I can take both on my own, like. I want Roxie and you to stay here to look after our stuff. Okay, Axle?"

"Sure thing, boy, anything you say. I mean, you got us this far I trust your judgment. But make it fast, hey? I hate being out in the open like this if we are not moving on our wheels, like."

26

"I'll be as fast as I can. I don't fancy having my face chewed off by those fuckers any more than you do, Axle. But do me one favour: look after my gal."

"You got it, boy. I won't be leaving her side, plus I got a twelve-gauge here that says no fucker is going to mess with us." He smiled as he clubbed his open hand with the muzzle of the shotgun. It had come off a dead policeman somewhere on their route.

"Thanks, butty. I'll throw you a signal once I've cleared the area."

Axle pitched him a nod of his shaven head, and Ollie kissed Roxie on her thin lips as he headed out of the crude hideout. He drew the holstered knife that lay at his hip as he went.

Ollie moved out of the green covering with stealth. For a big man he could shift; his knife in hand and the bedraggled bandana covering his mouth and nostrils so that no contaminated blood from a killed infected could enter him.

The two had now split up. One still stood by the door but the other had moved to the main window of the place. Ollie, after inspecting once again, found the area dead, apart from the two. But there could be more around back. He wasn't about to check that out just yet. He got up close to the one standing by the door and drove the tip of his blade deep into the back of its neck until the hilt met skin. A strangled gargle erupted before it fell forward and slammed its head against the door, alerting the other one.

Ollie tried to dislodge his knife but it must have been tangled in cords or vertebras, as it would not move. He saw the second close in on him through his peripheral. He turned to face it, and the "it" was female and naked. This was the first infected woman that Ollie would have to kill. He could see her enormous breasts wobbling as she ran; muck and grime coated her body and not much milky white skin could be seen. That of which could be seen had bruises, cuts and boils which leaked pus and blood. Her arms were outstretched, and her teeth were bared. Some of them were chipped and broken. Its tongue wagged. This gal has been through it, he thought.

God, Ollie had never noticed until now how terrifying their eyes were. They seemed wild with rage and strangely coloured, an amalgamation of burgundy and yellowish-brown. He realised that this thing was coming for him at breakneck speed and he had nothing to arm himself with.

There was nothing for it. He would have to fight it out with this one. Ollie got into a boxer's stance ready to deal the first blow, but she pumped right through his guard, placing a solid shoulder into his flabby gut. The air whooshed out of him. As he inhaled frantically, the fabric of his bandana was drawn in, causing difficulty to breathe. The next thing he knew he was grounded, with the thing on top of him. He managed to grab onto her wrists. He knew what these things could do at close range. He had seen some of his butties of the road have their faces melted by the acidic puke these things could unleash.

As he wrestled with the thing, screams and roaring gunfire could be heard near his crew in the bush. "Roxie," he said. He began to thrash about under his attacker, delivering a knee to the gut and a left hook to the jaw, which broke with a sickening *crunch*. The girl buckled from the combined blows and Ollie was able to throw her clear.

She was on her hands and knees when Ollie got to his feet and moved in for the kill. She then spewed acid-vomit, spraying the grassy area they had just taken a tumble on. The stuff was vile in colour – a pale purple and green. The blades of grass smouldered, hissed and issued off plumes of grey smoke. The bitch sprang back to her feet; Ollie had stopped dead in his tracks after the bile attack. She flung herself at him again. He dodged her, but pulled her in close by her hair, then snapped her neck in one swift movement. He let the bitch fall to the ground. Ollie could still hear wails, but no gunfire. He needed to get to Roxie.

Before he dashed off, he managed to draw his blade out of the dead thing's neck. The steel gleamed with blood and chunks of flesh as he pulled it from the crimson void with a sludgy noise. He ran off to the others. When he got there, there were three of them circling her.

Axle was dead on the floor; half his face ripped off. His body was leaking blood as a burst pipe leaked water. His friend was gone but he could still save Roxie, the woman he would give life and limb for. Two out of the three rushed him. One of them appeared to be wearing a black cloak, and Ollie could see a white collar around his neck. This was going to be another first. He caught hold of the tip of his knife and flicked it. He watched as the handle flipped over the point, time and time again, before it thwacked into its target, catching the vicar in the brow. Ollie turned just before being tackled to the ground by the second.

For the second time Ollie found himself wrestled, and this time it was more serious than the last. He was outweighed by a man that had the air of a butcher about him. A double chin and a stomach built for devouring meat, his breath stank of sour milk and his teeth were like grizzled tombstones – it was like having a repulsive lover on top trying to rape the hell out of you.

Ollie's bandana was snatched from his face by rancid claws – he cringed and turned his face as strings of crimson-purple saliva stretched down toward him from "the butcher's" mouth. A deafening blast boomed through the air, and when Ollie turned to look at his attacker, half of its head was missing, exposing cords and shattered bone. Ollie's face felt hot from gushed blood; made him felt sick. But he was also angry, as dirty blood could have got inside him. He couldn't feel any on his lips and nothing distorted his view. His luck was really working overtime.

As he lay there shell-shocked, wondering how it would all end, her sweet seductive voice came. "You okay, love? You didn't get any of his blood in your mouth or eyes, did you?"

"No, beaut, I didn't. Where's the other one?"

"I killed it."

"That's my girl," he said, and smiled for the first time in what felt like weeks.

Ollie rolled what was left of "the butcher" off him and got to his feet. He plucked up his bandana and retied it around him. Roxie looked good, Ollie thought. There was something about the way in which she held onto Axle's smoking shotgun. She wore a short tartan skirt on top of fishnet tights. Her Doc Martins were almost knee length; her hair plaited

31

into pigtails fell either side of her cherubic face. Her dark lipstick smudged, matching eye shadow a running mess, which left streaks down her face. Roxie's tummy was surfboard flat with small jutting hips; her cleavage petite, and sexy. Around her left knee was wrapped a Harley bandana. More bandanas jutted from the top pocket of her leather jacket. They were from fallen Boa's. Ollie looked on as she bent down and took Axle's from around his neck and placed it with the others.

Ollie got his knife out of the vicar, while Roxie gathered their stuff from the bikes. They headed down to the old cottage. Ollie pulled the dead thing away from the door.

He didn't bother rapping on the door. Instead he turned the doorknob, slowly. He was worried that maybe somebody else had happened across the place and was inside riding the storm out. The door was locked.

"Love, over here a minute," Roxie shouted.

Ollie followed Roxie around the side of the house. She had found an unlocked window.

"Nice once, beaut," he said. "You not only have looks, but the brains to go with them."

She winked at him.

He poked the muzzle of the shotgun out in front of him as he entered the place via the small window.

The air inside was stuffy and reeked of something dire. The place was in blackness apart from a fire glowing in the corner. Ollie could hear small flies buzzing around.

Keeping the gun trained with one hand, he searched the wall with his free hand for a light switch. He reassured Roxie with words of encouragement, "Come on, beaut. It's going to be okay. Let's just light this place u—" He flicked the light switch; nothing. The place had no electricity.

"No power, Ollie?" she said, not seeming bothered by the fact.

His heart hammered. "No, none, but there's a fire in here, love." And to his amazement the place was no more than a shell: no furniture, no carpets, no TV. In fact, no electrical equipment at all. The fire burned away slowly in the fireplace. A pile of fresh wood was stacked up in front of the flames, which lapped at an oak mantle. But where was the person who had started the fire? Then, his thoughts were answered by a loud crash from above.

The smash sounded like a heavy glass or piece of china breaking..Ollie and Roxie were fused to the spot, too stiff to move. Ollie whispered, "Bolt that window, love. I am off up the wooden hill to find out what just caused that racket."

33

He gave her the shotgun, and drew his Bowie knife. Roxie slammed the window shut and bolted it. Ollie decided to rush upstairs and take out the threat. It has to be one of those things up there, he thought. It didn't seem like a place a person owned, being so rundown. The sick must be there. It would explain the locked door. At the top of the stairs he was faced with three doors. He headed for the one right in front of him. Before heaving his leg up and kicking the door open, he paused and pricked his ears. He could hear muffled screams but couldn't tell which room they came from. He slammed his foot against the wooden door, which bucked in its frame before popping open. He had visions of it coming back towards him and slamming him in the face, but it stayed open. He entered slowly, knife in mid-air, ready to plunge into an attacker.

He walked over the threshold, his head bent to one side, trying to see around the door. He saw legs. They look young, he thought, as he watched the legs thrash about on the bed. As his eyes climbed the torso he could tell it was a girl tied to the bed. Just as he was about to reach her face he noticed a second person in the room, on an adjacent bed. This one was naked. Her throat appeared to have been ripped out. She too looked young.

"What the fuc…" His gaze settled on the squirming girl's eyes, which were flitting to one side madly, as though trying to tell him something. "FUCK!"

Eddie's straight-razor sliced open Ollie's left cheek. It cut through the air with deadly accuracy – *whoosh*. Before he could react to the first cut, a hot slash caught him across the right-hand side of his jawbone, sending him backwards, out of the room. Ollie's back found the corner of the banister, and the ball of solid wood there slammed into the small of his back – "*Aaaargh.*"

"Ollie. Are you okay, love?"
He gathered enough wind to be able to answer Roxie. "Stay down there, beaut, and don't come up here fo—"

The air was driven from him again by a hard fist to the guts delivered by Eddie. Pain tore through his scalp as he was pulled forward by his hair, and a knee forced into his stomach, again and again, before his face was rammed into the wall opposite. Ollie felt his nose crumble on impact. He felt three swift jabs to his kidneys which forced his legs to buckle. *I can't go down*, he thought. *If I go to ground this fucker will stamp my brains to mush.* Instead, he turned his body – it hurt like hell – and faced his attacker. A balled fist smashed into his left eye. Ollie collapsed against the wall again, but forced himself to stay off the ground. Eddie danced back from the fallen man, and looked around frantically. "I want to slice this scummy fucker to ribbons," he said aloud. "Where in the hell have you got to?"

Ollie leant against the wall, watching the fat man look about the floor. He knew what the man was looking for. His razor. Ollie had seen him drop it in the room.

"Over here, tubby. I got it."

The grotesque face of Eddie turned to Ollie. A tortured smile spread across his face.

"You have it? Well then, boy bach, best you give it back before I have to hurt you some more. Is that what you want then, is it?"

Ollie watched as Eddie walked over to him: the man's naked body reminded Ollie of a load of dough. Loose skin flapped under his arms, and his jowls wobbled; more chins than a Chinese phonebook, Ollie thought.

Eddie's limp, stubby dick looked lost between his tree trunk-like thighs; you couldn't see where his ankles were due to the fat on his calves.

"Why don't you come over here and find out then, pork chop?"

Ollie could see the man needed no invitation, and felt like a weak child standing in a giant's shadow.

Eddie grabbed Ollie by his jacket and pulled him forward.

"I'm going to dance all over your dead, fucking body. Then, once I'm done with that, I'm going to fuck your girl, see. How do you like that thought, then? I bet that pisses you off."

"Thought you'd only be able to get your kicks from screwing children, tubby," Ollie assumed. "That's why you got them marks all over your face, isn't it? I've met your type before, and I'm going to kill you, Fatso."

Eddie let out a bellowing laugh before headbutting Ollie square in the face, once, twice, three times. Ollie felt himself slipping into a state of unconsciousness, and tried to fight it.

"Kill me, will you? We'll see who kill's who."

Eddie began pressing his thumbs into Ollie's eyes, determined to pop them and drive his thumbnails into the biker's brain.

"Ha-ha, die, fucker, die!"

"Ollie! Are you okay, love?" her voice frantic. She began climbing the stairs.

"He's a bit tied up at the minute, slag. But I'll be down to give you my...*argh*!"

Eddie's chirpy tone changed as a vice-like grip on his balls became an intense, swelling pain. He had the urge to throw his guts up. He unplugged Ollie's eyes and grabbed hold of the hand that was attached to, and squeezing the hell out of, his private parts. Eddie's face lost its crimson colour and was now a bone white. Ollie gritted his teeth, ducked his head, and drove the back of his skull into the multiple chins of Eddie, snapping his mouth shut. A few bits of ivory ricocheted off Ollie's back. Eddie stumbled backwards, clutching his balls and chin as he did so. He smacked into the banister, which shook and threatened to give way. Ollie had just enough time to gather himself and get back into the fight. He grabbed a framed picture off the wall, which was shedding wallpaper, and flung it at Eddie. It flipped end over end but failed to hit its target as it flew over the wooden railings, and clattered to the floor beneath.

"Get the hell back downstairs," he shouted at Roxie, who was now at the top of the staircase, looking at Ollie.

"But—"

"Get back down, mun, *now!*"

"Ollie I…"

Eddie pushed himself off the banister and met Ollie in the middle of the landing in a bear hug. Both men had their arms wrapped around one another tightly. But the fat man had the weight advantage, and drove both himself and the biker back into the room where the one girl lay dead, and the other was still trying to free herself. Ollie spied the Bowie that he had dropped. It was in the middle of the room. First, he thought, I have to free myself from this bastard.

Both men grunted as they danced and twirled around the room like two mad ballerinas. Ollie stopped the blob's momentum, and stamped on his exposed toes. He was sure he heard a couple of them crack under his boot. The hug was broken and Eddie went for his toes, giving Ollie the chance to drive a few hard lefts then rights into his opponent's face and gut: left, right, left right.

Eddie stumbled into the bed behind him, the one that held the writhing girl, and flew over the top of it. He came back up holding his razor.

"Come on then, big boy," he spat, spraying blood from behind his clenched teeth. "Let's see you take me out now then, is it?"

Where the fuck did that come from? Ollie thought. Eddie slashed the cut-throat from side to side. Ollie picked up his knife. Again they went for each other, but this time Ollie went into a rugby tackle, thumped his shoulder into Eddie, and they crashed against a wall. At first neither man could get their knife near flesh. Then Eddie managed to get his blade close to Ollie's face, but Ollie pushed it to one side and out of the way. The stalemate was broken when Ollie managed to shove Eddie away from him. Eddie staggered through the door, and into Roxie. Ollie followed him out just as Eddie tried to slash at Roxie. This gave Ollie the strength he needed. He bull-charged Eddie and, on connection with the man, propelled him back with such force that both men went through the frail banisters and crashed to the floor below. Roxie let out a huge wail of fright, and rushed downstairs. The men rotated on the floor until Eddie managed to get the better of Ollie, and while straddling him, plunged his razor into the biker's gut, ripping sideways. Before he could get another stab at Ollie, a snapped spindle was thrust through his left eyeball. Eddie jolted stiff, relaxed, then slumped down. Ollie pushed the fat man off him and got to his feet. He clutched his side as he booted Eddie in the ribs, time and time again while cursing him into a heap.

"Oh, my God, Ollie." Roxie rushed over to him. She hugged him tight, but he had to ease her away from him.

"My side, beaut. The bastard got me good."

"I'll clean you up now, love. Let me—"

He cut her off. "Upstairs, fast. There is a girl tied up. Go and help her first. I'll be okay for a bit."

"But Ollie, bach, you—"

"Go Roxie, love, I'll be fine, honest." He smiled at her. He wanted to hold her, but he knew he couldn't. That poor girl upstairs needed their help.

Roxie rushed up the steps, and into the room she guessed Ollie had been in. There, on the bed, was a young girl of no more than twelve. She was thrashing around and wailing under her gag. Roxie picked a knife that she found on the floor and cut the girl's restraints. The girl – *Amy* – sprung up from the bed, ran out the door and down the stairs.

"Hey, come back. I was only trying to help you."

Roxie ran after the girl, who was now down the stairs and in Ollie's grip.

"Calm yourself, child," Ollie said. "We are not going to hurt you, mun. We just saved you."

Amy's eyes were frantically wild as she tried to be free from Ollie. She kicked at his legs and tried to bite his hands and arms. Roxie reappeared and helped Ollie try to get the girl to calm down.

After getting the youngster to finally relax, Roxie spent the next few minutes taking care of Ollie's injuries. From one of their bags she found tissue paper, gauze tape and some hand cream. She padded his side wound then taped it down. She dabbed at the cuts on his face with more paper and a bottle of water, cleaning them of blood before rubbing some cream into them. Ollie gritted his teeth at the stinging pain.

His eyes appeared slightly bloodshot, but nothing serious. He was still dizzy from the headbutts he had received, but knew he could cope with that. His nose was broken, but not shattered, which he had feared it would be. He crunched it back into position, causing it to piss blood.

As she patched Ollie up, Roxie kept an eye on the girl. She was sitting in front of the fire just gazing into the flames. Her eyes unmoving. Her state seemed catatonic. Roxie felt a pinch of sorrow for the child, and wondered where her parents were.

Roxie stripped her skirt off and got into a pair of jeans. She had brought spare clothes along with other bits and pieces. She placed all of the gathered bandanas from their fallen crew members into her holdall, then handed Ollie a box of headache tablets which she had had stashed away. He swallowed two.

While she continued to dress, Ollie gathered up all their weapons, placing them by the fire – Amy didn't flinch or move as he did so. He'd come across a hard wooden handle that looked like it had once belonged to an axe. The one end was stained red. He then fed the last of the shotgun shells into the shotgun, making sure it was ready for action.

As Roxie buckled her jeans, the front door flew open. Roxie jumped back out of the way as a man brandishing a machine-gun came rushing in and shouted, "*Freeze*." Ollie just stood there in amazement and shock. He knew that the person standing in front of him was not a threat; he wasn't military. Nor was he sick like the others.

"We are human," Ollie said.

The man breathed a sigh of relief, and started lowering the gun.

"Sorry, I thought you were like them," the man said.

Silence filled the room. Nobody spoke for the next few minutes.

"My name's Jeff," the man finally said, and offered his hand.

Ollie felt the rage build inside at how stupid this man had been coming in here like that, shouting in their faces. He looked at Jeff's outstretched hand, and then knocked the guy out with a swift couple of blows to the face and head.

Chapter 3

Jeff looked over at Maria – she was asleep. Her long dark hair covered her face. He could hear Ollie and his girlfriend, Roxie, talking quietly out in the kitchen. The young girl, Amy, sat by the fire, was still silent. She had spoken once since he and Maria had arrived, and that was only to inform them all that her name was Amy. He rested his head against the barrel of the gun, which was now cool, and let his mind drift.

"What're you thinking about, Jeff?" Maria's voice was soft, like that of a child.

He raised his head slowly, his damp, sweaty hair clinging to the barrel. He was too scared to answer back just in case his voice cracked, or he gave away his thoughts of leaving them to die in this Godforsaken hellhole.

"Jeff?" she pushed, her tone wavering.

Could she see the terror hidden in his eyes?

"That sound out there, it's getting to me." He kept his voice low, not wanting the two in the kitchen to hear him. "I wish they would just leave us alone, give us a chance to rest, for pity's sake." She became a slight blur in his vision. He wiped the sliding tears away. "Do they have to come after us all the time? Why don't they give up?" He looked over at the dead man in the middle of the room, the snapped banister jutting from his left eyeball. "Even though I know what that man did to those poor kids upstairs, I can't help wishing I was him, dead and out of all this. Out of this hell and back with my wife."

He was conscious of the fact that his voice had been getting louder as he spoke, and shut up. He didn't want Ollie back in the room. The man had too much strength and fight to burn. *Next time he might just pummel me into the ground,* Jeff thought. *Them outside I can just about handle – him I can't.* Plus he had nothing to say to the man. Not even when the biker had told Jeff his story. He'd just nodded his head and listened.

Maria swept most of the spent rounds of ammunition out of her way as she slid over to him; the bullets had come from Jeff's gun. He had shot a few that had been close to the windows. She put her arm around his back; he followed suit by putting his around her shoulder, drawing her into him until they were snug against each other.

"Don't talk like that, Jeff," she said, looking up at him. "If it had not been for you, then I would still be trapped in the petrol station. I was terrified." He felt her shudder, and applied more pressure to his hug. She looked up at him, and felt his blackening eye.

"Does it still hurt?" He could only nod. "They'll be gone in the morning, Jeff. Try not to think about them."

Her voice was soothing, he thought. Just like a mother's would be to her child.

"Do you live with your parents?" He felt her back stiffen at the question. "Sorry, I…I didn't mean to pry. Just, just…" He let himself trail off.

"It's okay. I haven't seen my mum and dad since I left for work the night of the attack." She began to weep. "I argued with my dad just before I left. Now I may never get to tell him how stupid I was. That I'm sorry for what I said."

Now it was his turn to coo. To settle her with a gentle voice. But what came out resembled a harsh rasp of a tone; his throat was dry. What a dumb thing to have said, asking about her parents with all this going on.

"I'm sure they managed to get free, or kept themselves safe indoors." He looked over at the main window to the cottage. He had crudely boarded it up with the aid of Ollie – they had used the table from the kitchen. It covered most of the big window, apart from a couple of inches either side, through which *they* could be seen wandering around outside. The window Ollie had climbed through had also been covered. Cupboard doors had been used for that one.

They had torn up some of the planks from the cottage-floor and reinforced the table with them. There was plenty of wood around the place. Hell, they could even take down some of the doors from the rooms upstairs and use them.

Jeff had parked the truck outside in such a way that the window and door to the cottage were blocked. The cab to the vehicle was opposite the front door, so if they *did* need to use the truck in an escape, they could. He and Ollie had also found and unloaded an ammunition crate from the back of the wagon. It contained bullets for their SA80s. They'd discovered a Browning 9mm pistol with three spare clips, which they had given to Roxie.

Out back was a small, overrun garden, sealed off with a very high stone wall. There had been a couple of *them* out there, which Ollie had blasted dead with his shotgun. Rickety old garden furniture lay strewn about, green as a result of being lashed by the weather. A small tool shed stood at the bottom, in which Jeff had found a few jars of rusted nails and a hammer. They had come in handy for boarding up the window. He'd also found various rusting gardening implements, such as a rake, spade, hose, shears and a gardening fork. The fork and shears they kept because they could be of use; even though the prongs were blunt and the scissors dull, they were still spare weapons.

There was no furniture inside the house, not a scrap. And the same went for food. The cottage was thick with dust and cobwebs. Rats could be heard and seen. No carpet lay on the floor, exposing damp, rotting floorboards. The pipes in the kitchen had either frozen, seized or burst, as no water came from the taps, just brown sludge that made the pipelines groan.

"We could take the truck to their house, you know? Pick them up and bring them here, or take them to safety. I have a…" He let himself trail off.

"You have a what? Jeff? Come on, tell me." A slight irritation in her voice. "What are you hiding from me?" She sounded like a teenager in mid-pout.

She twisted, loosening his grip on her shoulders, and looked him in the eye. "You can tell me, you know that. If you don't trust the other two you can just tell me, and I won't say a word. I promise. If you are thinking of leaving, I want you to take me with you."

"A plane, I have a plane." There, it was said. He instantly felt better knowing that she knew. "Before all this happened I was a flight instructor, based on the outskirts of Cardiff airport, working for a flying

48

club. The plane isn't mine, so to speak; it belongs to the club."

She felt that he spoke with a plum in his throat, that he may have been looking down on her and the others somewhat. "So how come you have the keys then, Jeff?" Her tone of voice was somewhat distrusting.

"I have the keys because when things started getting really bad I left work with them, hoping to fly my wife and myself out of danger. But she got sick, and I didn't want to take her from the house in her condition, so we did what we have done here, barricaded ourselves in in the vain hope of sitting it out. There's no hope of us outlasting this, this *hell* we are caught up in. Our only chance is to make it to my plane, and fly away from here."

"But fly to *where*, Jeff? This is happening all over Britain. I heard it on the radio. They advised people to stay away from big cities and towns. That locking yourselves indoors and staying put was the best thing to do."

"I already tried that, and it didn't work. I have a plan all mapped out."

"Huh, so you're going to take a small plane like yours and fly it to an island somewhere? Hmm, is that the plan? How many times would you have to stop and refuel? This thing, this…"

"Plague?" he interjected.

"Plague may have reached the four corners of the earth by now?"

"Not if we went to the place I have in mind, we won't. And besides, even if we did have to keep moving, I know mostly all of the small islands off Britain and Europe. I also know what airports to land at for fuel."

"Sounds to me like you've been working this out for a while? So tell me, what was or is your plan?"

"My goal was to fly to the north of Scotland, to Inverness. I have a sister living there in a small fishing village, with her husband James. The population is very low, and the chances of the place being overrun by *them*, is slim to none. She runs a fresh fish farm, and has access to trawlers. If push comes to shove she could take us over to the Shetland Islands or up to the Orkney ones where I am sure we would be safe. We could stock up on supplies and be safe." Jeff looked over at Amy, and was now worried that the girl may tell the other two. But she was still transfixed by the fire; she was in a zombie-like state. Poor child, he thought.

"But, err, Jeff? What makes you so sure your sister is okay up there?"

"I spoke to her before the situation got totally out of hand. She told me she would be waiting for us, that she would keep herself safe and wait for Kathryn and me."

"Oh, right, I see."

They fell silent for a bit before Jeff broke the silence.

"May I ask you something, Maria?"

"Yes, Jeff, of course you can."

"Where are you from?"

"From this area, but my parents are from Greece."

"So you are Greek?"

"Yes and no…"

Before she could finish, a shower of rocks and shrapnel bombarded the house. Jeff heard an upstairs window explode and rain onto the floor above him. More stones could be heard bounding off the walls outside and ricocheting off the army wagon. *Clink, clink clink…*

"They at it with them fucking bricks again, Jeffy?" Ollie yelled.

Ollie stood in the doorway to the kitchen, his shoulders near enough touching either side of the frame, with his dainty girlfriend standing somewhere behind. Lost at the back of Man Mountain.

He walked over to the window covered by the table, and looked out. He could just about see past the truck and spot maybe a dozen of *them* gathering things up to fling at the cottage. He could hear their

51

missiles roll off the roof and hit the floor below or find their way into the guttering with a rattle.

"Bastards. Maybe we should go back out there Jeff, boy. Take care of some more of them? Thin their numbers out, like."

"No, I think we should conserve our ammo; we might have to make a break for it."

The air felt tense. Jeff felt that the biker may come over and whack him again, just like he had done when Maria and he had walked into the cottage for the first time. He had not meant to brandish his gun in the big guy's face. He wasn't to know that Ollie was not sick like the rest of those things out there. He was just being cautious. He'd smashed Jeff in the eye, knocking him out. When he had finally come around, Ollie had had a hold of Maria by her jumper, lifting her off her feet and holding her close to his scarred face. He didn't know what had happened between the two of them while he'd been out cold. He eyed Ollie now, unsure whether his comment about saving bullets had gone down well.

Then the lines in Ollie's pulled face relaxed.

"Good idea, Jeffy. But I think we should make a move soon, like. Maybe tomorrow morning we can make for the hills in the truck you brought? This place isn't going to keep us safe for much longer, and besides, we've no food or water."

"Yes, you're right," he said with a false smile. God the man's a vile pig, Jeff thought. But Maria and I are going to need him to help us get out of here. Jeff had seen the man take out a few of them with his bare hands, just before they had put the truck across the face of the cottage; a couple had managed to get in through the door because Jeff had broken it down to get in. Ollie had broken their necks. He didn't technically need a gun. But he was nursing a wound to his gut that he'd picked up whilst fighting the guy now lying dead in the middle of the room. He'd stuck Ollie with a straight razor, just before Ollie could get him with the broken banister.

"We could just leave right now, I mean we have guns. The truck outside is all fuelled up, right Jeff?" Roxie said. "We could even take the bikes with us, Ollie. Put them on the back of the wagon? I know their tanks are dry, but they may come in handy at some point."

"That's a sweet idea, love," Ollie said to Roxie. "But what about Amy? Look at her. She is in no state to go anywhere."

"But—" Roxie was about to protest.

"But nothing, love. I think leaving in the night is stupid, anyway. Where are we going go to? We've got no plan, no food and no water. At least in the day they're not about, which will give us a chance to look for supplies. I think we should ride the night out and leave very early tomorrow morning."

"I…I'm scared, Ollie, love," Roxie said, snuggling herself into her boyfriend by wrapping her both arms around his one, huge tattooed arm. "What if they manage to get in here in the night, like, and take us by surprise?"

"That's the last of your worries, beaut. Jeffy and I will take turns guarding the place while you sleep. Innit, butty?"

Jeff put the thought of telling them about the plane to the back of his mind. "Yes, Ollie. Good idea." He truly thought it *was* a good idea; it was stupid all of them trying to stay awake when three could sleep and one could stand guard. "I don't mind taking first watch." He felt he had to; he'd only known these people for a few hours. He was pretty sure he could trust Maria though. "I could watch for most of the night then wake you, Ollie, so I could get some shut eye before morning. And maybe by that time Amy will have come out of shock."

He looked at his watch, and not at the wall-mounted clock with its cracked face in the empty room. 00.02. Precisely three hours he'd been here, most of them spent sat on the floor with his head bowed. He hadn't even bothered to give the place much of a look over.

"OK, butty. Do you and your girl want to take the beds? I don't think Amy is going to want to sleep…"

"Now listen here, Ollie," Jeff butted in. "She is not my 'girl', as you put it. I'm a married man." He flashed his third finger at the biker.

Ollie shouldered his machine-gun by the strap, and marched over to Jeff. "Don't piss me off with that hoity-stick-it-up-your-toity-tone, Jeffy, bach." He dragged Jeff from the floor and rammed him against the wall. The back of his skull *thwacked* the brick. "I was only trying to be nice to you." Spittle found its way into Jeff's mouth. The biker's hot breath fanned his face. Roxie and Maria tried pulling him free of Jeff, shouting at him to stop, that he was hurting him. "Next time I won't be so nice," Ollie spat, letting Jeff go and watching the man slide down the wall

Jeff narrowed his eyes as he looked up at Roxie and the brute. "Well, I'm sorry you feel like that. Maybe I should just take my plane and leave you two here to rot in this fucking place." He could feel the small hairs on the back of his neck stand on end. It was the first time he had lost his cool and used such distasteful language in years. "Maybe I should just stick to my plan and sneak out in the middle of the night and leave you fuckers here to die. Hmm? Is that what you want?" He found strength in his legs, and stood up. He looked up at Ollie, and jabbed his finger into the man's chest. "Just maybe, I should take that truck *I* brought here and go with my 'girl'?"

Ollie swatted the stiff finger away. "You're bluffing, boy. You haven't got a fucking plane. And if you did, you'd have made straight for it instead of coming here. You—"

"Ollie, please," Roxie protested, tugging on his arm. "Perhaps he does have a plane, mun."

"Don't go buying into his bullshit, love. He's full of it."

"He does have a plane," Maria said softly. "He told me earlier about it."

Jeff's mouth grew into a wry smile as he pulled the keys from his back pocket and dangled them in front of Ollie's nose. "What the *fuck* do you think these are? Why don't you have a read what it says on the fob?"
Ollie slowly tilted his head to one side, the way a dog would when trying to work something out. He scanned the dangling key ring, and mouthed the words, "Wings Flying Club, Cardiff, CF62 3BD – Instructor's Key, plane 6." Ollie looked up and Jeff could see the man's half-witted brain searching for an apology. His smug, angry expression had been wiped from his face. Roxie could do nothing but look on in agony, for she knew that Ollie had hit and abused the only person in the house with a solution to their fucked-up-situation.

"Don't you think you should at least say you're sorry? Sorry for hitting Jeff and calling him names?"

The stunned man looked over at Maria. "I…I…"

"Well?"

"Come on Ollie, mun. Tell him you're sorry." Roxie's tone wavered, portraying her terror for the first time.

"Look, Jeff, butt. I'm…is there any point in me trying to say sorry to you?"

Jeff closed the gap between the two of them

"Why don't you have a go? You don't exactly strike me as the sort of person who's capable of saying sorry. And even if you did, and it sounded half convincing, why would you want to anyway? You don't want my friendship, do you? You just want my plane. So here's a bit of free advice for you Ollie – keep your damn hands and comments to yourself in future. And stop bloody well calling me *Jeffy*. It's Jeff. Or can't your minuscule brain get that?"

The big man was stunned, rocked by the fact that Jeff had had the balls to stand up to him and by the realisation that it was he who needed Jeff, and not the other way around.

"Look, I'm sorry. I'm sorry I punched you in the face earlier, but how was I to know you thought I was one of them, innit?" He resembled a naughty child who had just been told off by his mother. The only

57

thing missing was that his hands were not buried in his pockets. "How would you feel if someone had shoved a gun in your face, just after you'd been stabbed in the gut by a fucking perv? Come on, mun. Give a man a break, yeah? It's been tough on all of us. We need to work together, not go at each other, innit? The fight is outside, all around us. Please, look, I am truly sorry. I'll try and control my temper from now on."

He stuck his hand out for Jeff to shake. They stood there looking at each other for a couple of moments, before Jeff finally took the offer of friendship.

"And in answer to your question, we'll stay down here with Amy. You two can have the beds up there. To be honest with you, I don't think I could sleep next to a room with a dead child in it. Makes me go cold just thinking about it," he said, almost mouthing the last part.

"Ollie, do you mind if we stay down here too? I'd like to stay with Amy." Roxie looked at him with pleading eyes.

"I think it would make sense if we all stick together in this room. Plus you'd both be much warmer with the fire."

Jeff couldn't help but go to Roxie's rescue. He liked her – the daughter he'd never had.

"Okay." That's all he felt he could muster, and he left it at that. He'd been a fool. He knew that.

Before they settled for the night, both men carted Eddie's body upstairs and put it with the other one.

The others had been asleep for almost two hours, Jeff thought, looking at the time on his watch. Ollie and Roxie lay in a lover's embrace on their jackets in front of the fireplace, with Amy cuddled into Roxie. A duvet from upstairs draped over them. They'd fed wood to the fire shortly after one, just before they had settled there for the night.

Maria lay close to them with a quilt of her own. They had talked about bringing mattresses down too, but had decided against it in the end. Jeff sat by the window and watched Maria. Her breathing seemed controlled, rhythmic. It was a peaceful sleep for someone who had been 'too terrified to sleep', even though *they* had gone a bit quiet outside. The odd brick would pang off the house now and then.

Jeff got up on the hour every hour to walk around the cottage and check on the activities outside. He'd start upstairs, avoiding the room with the dead girls, and make sure those outside had not managed to scale the walls and slip in through a window. Once done up there, he'd look out in the kitchen, then garden. This would take Jeff around twenty-minutes to do. On completing his perimeter check, he'd settle back by the window, and watch them.

But now he watched Maria, the twenty-something student, sleep. He kept his eye on her, and the way her face twitched every so often made smile. How could she sleep so peacefully with what was going on in the world? He looked back out through the glass.

He was sure there were more of them out there now. He pushed his face close to the window, until his breath misted the glass slightly. There was one standing right in front of him, about twenty feet away, holding a baseball bat at his side. The lone figure stood unmoving, just watching. *Can he see me?* Jeff thought. *No, impossible. There is no light on in here and it is too dark out there.*

The silhouette started to rotate the bat. Thin trails of air issued from its mouth, reflecting just how cold it was out there. Then, the thing waved over at Jeff.

"What the hell is…did it just…just *wave* at me? Impossible. They're brain-dead?"

A tap on Jeff's shoulder almost made him scream out; he flew around, fist clenched.

"Shh, it's only me, Maria."

"What the heck are you doing up? You were sleeping a moment ago."

She shrugged her shoulders, unsure of what to tell him.

"I just woke up and saw you sitting over here. Thought I'd come and join you."

She settled down by his side.

"What were you looking at?"

"There is one standing out there. It's got a baseball bat. Look, out by the back of the army wagon. It…" He trailed off.

"It *what*, Jeff? I can't see anyone. I can see a few moving around by the trees, but that's about it."

He looked himself, and sure enough, the one he had been watching had gone.

"It…it…nothing. It doesn't matter."

She nodded.

"Are you cold?" he asked.

"Not too bad."

"You should try and get some rest," he said.

"Their movements are keeping me awake. And that growling they do, it's awful. It's as if…as if they are…"

"Communicating with each other," he said, and shivered.

"Try not to think about it, Jeff, that's what I am trying to do."

"Talk to me then. Tell me something to keep my mind off it."

"Mm," she thought. "Remember you asked me about Greece and my family?"

He nodded.

"Well I never did get the chance to tell you, did I? See, the thing is – my mother and father came to Britain before I was born. They had me when they were very young, before marriage. When my mother's mother found out, she wouldn't have anything to do with them." Her eyes glassed over slightly, and her mouth started to wobble.

"It's okay," Jeff said. "You don't have to tell me."

"But I *want* to, Jeff. She cursed them, and their unborn baby, for having a child before getting married. She told them it was a sin, and that she didn't want the wrath of God brought down on her house, so she banished my mother."

"So what happened? Did your parents stay together?"

"My dad brought my mother to Wales where he had a brother to stay with. Soon after he found a job, and started to support his family. He moved us into a house. My mother tried to keep in touch with her mother, but her calls and letters were unanswered."

Tears slid down her cheeks as her fingers fumbled with a corner of the quilt. Jeff drew her in and held her.

"That's a horrible thing that your grandmother did to your mother. But your parents' love for one another, and you, pulled them through it. I'm sure they have survived this."

"I'm sure you're right, Jeff. I just wish I knew for sure."

"Of course I am. It sounds like your father is pretty resilient, and good at handling difficult situations."

They sat there in silence for a bit. Jeff fingered his wedding ring.

"Will you tell me what happened, Jeff? To you and your wife, I mean?"

He'd been waiting for that question all night. He knew at some point he would have to relive the story. But before he did, he noticed something; a room he had not yet checked – there was a door under the stairs, as though there was a cubbyhole there. He slowly got up and walked over to it.

"Jeff, what's the matter?"

The worry was back in her voice.

"It's okay, stay there. I just want to check something."

He approached the small wooden door, and caught hold of the brass handle. He readied his gun and gently pulled his arm back, but the door didn't budge. Locked. She saw his shoulders slump. Jeff returned to where he and Maria were seated, and sat back down by her.

"I had to kill my wife…"

Chapter 4

Ollie stood with his back against the passenger door of the army truck. His machine-gun pushed into his back, but he ignored the pain. He slowly drew at the cigarette in his mouth, while lazily plucking it from his mouth to blow out the smoke every now and then. He smashed his balled fist into the door behind him and shouted, "*Fuck!*"

"Ollie, love, is that you out there?"

He rolled his eyes, and gulped down the tobacco-tasting spit gathering in his mouth.

"Yeah, it's me, beaut."

"What you doing out there at this hour, mun?"

He put the cigarette out on the sole of his boot, and called back to her. "Was just taking a look around the place. I found a water pump around back. It must be hooked up to the mains – looks like it is pumping fresh water anyways."

"So what's all the shouting about?"

"They've done our fucking bikes in. Taken knives or something to the tyres and slashed them to ribbons, like. They have even battered the bodies bad enough to crack the fuel tanks. Bloody bastards."

"And the truck, is it okay?"

"Two tyres have been cut on that. We won't be going anywhere this morning. How did they know to do this? I think they are getting smart, Rox."

"Oh," was all that Roxie could come back with.

"Yeah, 'Oh' is right, beaut. Are Jeff and Maria awake yet?

"Not yet, you want me to call them, do you?"

"No, leave them sleep for a bit." He paused, then spoke again. "What about Amy, beaut?"

"She is still sleeping, bless her."
"Why don't you come on out here and join me."

He heard her scramble up and over the driver's seat; she made her way on hands and knees to the passenger door. Ollie turned and helped her down. She saw that the skies were still grey and heavy. No wind stirred the grass, or ruffled their hair. It had been like this since the outbreak began. The sky had lost all of its charm. No sun, no rain, no nothing. Just night and day. A sense of time lost.

"Any idea of the time, Oll, love?"

He shook his head slowly, "Nope, none. I came out here just as it became light. I took over from Jeff at around six-ish. Been out here for about an hour or so I'd say, beaut."

"Had they gone by then?"

"Yeah, well, some of them were still hanging about; it was still a bit dusky out here, you know?"

"What we going to do about the truck then, Oll? We've got no way out of here now the bikes have been wrecked as well, like"

He could hear her starting to snort back tears; he turned and pulled her in close to him.

"Hey, come here, mun. We managed to come this far, didn't we? And you heard Jeff last night: he has a plane. All we have to do is make it to that hangar in Cardiff, and we are out of here, innit?"

He kissed the top of her head. "Come on. We'll be fine. I know I was a bit short tempered last night, but I was pissed off." He gripped her at the top of the arms, and slightly pushed her away from himself. Seeing the tears in her grey-green eyes made his throat tighten; he had to gulp several times to get rid of it. He drew her back to his chest. "Please, Roxie. Don't upset yourself anymore. Tell you what, you go and call Jeff and ask him to come out here to me, okay?"

"Okay," she managed. Her voice sounded harsh and rasping, the lack of fluid beginning to show.

"Thas my good girl." He watched her climb back through the truck, and heard her go into the cottage. "What the hell are we going to do?" he spat, looking at the two huge rips in the truck's front and back tyres.

He surveyed the scene about him – from where he stood he could only see woods. Not totally dense, but quite thick. The garden that Ollie stood in was overgrown with weeds and grass that stretched to his knee. A picket fence had once stood erect, but Jeff had smashed through it with the truck. Some of the strewn planks were visible in the knee-high grass, their timber brittle and flaky.

In-between Ollie and the woods was grassland. It gave the impression that it had once been a place of work, because to the right stood a rusted barn. Within its decaying walls of tin and timber were a corroded tractor and bailer. So maybe this cottage once belonged to a farming family?

Just past the barn was the brow of a hill. Ollie's inquisitive mind managed to get the better of him, and he decided to walk the quarter of a mile or so to the top, to find out what was on the other side.

Roxie gave Jeff a rough shake by the shoulder. He was huddled by the window in the corner of the room; Maria snug under his arm, a jacket over the top of them. The machine gun stood by his side against the wall.

"Jeff, Jeff. Wake up, mun," she called. She looked over at the child, who was still sleeping. Roxie had spent the night by her, her arm around the girl. Amy hadn't protested against it, just snuggled in closer to Roxie.

"Mmmm," he managed, before finally coming around. He squinted his eyes open, yawned, then said, "What time is it, Roxie?"

"Time you got up, I think, bach. The tyres have been slashed on the truck, Jeff. I'm worried, but Ollie seems alright about it. He's outside waiting for you."

"*They* have gone then, I take it?"

He yawned again, rotating his neck to ease the stiffness. Maria stirred and murmured with his movements. Jeff took his arm from behind Maria, and worked the pins and needles out of it by shaking it. He slowly lifted her head from his chest and gently put her to rest on the floor. She didn't wake.

He got to his feet, arched his back and moaned with delight as his back clicked. He went to the front door and opened it. The light from outside hurt his eyes. Roxie stood behind him.

He climbed into the truck, and shuffled over to the passenger side. He looked first, before jumping out onto open ground. Ollie was nowhere to be seen. Jeff turned back and told Roxie, who immediately flew through the truck, pushing past Jeff at the other side to start looking for her boyfriend. When she couldn't see him, she began calling his name.

"Ollll, Olllllie. Where are you?"

She scanned the area with frantically before Jeff finally put her mind at ease.

"He's over there, look, on top of that small hill."

"What does he think he's playing at, mun? Going off like that and not saying anything to us. For-fuck's sake, he wanted me to wake you so he could have a chat with you. So why go bloody walking off like that?"

"Couldn't tell you, sorry, Roxie. The man must have something on his mind. Let's just wait here for a bit, he will come back soon enough."

Jeff and Roxie watched as Ollie crossed the field towards them. He'd done nothing but stand at the top of the hill, before turning around and coming back. While they waited for the big man to get back to them, Roxie showed Jeff the ruined tyres of the truck.

"Well, I think there's a spare underneath," Jeff said. "There should be anyway. Depending on how far out of Cardiff we are, we could drive there on one crippled tyre."

"But that will do damage, won't it? Roxie said.

"We may end up destroying the wheel, but that won't matter."

"We'll have the plane when we get to the hangar, anyways," she said.

"Totally fucked, innit, butty?" Ollie sounded slightly out of breath as he spoke.

"I was just telling Roxie, there should be a spare underneath."

"That's only one though. We'll need two, like?" Ollie said

"Not necessarily," Jeff said. "I think we could make Cardiff on the rim."

"Not sure, butty," Ollie said. "I do have some good news though. There's a town just over that hill."

"Is there?" Roxie said.

"Yeah. A town by the name of Twsc, I think it said – couldn't quite make it out."

"Hmm. Maybe we could spend the night then," Jeff said. "Get some supplies in."

"There might be survivors down there, like?" Roxie said.

"Damn, I never thought about that?" Jeff said. "So why don't we go and have a look?"

"An idea just came to me," Ollie said.

"What?" Jeff said.

"We got ourselves a town over there, right? So why don't we find a nice 4x4, or something like that, fill it with what we need, then drive it to that hangar of yours?"

"Hmm," Jeff said, rubbing at his chin.

"I guess this truck is not our only ticket out of here, boys," Roxie said. "But I suggest we stock the car up and leave it in town somewhere."

"Yeah, okay," Jeff said. "We could bring food back here for the night, and then leave early tomorrow. What do you two think?"

"Yeah, good plan."

"I'm up for that too," Ollie said.

"One more night is not going to harm us," said Roxie.

"Sounds like we have plan then, guys?" Jeff said, smiling.

"Yeah, butty, we do," Ollie said.

"Wait a minute. *Amy*. We will have to take her into town too."

"Shit, I forgot. Damn," Roxie said.

"It would be too dangerous to leave her here on her own," Jeff said.

Before heading out later that morning, Jeff woke Maria, and the five of them washed with fresh water from the pump at the rear of the cottage.

The five of them set out from the cottage. As they crossed the field, Ollie covered the rear while Jeff led the way, leaving the women and child in the middle to keep their eyes peeled for any trouble. Amy had come along without any fuss.

They took their time crossing the muddy field, in case one of them slipped and hurt themselves. At the top of the hill, they looked down to the town of Twsc – the place appeared nothing but an empty wasteland, dry of any human life or activity. Burning wrecks littered the streets, along with dead bodies. Buildings smouldered, and thick plums of grey smoke blanketed the town. Debris and rubbish filled the main road through the large town, and mangy dogs nuzzled at the dead. Their hungry growls and the sound of teeth gnawing on flesh were audible over the roaring flames.

"If anyone is alive down there, I'll be shocked," Jeff said.

The dense smoke burned their eyes, and brought tears on. Maria had a headache developing, but said nothing to the others. The heavy smell of burning petrol and charred bodies clung to the air, sickening her to the core.

"Yeah, me too," Roxie said.

"We'll have to watch the dogs, boys and girls," Ollie said.

"Let's just get this over with," Maria said.

As they walked into town, Ollie spotted a Toyota, Hilux Surf 4x4, mounted on a kerb just opposite a newsagents'. The driver had been pulled from the jeep, his face smashed in. A pool of dried blood had gathered on the concrete. The windshield had small flecks of crusted blood on it. Flies were hovering over the body to feed.

Ollie stepped over to the 4x4 and pulled the dead man free, leaving the body to slam to the floor with a dull *crack*. Ollie couldn't bear to look at the caved in face.

"I think I can get this thing going. Keep Amy back there with you lot."

He jumped in behind the wheel, only to find the key barrel empty. He searched the dead man, but the key didn't turn up – it was nowhere to be found.

"Oh, *fuck*!" Ollie shouted, as he kneed the wing of the jeep.

Maria walked over to Ollie, and put a hand to his shoulder, "Let me try. I used to be pretty good at hotwiring cars at one time." She turned back to Roxie and Jeff, who were looking at her agog. "What can I say, I had a misspent youth," she said smiling. She faced Ollie again, "I might need your help."

"Okay, what you want me to do then, beaut?"

"Hey, Jeff, why don't you take Roxie and try to find us some supplies, this may take me awhile. We'll keep Amy here with us."

"Okay, we'll meet you back here in about an hour or so."

"Hey, butt, pick me up some cigarettes if you come across any. I'm busting for one."

Jeff couldn't help but smile, "Sure thing."

Ollie watched as his girlfriend walked off with Jeff. He felt uneasy. *Maybe I should be the one going with her?* No, Jeff was more than capable. But the worry remained.

Chapter 5

Amy sat in the backseat of the 4x4, her head bent. She wanted to speak to them, she really did. She just didn't feel up to it yet. But she knew she needed to talk to these people, maybe Roxie first. But every time she went to speak, she had to fight back tears. All she could think about was her dead parents, "Cut into pieces," as Eddie had said. Then Ollie caught her eye – he winked at her and mouthed, *Are you okay?* She held back tears, smiled and nodded at him. His smile was warm, inviting.

Ollie turned to Maria, who was now inside the jeep and bent over. "So, what's your story, Maria? How comes you and Jeff managed to hook up? Were you with him at the start of all this mess?"

Maria grunted, pushed herself up from under the steering column, and sat up, facing Ollie so that she could speak to him. "I'm not sure you want to know, Ollie. It was not a pretty sight. I saw people die." Tears gathered at the corners of her eyes, and Ollie stepped closer to her, putting a hand to her delicate shoulder. She looked up at him, and for the first time she saw the good person in him, his soft nature. Sure he was hot-headed and rough. But deep down, he was like the rest of them. Scared. "Sorry, I…I…"

"Hey, it's okay, gal. We have all done things we didn't want to do. That includes me, like." He rubbed her shoulder.

She smiled at him, knowing that she could open up to him, and began to speak.

"I work at a petrol station in a small town by the name Porth, and the night before last I came under attack by the infected," she said. She bent back down under the steering column as she continued to speak. "I had pulled the nightshift again, because the other girl I work on rota with, Sara, hates doing them."

She paused, and got back up again. She looked back at Amy; the child seemed transfixed on something and appeared not to be listening. Even so, Maria lowered her voice. "I'm pretty sure she was giving our boss, Jim, sexual favours to get out of the nightshifts."

Ollie choked out a laugh at this, but said nothing. He kept listening to what Maria had to say.

"I got to work and Jim was pissed off with me about being late again, he gave me the same old crap about 'did I want to keep my job' and shit, blah, blah, blah. When I took the keys off him, he was attacked as he walked to his car. They came from nowhere." Again she kept her voice low, not wanting Amy to hear everything she was saying. "Must have been at least six or seven of them, and they just laid into him with all sorts of weapons – axes, knifes, hammers, chains the lot. It was horrible.

"I wanted to rush and help him, but I knew I would be no good. Besides, Jim was dead before he even hit the floor. So I locked the door, and just prayed they would go away, I had no idea what the hell was going on. Fucking brutal pigs," Maria snapped, then continued work on the multicoloured wires.

Ollie looked on in shock. It was the first time he had heard her truly swear since knowing her. But he guessed she had every right. Fancy seeing your boss slaughtered like that? Even if he *was* a bastard, he didn't deserve to die that way. Chopped and hacked to death.

"Hey, come on, it's okay," he said, his tough-man image now totally gone. He put a hand to her back, and soothed her. He heard her take a deep breath before starting to talk again. He had to bend slightly, as her voice was muffled.

"Then the whole place plunged into darkness, because they were tampering with the fuse box outside. But the back-up generator kicked in, which gave me some light. I'd lost the TV monitors too, so I couldn't really tell what some of them were up to out there. And the phone had gone down. I was totally cut off."

Ollie took the weight off his feet by leaning against the 4x4. He kept scanning the town, but nothing seemed to move.

"When I knew I was finally safe inside, I put the radio on, and was shocked at what I was hearing. It said that most of South Wales had succumbed to some virus or other and that people should stay inside. But deaths and injuries were rising by the hour. A few hours later, I thought I heard the army break into the building that the news programme was being reported from, and gun down the presenters.

"It was bad, Ollie. I think that was the longest night of my life trapped in the station, with nothing to keep me company but *them* and their groans. When morning came, it was no better. Even though they had gone, I didn't want to go outside – I was too scared of *them* still being there. I didn't know then that they didn't like the daylight. So I stayed inside, and watched as the crows pecked away at Jim's body. I looked for weapons, but only managed to find a skewer from a throwaway BBQ set."

Ollie pushed off the 4x4 and circled the jeep. He looked at the tyres, making sure that they were all in good shape. He lifted the bonnet, checked the oil and water. Satisfied, he went back around to the driver's side, all the while keeping his eye on his surroundings.

"Jeff showed up the second night, which was a good thing, because I had planned to leave the next day at first light. He came at the petrol station in the army jeep and shot them all."

"Lucky he didn't hit one of the petrol tanks, beaut? Or you would have all gone up," Ollie said.

"Yeah."

"Bloody lucky, hey?" Ollie laughed out.

"Yes, I guess so. So after he killed them all I let him into the shop. I was a little wary at first, but the man had just saved my life."

"Thas one hell of a story," Ollie said.

"Yeah. I'm just so glad it is over."

"Fuck, it sounded as though it was right mayhem."

"It was. And after I let him in, we gathered a few things up and I switched the pumps back on so that he could fuel the truck up with petrol." Just then, the Toyota fired up, and Maria smiled. "Got it."

"Well done, beaut. Now all we have to do is wait for them to come back."

"I'm hungry," a voice said.

Ollie and Maria both turned to Amy, and smiled. It was the first time she had spoken since she had told them her name last night.

Chapter 6

Jeff and Roxie began searching for shops that would be useful to them. Twsc appeared to be a big town, and took a bit of time to investigate.

The first thing they came across was an Asda superstore. The green lettering of the shop didn't make the place look inviting. The car park was amassed with jammed cars; it looked like the drivers had been trying to leave in a hurry. Dead bodies lay everywhere, and the stench of death hung in the air. Blackbirds sat on the roofs of the trolley bays, and on the store itself. Some could be seen pecking and tearing away at the flesh of the dead. The sight of their claws dripping red was chilling.

Jeff and Roxie entered the shop. Roxie drew her 9mm Browning from behind her back, while Jeff lowered his machine-gun as they went inside, unsure of what they might find.

Inside was no better than the outside. The aisles were littered with the dead, and the air smelt of rotten food. Some had been attacked by knifes and broken bottles. One man lay amongst the vegetables, a cleaver buried deep in his forehead; his eyes rolled into the back of his head. Some were slumped over trolleys, others draped over freezers. The floor was awash with dry, sticky blood – which, when trod on, made a scratching sound like a Velcro strap. A low hum from the backup generators could be heard, and eerie elevator muzak played over the carnage.

"They're in here, Roxie. I can feel them all around us, hiding in the darkness, in the walls, scratching and sniffing. The daylight is the only thing keeping us safe."

"Please, Jeff, keep those bloody thoughts of yours to yourself mun, is it?"

"Sorry, I…I, didn't mean to s—"

"I know. But let's just grab a trolley or something, and fill it. That way we can wheel it over to the jeep."

"This is a customer's announcement. We are pleased to inform our shoppers today of the offer on our dairy products…"

The burst of a human voice from the amplifiers around the store caused Roxie to shout out. Jeff turned and rattled off a few rounds, sending cans of pop fizzing into the air. The crack of gunfire quickened his heart, making blood rush to his ears and flare with heat.

"Fuck, fuck, fuck," Jeff panted. "Shit, sorry, Roxie."

She didn't reply. Jeff turned to find Roxie huddled in a ball, pushed tight against one of the aisles. Hands over her ears; the 9mm by her side. Jeff shouldered the gun and crouched down by her side, carefully putting his hands to her arms.

"Hey, come on. It's okay. I just freaked out, that's all. There's nothing living in here except you and me, Roxie. Come on," he cooed. "Let's get cracking, no need for us to be in here longer than ten minutes."
She looked up at him, the vagueness gone from her eyes.

"Come on," he mouthed.

Roxie took hold of her gun, and got to her feet.

"Sorry, Jeff, I…I don't know what came over me. I just thought that, that maybe it was our end."

"No, nothing like that, I just got jumpy. That bloody announcement flustered me."

"Hmm, me too," she said, letting a small laugh slip. "Do you mind coming with me to get a trolley?"

"No, not at all."

They skirted around the bodies in the aisles as they loaded the trolley with bottled water, tinned foods, such as soups, and packet goods – biscuits, pastas and other bits and pieces. They found disposable BBQ sets that would come in handy to cook on. Both of them picked up toiletries and Jeff got a sleeve of cigarettes for Ollie. Backpacks, candles, torches, batteries, lighter fluid and various other things were tossed into the metal trolley, along with a map of the immediate area that Roxie had managed to find, and a radio.

Once they had finished inside, they headed back over to Ollie and Maria. But not before stopping at an Army and Navy Surplus Store they came across. Jeff looked down at his feet; the old trainers he wore were coming apart.

"Do you want to wait out here, or do you want to come in with me?"

"That's a bit of a daft question mun, Jeff."

The inside of the small shop was stuffy, and dusky. Not much light came through the window, which was filled with mannequins dressed in military garb, displaying some of the foldaway knifes and axes that were sold here. Roxie led the way into the shop, the Browning pointed out in front of her with stiff arms. Jeff followed close behind.

"Let's just grab a bunch of shit, and get out of here," Roxie said, her voice quivering.

"I'm with you on that one."

Jeff headed straight for the boots and grabbed the first pair of size tens he came across. Discarding his trainers, he slipped his new footwear on. Roxie picked up a military-style rucksack and begun filling it with what she thought they would need. A compass, Buck knives camp axe and Buck Knives folding saw, a

Kelly Kettle, a Billy Can Nesting Set, along with some glow sticks.

Jeff followed suit, and grabbed another holdall. He filled his with a duel fuel stove, another axe, a couple of warm padded shirts, trousers and thick socks. He went outside and placed his bag by the trolley, as did Roxie. They went back in to have another go, and were greeted by a guy well over six feet tall, wearing combat trousers and a flask jacket that had *Property of the United States Army* inscribed on it. His face was an oozing mass of multicoloured pus. His eyes were a dull white, which stared vacantly. In his hands he held a Bowie knife. Second and third knives were sheathed at either side of his hips. He began to growl from the pit of his gut. His mouth opened slightly, exposing bars of saliva that stretched from one side of his mouth to the other. He charged at them.

Jeff was quickly up with his gun, but it jammed. Beads of sweat burst on his brow. The soldier wannabe closed in on him.

"Come on, come on, work," he shouted as he rattled the cocking mechanism.

Then three loud cracks blasted in Jeff's ears; they had come from behind. Jeff watched the 'weekend warrior' take two slugs to the chest. The third found his gut as the man was propelled backwards toward the counter. He smashed into the glass of a display case.

He fought to get back to his feet, but Roxie made sure of the job. She emptied two more bullets into the guy's skull. Bone, brain matter and blood spurted across the wall.

Jeff could taste the burnt gunpowder of the exhausted shells, and smell the gun oil. He felt sick at the sight of the man's open head, which looked like a cracked egg. Roxie looked up at Jeff. A thin stream of blood had snaked its way up her clothes to the bridge of her nose. She was panting hard.

"Come on. Let's get the bloody hell out of here, before more of them turn up."

"Wait," she said, heading back over to one of the shelves. There she holstered her gun behind her again, and picked up two Jerry cans, capable of holding up to twenty-litres of fluid each.

"We could fill these with petrol. That Asda had a petrol station. You never know, Jeff, we may need some along the way, like."

He knew she had a point; the thought of going back to that dead place was chilling. But he knew they had to. He also grabbed two Jerry cans. They headed out of the shop to their trolley.

"We should be able to get at least three of these cans in there. I can carry the other two."

Roxie nodded.

Jeff pushed the trolley back to the petrol station, while Roxie guarded them. The sky was beginning to lose some of its light, and that worried them. But they said nothing.

The forecourt to the petrol station was jammed with cars and their dead owners. A woman clutching a child close to her chest could be seen huddled against a car. The sex of the child couldn't be determined, as its hair was matted to the skull, which appeared to have been kick or bludgeoned open. The mother's face was badly beaten, suggesting that the pair had indeed been clobbered to death.

"Let's not hang around, Jeff, love. This place is beginning to give me the willies."

Both Jeff and Roxie went to different pumps. They filled two of the Jerry cans with diesel for the plane. And one each full of leaded and unleaded, not knowing what the Jeep took.

They took their haul back to Ollie and Maria, who were waiting on them. Amy got out of the 4x4 and went to Roxie. The young girl put her arms around Roxie.

"Hey then, what's all this about, bach?" Roxie said.

"Glad you're back safe," Amy said.

"Aw," Roxie said, stroking the young girl's hair. "Hey, I brought you some sweets and some warm clothes to change into."

The young girl looked up at Roxie, and smiled. Ollie had to gulp the wedge out of his throat on seeing his girlfriend interract with the youngster. He walked over to them and kissed Roxie on the forehead. "What took you so long, then? I was getting worried, beaut," Ollie said.

"*Were* you worried?" Roxie said.

He nodded, and pulled her close. "Next time, I'm going with you."

"Hey, Ollie," Jeff called. "I got you some cigarettes." He threw the sleeve over to Ollie who, on catching them, thanked Jeff.

"I got this baby going," Roxie said.

"Great," Jeff said. "Let's fill and get out of here."

The four of them filled the Hilux with the gear Jeff and Roxie had managed to get, apart from some food and the duel stove which they filled with petrol to take back to the house. They waited as Ollie parked the jeep in a nearby street. Happy that their vehicle was safe for the night, they headed back before light was totally lost, and the streets were filled with *them* once again.

Chapter 7

They sat around the makeshift table with a couple of candles in the middle. The sun had set, and the moon had moved in for the night. Ollie popped the cork on the bottle of wine Jeff and Roxie had picked up earlier; he passed it around the table for the others to take a swig.

They'd set the small radio up at the side of them, but nothing could be found on any of the channels. Roxie had made a sweep of the radio bands almost as soon as they had got back from their scavenger hunt. Nothing but dead air blasted out at them – *hisssss*; Jeff had received the same response from the army truck's CB radio. They appeared to be totally alone.

"I thought we might have found someone down in Twsc, today." Maria shook her head in disbelief. "What a shambles it is over there. I've never heard of, let alone seen, so much death and destruction in my life." She felt sick, and pushed her plate away. "I can't stomach anymore, sorry. The thought of all those dead people being pecked at by hungry birds gives me the…It reminds me of Jim…" She trailed off, and shuddered.

"You should eat, Maria. It'll help keep your strength up," Jeff said.

She again shook her head. "No, I can't touch another bite."

Ollie also looked sheepish – he was drinking and smoking more than he was eating. He had hardly touched his meal, and as a big man he needed the energy more than any of them.

"I think I've had enough too, love," Roxie said to Ollie.

Ollie grabbed her hand, and squeezed it. "You feeling alright, bach? You're looking a bit pale. Come here, and let me give you a cwtch."

"I'm fine. I've just had enough."

"I think today may have been a lot for us to handle. The sight of such... *slaughter*," Jeff said.

"You must have seen a lot worse when you were making your way here, Jeff?" Ollie said.

"Yes, I did. I saw a lot of bad things out there."

He took a good swallow of wine before handing it to Maria, who also took a good drink. "I...I had to kill Kathryn. My wife. She became sick."

"Fucking hell," Ollie said, closing his hand around Roxie's.

"Ollie!" Roxie said sharply. "Don't swear in front of Amy."

The young girl was sat between them, slowly picking away at her food, seemingly oblivious to it all.

"Sorry, beaut. But the thought of having to do you in is…is…well, *awful*." He felt his throat tighten.

"I'm just glad I didn't have days to ponder how I was going to kill her. The sickness came on fast. *Very* fast."

"I'm sorry to hear that, butty. I had to kill a few of our friends when we were on the road. Done my best mate in, like." A tear rolled from Ollie's left eye. "I've known him for years, since we were kids. I see him in my nightmares, mun." He took a deep breath before speaking again. "So how did you manage to get from your home?"

*

He stood over her dead body – a lump of wood in his left hand. She lay naked and twisted to one side on the soft white carpet. A pool had gathered from her blood; it was becoming a brown mustard colour. Her long brunette hair rested in lazy, rusty coloured ringlets to her left side. The right-hand side of her skull was caved in. Now Jeff stood in his worst nightmare: he had killed his own wife.

He raised his right hand to his face and pinched his thumb and forefinger into the corner of his eyes to stop the tears. His shoulders jumped and his body quivered. Without looking up, he pictured the photo on the nightstand at the side of their bed. The frame held a caption of them strolling along a beach in

Hawaii; it had been taken by a young boy for three dollars. The holiday had been their honeymoon. God she had looked beautiful that day on the sands, he thought.

The disease had taken her fast; Jeff never even saw it coming. He thought they were safe penned up in the house. But then she became sick, only slightly at first. Within hours her skin had become blistered – then the aggression started.

He threw the plank to one side and fell to his knees by his wife's side. He scooped her up into his arms and held her close to his chest. He whispered, "I love you". His weeping was uncontrollable as he gripped her tight to his body.

A roaring smash from downstairs brought him out of the loving embrace – Jeff listened. He could hear one of *them* shuffling around down there. His heart raced and thudded against his ribs. He gently lowered Kathryn back down onto the carpet. Strings of blood pulled away from her lips, the other end of which were fused to his chest.

He picked up the wood again and headed to the bedroom door. Out on the landing, Jeff stood and listened to the noises downstairs. How in the hell did they manage to break their way in?

Low growls and hissing sounds could be heard down there. He looked at his trembling hands, and clutched tightly at the clubbing instrument, determined to shake the quiver. He could feel the pine bore into his skin. Beads of sweat began to trickle down his temples – his mouth arid; Jeff could feel his tongue becoming bulbous through the dryness.

He edged along the corridor, and as he neared the top of the stairs he was able to peer around the balustrade. His bladder clenched.

Jeff placed his right foot on the top step, which barked with his weight. A face appeared around the corner of the door jamb to the living room. Its head was bent, and greenish-yellow dribble hung from the lolling jaws in chunky threads; the tongue bobbed on its cord. *It* didn't so much as hear or see Jeff, it just sensed his presence. Jeff drew in a gasp of breath as the dead eyes turned his way; it was Ted Ebbing from next door.

Ted's face blistered and popped with bubbles of God knows what kind of fluid. His forehead and jawline pissed fluid. Ted's mandible suddenly became strong and brutal-looking. A low-sounding growl found its way out of his mouth; a thin smile appeared on the lips.

"Stay back, Ted, stay back or I will be forced to take you down."

Jeff brandished the wood out in front of him, but Ted didn't seem to care as he began to ascend the stairs.

"Please, Ted, don't come any closer, or I *will* be forced to hit you."

Ted reacted by bounding up the stairs like a rabid dog. Slobber found its way onto the walls as Ted headed straight for his target. His actions were more like a Safari predator than a man of eighty.

Instead of lashing out with the full-bodied stick, Jeff stuck out his foot; the heel found the side of the Ted's jaw, sending the head sideways and snapping his brittle neck. Jeff jumped back as Ted just stood there for a couple of seconds with his head rolling around on twisted neck muscles before finally collapsing backwards. The tumble was hard; he bounced off the wall and crashed through the banisters. He came to rest at the bottom, his face peppered with splinters. Christ, Jeff thought, I've just killed an old man. Snap out of it, he told himself, everyone is killing one another out there. Chances are Ted has already killed Angharad.

He knew now that boxing himself in the house had not been such a good idea, because *they* could clearly get in. He decided there and then that he had to make it to his car out front and get the hell out of here, but go where? The world was crumbling from

94

this disease; there's an army of sick people out there, waiting in the shadows to take a chunk out of you whether or not your back is turned. The law and army had been shred to nothing; phones were down, T.V stations also. It had been a joke how the army had tried to stamp the problem out; their heavy-handed tactics had failed. Jeff remembered Ann Swiss, local DJ, on the radio telling people to stay indoors, and discussing the issue with people on a phone-in. The army had broken in and told her to shut down. On refusal, they'd shot her and the rest of the morning team dead, live on radio. That had been just a day ago, right at the beginning of this mess; but Jeff could still hear how that dead air had sounded, almost deafening. Then the plugs had been pulled. The phone lines had gone around the same time. The reports of killings soared by the hour. Reports of babies being slaughtered by loving parents; wives battering husbands to death and vice-versa. A story of a gun club owner who went into his local pub armed with a shotgun, and rattled off twelve rounds of ammo, before being stabbed in the throat and killed by the landlord.

Jeff shook his thoughts free and went downstairs – his heart still pounding. He winced at the cruel noises escaping from the boards. But Jeff was pretty sure no more of them were in the house. At the bottom, he peered around the doorframe and into the living room. One of Kathryn's two-foot-high plant pots lay in the middle of the room; red and orange haze snaked its way in through the gaping hole. Jeff tiptoed to the window, being careful not to tread on any of the scattered glass; bitter cold wind whistled through the room. Through the tattered glass, only burning buildings and ruined valley towns could be seen for miles around.

Jeff turned and ran for the bedroom – he half expected Kathryn to come at him again, but she was dead; a harsh reality. He placed the wood on the bed and pulled his rucksack out of the wardrobe – beginning to pack it half blind. He plucked the photo frame off the stand, buried his fist into the glass and snatched the photo from inside..He threw on the rumpled clothes that had been lying at his side of the bed. The old blue faded jeans felt good and snug.

He snatched up the bag and stomped out of the room. Downstairs in the kitchen, he armed himself with a butcher knife from the knife-block. He moved swiftly from kitchen to hallway. With the rucksack on his back, he had one hand free; the other brandished the blade.

Jeff snatched his car key, and the keys to a light aircraft he had stored away in a private hangar on the outskirts of Cardiff, from off the wooden holder in the hallway. He counted to three – *one*, *two*, *thr*...then threw the front door open; it didn't protest. He gulped his breath down and eased his way out the door. The street appeared empty. Keeping low, and hugging the wall of greenery, Jeff pushed on, now only inches from his car. No attack seemed impending as he made it out of the garden and to his car. His fingers struggled with the key. He kept missing the slot in the darkness, and scraping the paintwork. Something moved to his left, and his head darted to find a pack of *them*, maybe eighty-feet away, mauling a body on the floor. His gut clenched. The key found its home, *clacked* as he twisted, bringing *their* attention to him.

"Shit!" He flung the door open and threw himself behind the wheel. He slotted the key home and twisted it in the barrel, causing all doors to lock, but the engine failed him. Two of them flung themselves onto the bonnet. The noise was horrendous: the crashing bodies sounded like a shower of rocks pelting the car's body. Jeff kept trying the engine – but it was now drowned. He sat there, praying they wouldn't get in while he waited for the motor to settle. The two on the bonnet were disgusting: their faces were covered in air bubbles full of pus and the hair on their heads fell out as they thrashed.

They began raining blows down onto the windshield, and each time they pulled back their fists, chunks of flesh were left behind on the glass. The flesh of their knuckles was falling apart like well cooked beef. Their snarls lashed blood over the window; trails ran down the glass, washing the skin away.

While they pounded on the glass in front, the three behind hammered at the car with various objects. One held part of a picket fence in his grasp and battered the bodywork. Another stood directly behind the rear window – he bashed away with a dustbin lid. The one by his side just clawed at the wagon, snapping all his nails off.

The windshield began to crack and give way. He turned the key once again and the engine kicked to life. Dropping the handbrake, Jeff punched the accelerator to the floor. The back wheels squealed and the car lurched forward, throwing the two on the bonnet over the roof and onto the floor behind. The tires screeched and kicked off smoke and dust as Jeff pulled away.

He climbed out of the war-torn car, with knife in hand, to inspect the camouflaged vehicle for weapons. Vigilance was of the utmost importance. The orange glow of the truck's signal lights burned with an eerie rage, and the dead night air whistled with sad song. Tonypandy: the town in which the truck was on stop, seemed deserted; newspapers and other bits of rubbish blew past his legs like tumbleweed..The shops and houses looked barren, but hostile. The darkness stretching out from the shop windows seemed bottomless; Jeff shivered and wondered if eyes looked intently back at him from all the hidey-holes of obscurity. The road had abandoned cars on it, and dead bodies littered the streets and avenues.

On approaching and opening the truck's door, Jeff found a dead soldier in the cab; the face burnt away as though acid had been thrown into it. The body was slumped over the wheel and its hands rested at its sides. Flies lightly buzzed around and landed on the carcass to eat away at what was left of the mushy face – Jeff turned to spew on the floor.

After regaining his composure, he searched the reeking cab and found a flashlight and a holstered 9mm Browning on the waist of the dead fighter; he swapped the knife for the gun. Then it was time for the most daunting of tasks – to search the back. But before Jeff did, he made another sweep of the town. The wind still whistled sombre; the debris still danced to its tune and those windows, God those windows – so black and hellish.

The camouflaged canvas rippled in the breeze and gave the impression of movement in the back. Jeff held the gun ready in his right hand, the left carrying the torch. As he edged closer to the rear the flapping hessian seemed to wave more violently – it's just my imagination, Jeff thought. Standing at the foot of the canvas, he pulled the cocking device back on the Browning, clicked on the torch, and pulled quickly at the flaps.

He'd expected his mind to have been playing tricks on him. Some kind of sick joke, but no, he was wrong and that wrong suddenly flew at him with clenched teeth and flying spittle. Its torn military outfit flapped in the swift advance. Jeff leapt back and let rip with the Browning. The muzzle flashes seemed to light up the whole town. It was the first time he had ever fired a gun before.

The shooting seemed to cease before it got started, and the gun soon clicked on empty. The soldier had been propelled backwards, and now lay slumped against one of the truck's sides. He'd taken six slugs to the chest and not one elsewhere. Jeff felt he needed to five-minutes to compose himself, but he had no time to; the infected came from everywhere, as though the handgun had served as a starter pistol, or a dinner gong. He felt his gut fall into a void as they rushed at him like rats from a hole, screeching a jungle tribe war cry.

Jeff scurried into the back of the truck, where he found, and picked up, an SA80 assault machine-gun. He just about had enough time to make it back to the passenger side of the cab, and get himself inside before one of *them* managed to grab hold of his ankle and start to heave him backward. Jeff yelped in shock as he began to slip, but he managed to regain control over the situation, and jabbed the butt of the lightweight machine-gun into the mouth of his attacker; blood jetted from its split lips. This enabled Jeff to scramble inside and shut the door as they closed in all around him. The wagon began to cover like a beehive as Jeff slammed the locks down on both doors.

He struggled to swap seats with the melted commando, but when he finally managed to, he got the truck started and bulldozed his way through the myriad bodies clinging to the wagon – crushing heads and body parts like melons with the robust wheels.

A partition separated him from the back. But he knew some had climbed on board. Jeff could hear their growls and the Godawful scraping of nails on the panelling, which chilled him. He thought of stopping once clear of the town, and getting out to riddle the canvas with shells, but decided against it.

He might need the bullets later on.

*

A crash from behind startled them all. The men went for their machine-guns, and Roxie drew the Browning. A man spewed from the door Jeff had failed to open last night.

"Please," he panted. "Don't shoot. I'm not like them."

"Best you start talking, boy bach. Or I'm going to put a burning hot slug between them eyes of yours," Ollie said.

The stranger scrambled to his feet. "Water, p…p…please." He held his throat. "I've been down there for days, mun, with de…dead… people. I…I need something to drink."

Ollie stepped around the table, gun still trained on the man as he walked toward him.

"You don't get a fucking drop of anything, boy, until you tell us what the fuck you've been doing down there. You hear me?"

"I don't want a f…fight," he gasped. "Just give me some water. I'll tell you all you want to know. Duw, please."

"Don't come all attitude with me, boy, or you're likely to end up hurt."

The man cowered away from Ollie's advance, and tried to defend himself with words.

"I only want some water. What's your problem?"

Ollie lowered the gun and stood toe-to-toe with the other man, jabbing his finger as he spoke.

"I'm trying to keep my arse alive, and I don't like it when people pop out of nowhere. For all I know, you could be like one of them outside, see, boy bach."

The man swatted Ollie's finger away, and Ollie grabbed the (not much smaller) man by his T-shirt, driving him back against the wall, cocking his fist in readiness.

"Ollie," Jeff shouted. "Wait. Let's hear what he has to say first."

Jeff could see Ollie was about to jump down his throat, but then the rage cleared in Ollie's eyes. He let go of the man's T-shirt.

"I'm sorry Jeff, you're right. I don't know what came over me." He turned to the man he had just pinned against the wall, and nodded his head in way of apology.

Maria brought him the wine, and let him drink greedily from the bottle, stopping only when he had drained it. He gulped hard and wiped his lips clean.

"I was cuffed and shoved down there."

"By who? Who did that to you?" Jeff said.

"I'm not sure, I don't remember much. All I know is I've been down there for God knows how long. I came around a few hours ago with my hands like this."

He raised them into the air for the others to see. They were cut and bloody. One hand was cuffed, whilst the other was free. The bracelet for that hand hung loose.

"It must have popped free as I fell." He rubbed at the back of his head. "I think I hit my head, too. I can feel a lump there."

"How comes you never shouted out, then?" Roxie said.

"I was too scared to I guess, mun. I don't know," he said.

"There is no need to be sharp," Jeff said. "She was only asking you a question."

"Sorry, it's...I...I...I'm hurting," he said. "Where is he?"

"Where's who?" Roxie said.

"The freak that did this to me. The one that killed those poor people downstairs?"

"Mammy, Daddy," Amy shouted, and ran for the cellar stairs, only to be pulled back by Ollie.

"No, beaut, don't go down there," Roxie said.

"Did you kill this girl's parents?!" Ollie roared, his face twisted with rage. Amy bucked in his strong clutch.

"Mam, Dad," she shouted hysterically.

"No, mun, I swear. It was someone else. Please, you have to believe me," he protested and backed away slowly.

"Jeff, boy, I think we should tie him down for a bit until we have made our minds up. We may have another killer on our hands."

"Please, come on, mun, I…it's the truth."

"Okay, Ollie, I think that's a good plan; we can't be too careful," Jeff agreed, ignoring the stranger's pleas.

"Roxie, come and have Amy, gal," Ollie said.

While Roxie and Maria looked after Amy, Jeff and Ollie strong-armed the other man into a sitting position by the fire, and fixed the loose handcuff to a pipe on the wall.

"That should hold him," Jeff said.

"Yeah, should do, like," Ollie said. Then he looked down at the man and grabbed him by the hair, pulling his head back. "I hope you didn't kill that little girl's family, because if you did, I'll kill *you*, just like I killed the fat *freak* that was here yesterday."

"Dead? Aw. That's a relief."

"What do you mean?" Ollie said.

"That sounds like the guy who threw me down the cellar," he pleaded.

Ollie didn't like what he saw in the guy's eyes. He had a shifty look about him. Ollie didn't trust him.

"Yeah, maybe he did."

"You can't just leave me cuffed to this pipe, mun. I need food, water!"

"We can do what we want – we run the show in here, boy," Ollie said.

"What's your name?" Roxie asked, still clinging fiercely to Amy.

"Dylan," he said.

"What's his name got to do with anything?" Maria asked. "He may have killed Amy's parents."

"But I *didn't*."

"Shut up," Ollie shouted.

"Maybe we should just let him go," Jeff suggested.

"Are you fucking *mad*, Jeff?" Ollie said.

"No, of course I'm not."

"Well, what you on about then? We can't just let him go."

"What choice do we have, Ollie?"

"We can let the fucker die cuffed to that pipe."

"But he could be an innocent man. Have you thought about that?"

"Jeff, mun. Look at him."

"What am I looking for, Ollie?"

Dylan watched with frantic eyes as the two men decided his fate. All the while he tugged at the pipe, testing its durability. It was weak; rusted. Much like everything else in the cottage. With one hard tug, maybe two, he could be free, and away from here.

"He looks crazier than a shithouse rat," Ollie said.

"Don't you think you would look like that after spending time in a dark hole with nothing but dead people for company?" Jeff said.

Ollie backed down momentarily.

"So what do we do with him, Jeff? Ollie might be right. We can't be too careful," Maria said.

"I know," Jeff said.

"I am here…" Dylan started.

"Pipe down," Jeff told him. "I need to think."

"Well don't think too long, Jeff, butt," Ollie said. "We have to get out of here in the morning."

"Yeah, I know, Ollie."

"And we ain't taking this knobhead with us."

"Okay, okay. I realise that. I don't want him with us either."

"But why? I ain't done anything, like. You have to—"

"I said, shut up!" Ollie roared. Roxie and Maria flinched. Amy began sobbing harder against Roxie. "One more fucking peep out of you, and I'm going to smack your lights out," Ollie warned.

"Ollie, calm down, you're scaring Amy. Please," Roxie said.

"I…" Ollie didn't bother finishing.

Jeff put his hand on Ollie's arm, and clutched it. "We're all scared, Ollie. We can't let our emotions get the better of us. All I was going to suggest was that we let him go. Let him walk out of here. He doesn't have to be a part of this group. He can find his own."

Dylan looked up with pleading eyes, and said, "You can't just send me out there."

Ollie seemed to simmer. Jeff could feel the big man relax. "Okay," Ollie said.

"First light, we'll send him on his way," Jeff said.

"First light? You want to keep him in here with us until morning?"

"We don't have much choice."

Ollie looked over at Roxie and Amy, then to Maria before finally turning back to face Jeff. "Okay, first light it is. But I want to guard him first."

"That's fair enough," Jeff said.

Ollie nodded at Jeff, then walked over to the cellar door to close it. But, before he did, he went down there, telling the others to stay put, and to keep Amy back. When he returned, he shut it with force, jamming it shut so that Amy wouldn't be able to go down there.

"Are my mam and dad down there? Are they dead?" Amy asked with a sob.

Ollie rested his head against the door. "What was your mam wearing?" Ollie asked.

"A dress; pink with flowers."

"And your dad?" Ollie asked.

"A blue shirt and jeans," Amy said, her lower lip shaking. "Is…is it them down there?" she asked.

Ollie nodded his head.

Amy buried her face into Roxie's body, wailing and crying.

Dylan wanted to say something, to try to plead his innocence again. But there seemed little point. The group had made their mind up: he was to be kicked out at sunrise to fend for himself. It could be worse, he thought. They could be kicking me out now.

"Jeff, butt. Where's that map you picked up earlier?"

"It should be in one of the rucksacks."

Dylan watched as the two men spread the map out across the table the girls had cleared, while Amy searched through some clothes Roxie had picked up for her at Asda. All the while he kept gently pulling at the cuff. He could hear the pipe creak under the pressure, which he applied every so often.

"It looks like the airport is only about five to eight miles away from here, Jeff."

"Hmm," Jeff said. "Maybe we could cut through here, Ollie?" Jeff indicated to an old B-road on the map.

"Yeah, seems like a solid route."

"We shouldn't encounter much trouble out on those roads."

"All farms and fields, butt. Not a town in sight," Ollie said.

"Guess our luck is getting better. I thought we were the other side of Cardiff."

"Yeah, that's going to save us having to go through the city centre."

"I bet the place is nothing more than a dead city, like Twsc."

"Could be highly populated by *them* though, Jeff," Ollie said.

"I guess it doesn't matter now, either way."

"True."

A burst of laughter erupted from behind Ollie. He turned to see Roxie tickle Amy and wrestle the young girl to the floor. Jeff hadn't noticed, and was now engaged in a conversation with Maria. Ollie watched as his beautiful girlfriend played big sister to Amy, who now seemed resilient to what was going on around her.

Ollie knelt by their side, and kissed Roxie.

"Ugh!" Amy mocked. "Boys got germs," she said.

"Not this one," Roxie said.

"And what would you know about boys then?" Ollie said, smiling.

Amy blushed, and turned away.

"Ha-ha. Made her blush," he said.

Roxie lightly slapped Ollie's arm. "Stop it, mun. Poor dab is all embarrassed now."

"I think this one will take some embarrassing, won't she?" he asked, and then began tickling Amy's side. She let out a shriek of laughter, and pleaded with Ollie to stop. "You'll take some embarrassing, won't you, crwt?" he said.

"He-he, yes, please, stop," she begged.

Roxie giggled. Watching the way Ollie was with the young girl almost brought tears to her eyes. Turning thirty had made Roxie think about her and Ollie's future together. They had spoken about giving up life on the road a few times, but she knew how loyal Ollie was to Dutch, and the rest of the Boas. Ollie had told her that he would give it all up for her, that he too wanted to settle down.

"I love you," Ollie said. looking over at Roxie.

She smiled. "Me…"

Loud guttural growls from outside, followed by thumps and slams at the main window, stopped Roxie talking. Ollie went for his machine-gun, as did Jeff. Roxie drew her pistol, leaving Maria to arm herself with the shotgun. Amy stood behind Roxie, whimpering. Dylan raged on the floor, as he pulled and tugged at the pipe, aching to be free. But the pipe was much more solid than he'd first thought.

"Help me," he shouted. "Please, for fuck's sake, help." The veins in his neck stood out, and his face became beetroot red. "Please, you've got…"

Jeff clamped a hand to the man's mouth. "*Shh.*"
All Dylan could do was mumble under Jeff's hand.

"Whack him, Jeff." Ollie said.

Jeff removed his hand from Dylan's mouth. "Shut up, we won't let them harm you."

The front door came under severe blows as it rattled in the jamb, and Ollie could hear them out there, growling with excitement. They were close to getting in. The table came away from the window and crashed to the floor. A lump of granite came hurtling through the exposed window pane. Glass exploded. *They* were in.

Jeff let rip first, mowing three of them down as they tried to scramble through the window – the door appeared to be holding, for now.

"We've got to get that table back up, Jeff," Ollie shouted across the blazing gunfire.

Roxie and Maria joined the fray, emptying slug and shell into the hordes starting to gather at the window; Amy was now screaming as she hid under the table. Maria blasted one which managed to escape Jeff's bullets, and was in the living room. Her bullet caught it in the chest, pushing it back and out the window. Roxie also killed one, pumping three bullets into a teenage girl holding a sickle; she fell within the cottage, and wriggled about on the floor before coming to rest face up. Her blood drained out, soaking the boards beneath.

When there appeared to be no more movement outside, they all stopped shooting. The room was filled with gun smoke, causing Ollie to cough. Jeff walked to the window with caution, and peeked out. Bodies lay scattered across the ground.

One was still moving around on the floor. Jeff put a bullet in its head, spraying the grass with brain and blood. Jeff called Ollie closer.

"Look, out there," he told Ollie. Ollie poked his head out the window, and felt the cold night air cool his face. The army truck had been moved out into the field.

"How?" he said.

"Good question, because I have the keys to it."

"They must have…have…lifted the handbrake and pushed it out of the way?" Ollie said, a baffled look on his face.

"If that's the case, then they are getting much smarter," Jeff said, his tone sombre.

"Now you come to mention it," Ollie said. "They did cut the tyres on our bikes, and the truck."

"True," Jeff said.

"And they managed to kill the power in the petrol station," Maria added.

"I didn't want to say anything last night," Jeff said. "But I'm sure I saw one of them wave at me when I was on guard last...shit!"

One jumped from out of the darkness, its face a blood-soaked mess. He swung at Ollie with a baseball bat, but missed, giving Jeff the opportunity to plunge the small, lethal bayonet on the end of his machine-gun deep into the thing's neck. Jeff twisted the steel to one side, and on retraction, a chunk of the thing's throat came away with the knife; blood spattered Jeff's face.

"*Shit!*" Ollie shouted. His face had lost its colour.

"We have to go out there and get the truck back in place," Jeff said.

Ollie looked at Jeff, and knew that it had to be done.

Chapter 8

Ollie and Jeff looked at the teen girl lying dead on the floor. Roxie had managed to hit the girl twice in the chest area, and once in the face; half the girl's jaw was missing. The two men caught hold of an arm each, and dragged the body to the window, throwing it outside with the rest.

Ollie unlocked the door, and peeped out. The coast seemed clear at the moment.

"Jeff, toss me the keys to the truck," Ollie said.

"You can't go…" Jeff tried to protest.

"Quick, we don't have much time, mun."

Jeff dug the keys from his pocket, and threw them over to Ollie.

"Get that table back up on the window, butty."

"Ollie, please, love, let someone go with you," Roxie pleaded.

"No, it will only slow me down. I'll be faster on my own."

"But—" she tried to argue.

"But nothing. I think you, Amy and Maria should go upstairs out of the way."

"Yeah, me too," said Jeff. "Just until we are safe again."

"What the fuck about me?" Dylan shouted.

115

Ollie stormed over to the man on the floor – his temper lost – and slammed the butt of his gun into Dylan's face, knocking him out.

"Ollie!" Maria shouted.

"Get upstairs, now, the three of you," Ollie shouted.

Jeff didn't protest. As he picked up the table, blood-stained glass slid off it and sprinkled the floor. He saw Ollie leave the cottage as he heaved it up against the window.

"Maria, pass me over the jar of nails and the hammer, please."

"Where did you put them?"

"I think Ollie took them out to the kitchen last night," Roxie said.

Once Jeff had the hammer and nails, he told the women to go upstairs with Amy, saying that he would look after the unconscious Dylan, and wait for Ollie to get back.

*

Ollie made his way over to the army truck which had been pushed a good twenty feet from the cottage. Nothing seemed to move in the field, which was lit up by fires burning in nearby Twsc. It appeared they had killed all that had been outside. But Ollie couldn't be sure of this, so he commando-sneaked through the long grass, keeping his ears pricked.

116

He turned slowly upon hearing a thumping coming from inside the cottage, and remembered that Jeff was placing the table back over the window. Ollie reached the back of the truck, and looked in. Nothing. Standing with his back to the truck, he held the gun upward and tight to his chest. He counted – one, two, three. He looked around the corner. Nothing. He shuffled over to the other end of the truck and, without counting, peered around. Two eyes glared back at him, and Ollie shouted as the thing winked at him.

Ollie jumped back, trying to lower his gun to shoot, but the thing leapt onto him, the weight almost crushing him. Hungry fingers dug at his eyes, pulled at his hair and found their way into Ollie's mouth, pulling at his tongue. Ollie tried to scream, to force the dirty digits out of his gob, but failed. The thing was drooling all over him. Ollie managed to stay upright, and tried ramming the thing against the truck, again and again and again, until eventually it lost its grip on him and fell to the floor.

Ollie took full advantage of this – kicked the ageing man in the teeth, which flipped him over onto his back. He growled up at Ollie, spitting chippings of broken teeth and blood at him. Ollie didn't hesitate, using the bayonet on his machine gun. He stabbed the steel into the man's heart, then stepped on the body to help yank the blade free. "Got you," he spat.

He made his way to the cab of the truck, and opened the door slowly, pointing his gun out in front of him. It was empty. Ollie jumped in behind the wheel and started the truck. He reversed it back as far as he could, before the dead bodies outside the cottage stopped him.

Jeff came out to see Ollie rush from the truck's driver side.

"I have to move these bodies out of the way, Jeff, mate."

"Okay, I'll give you a hand."

"No, mun. Keep me covered while I do it. I've already almost had my arse chewed off."

As Ollie started dragging the bodies away from the window, Jeff swept the field with his gun. He could hear the grass rustle in the distance. Then, whatever was out there, came closer. He trained his gun in the direction he thought it was coming from in the darkness, and walked toward it. A low snarl filled the night.

"Jeff, where the fuck are you going?" Ollie snapped.

"Shh, I hear one over here. Keep going, I got you covered."

Jeff waded out into the darkness, and by the shadow light of the fires, he saw something low and moving in the grass in front of him, less than thirty feet away. Then movement to the right – then left.

"Shit, Ollie, I got three or four of them coming at us."

"Kill the bastards, mun. Don't worry about ammo, we have plenty inside."

More snarling – louder, closer – on top of him. Jeff hunched lower, trying to see between the blades of grass. He lifted his gun and peered down the sights. Directly in front of him the grass moved – he fired a burst of rounds then ceased fire. He heard his target whine and flop in the grass.

"Fuck, fuck."

"What's wrong?" Ollie called.

"Dogs," Jeff said. "And lots of them."

One sprung out of cover at Jeff, its face ravaged and pulpy. Its eyes black like tiny cuttings of coal. Its body filled with welts which seeped blood. Jeff jumped back out of the leaping dog's way, but his feet got entangled in the grass, and he fell backwards, losing his grip on his gun, which flew into the night.

The dog was on him, trying brutally to rip his throat out. Jeff managed to get his hands on the mutt's snout, and clamped its jaws closed.

"Ollie, help, help, for Christ's sake, help," Jeff screamed. His lungs burned. Tears stung his eyes, and his body hurt from the ripping claws of the dog.

Jeff didn't hear Ollie rush through the grass to his aid, nor did he see him grab the dog, but he did see the way in which Ollie snapped the dog's neck in one swift move. The hound yelped, just the once.

"Get inside, Jeff, bach," Ollie shouted. "I've cleared the bodies."

Jeff watched as Ollie shot another approaching dog before jumping into the truck. He got to his feet, found his gun nearby, and headed into the cottage. He heard the truck scrape the walls as Ollie parked it up tight to the building. He went to the door and saw Ollie rip the wires from under the steering column and slice them up with his knife. He then shuffled over to the passenger door, and started to get out.

"Where the hell are you going?" Jeff asked.

"To make sure."

"To make sure of *what*?"

"That they can never move this thing again."

Ollie got out of the truck and went around the front. He opened fire on the tyre that had not been punctured the previous night, then did the same to the back one.

"Let's see them push it on four flats," Ollie said, and smiled.

He got back into the cab, shuffled over to the driver's side door, got out, and went into the cottage. He shut and locked the door behind him. Ollie looked at Dylan – the man was still out cold; his head hung low. A thick line of saliva hung from his open mouth. A bruise was forming at the side of his temple.

"Shit," Ollie said. "I shouldn't have hit him like that."

"There wasn't a call for it, I agree. But I'm not sure I trust him that much either," Jeff said.

"Hmm. Where are the girls?"

"They went upstairs, out of the way," Jeff said.

Ollie walked over to the bottom of the stairs, and shouted up. "You can come down now, the coast is clear." Ollie made his way over to Dylan, slipping on the blood and glass as he went. "Damn it," he said, but he managed to steady himself. He bent over Dylan, and shook the man by his shoulder. "Dylan? Dylan?" Ollie called. "Hope I ain't killed him, Jeff."

"Let me see." Jeff grabbed Dylan's wrist and felt for a pulse. "He's fine, just out of it."

Roxie, Amy and Maria came rushing down from the second floor.

"Are you two alright, then?" Roxie ask.

"Apart from my sides," Jeff said. "A dog attacked me out there. The bloody thing stamped all over me, dug its claws into my sides and chest."

Maria pulled Jeff's jumper up, and examined the areas. "The pooch didn't appear to break any skin. You have scratches, but that's about it. You'll be fine."

They all sat back at the table, and Amy drank some fizzy pop while she chatted quietly to Roxie. They all discussed what had just happened, and what they needed to do next.

Ollie had taken first watch, just as he'd wanted. Dylan had taken a few hours to come around after Ollie had hit him, and his mood had been foul. He'd refused to even look at Ollie, or answer any of Ollie's questions. Now Ollie was sitting opposite his prisoner, who was asleep.

Ollie got up from where he was sitting to make a sweep of the house, his machine-gun strapped to his back. He firstly checked upstairs, then out the kitchen, then finally out the back. There didn't seem to be any of them hanging around outside, certainly not at the rear of the house. Maybe they had killed all of the ones in the nearby area.

Once he was finished at the back of the house, Ollie went to the main window. He could feel a breeze coming through the hole there. He sighed with relief, and sucked in the cool air; there were none out front either..*That will make escape easier tomorrow*, Ollie thought, looking behind him for a moment – Dylan was still asleep. Everyone was asleep.

Jeff and Maria were propped against the wall next to the fire with a blanket over them; they looked so peaceful. It was going to be a shame having to wake Jeff for his turn to take watch. Maybe he would give it another half an hour before he woke him. The guy was starting to get on a bit; Ollie sniggered at that thought.

Then he looked over at Roxie, who was snuggled up to Amy in front of the fire. They too looked still amidst everything that was going on in the world.

He sat opposite Dylan, and cast his mind back to Roxie playing snap with Amy. She had really managed to bring the child out of her shell, making her forget the horror she had been subjected to the day before. Then his mind wandered to how lucky they had been with the infected, and how they could all have been killed.

Were *they* getting smart? Was that possible? He ran over the facts in his head. Maria had told him that they had pulled all the wires out of the cameras at the petrol station. But that could have just been luck, right? After all, they were just wrecking the joint in a mad way. They couldn't possibly know how to bring the power down, their minds are just mush? Then how do you explain one waving at Jeff the other night? *And the one that winked at me?* Ollie thought. They could be becoming intelligent – evolving into something different, somehow. But if that's the case, then why don't they know what they are doing, for fuck's sake? And then there was the tyre slashing, and the moving of the truck. They must have been working together to have moved it. Communicated with each other. In grunts? "Huh," he scoffed.

Ollie didn't want to think about it anymore, he was scaring himself. He wanted sleep. He needed to hold Roxie. He got up and headed over to Jeff, throwing a few logs onto the fire as he did so, and shook the sleeping man by the shoulder.

"Jeff," Ollie whispered. "Jeff, butt, wake up."

After another couple of shakes, Jeff blinked his eyes open. "I'm awake," he yawned. "How long have I been out?"

Ollie looked at the small clock they had picked up. "Around four hours, mate."

"Oh, God, my back."

Ollie smiled, "Yeah, well, you ain't getting any younger to be sleeping around on floors, are you?"

"Bloody cheek. Go on, go and get some sleep, Ollie. We need to have our wits about us tomorrow."

"Aye, we will, mate. I don't think you'll have much trouble out of Dylan – he hasn't moved since we settled down."

Both men spoke in hushed voices so as not to wake the others.

"Right, I'm off for some kip," Ollie said. "Oh, and I think we may have killed all the infected that were hanging around this area."

"Hmm," Jeff said. "Are you sure about that?"

"Ain't seen any for hours now, butty. I'll have one more look upstairs now before I head off to bed."

"Okay, but it sounds promising," Jeff said.

"Yeah, it does. Right, I'm heading upstairs for one last sweep."

Jeff nodded, and went to sit over by the window. He liked it there; he could see out. He had nailed the table up in such a way this time that he had more of a gap his side to see out of. He looked over at Ollie, who was heading up to the second floor. Roxie began to stir. He gave Dylan the once over; he didn't move.

Outside seemed to be deserted, and a cold, harsh wind blew in through the hole in the glass, fanning Jeff's face. He didn't mind it – it was nice to be able to cool down after being in front of the fire for so long. He'd move in a while, but first he wanted to sit and think.

Ollie went into the first room at the top of the stairs. He didn't hesitate, knowing there was nothing up there. The room was empty: no furniture, no beds. Nothing. He went to the window and looked out. The field outside was empty. He turned and headed out the door and into the next room. On the landing he could hear Jeff tell Roxie that he was upstairs. Ollie didn't pause, and instead went to the next door, into a box-sized room with a double bed and a dirty duvet. He went straight to the window. The scene was the same – there were none of those things left alive.

"Ollie?" Roxie's soft voice called. "I love you," she whispered.

He gulped. "Where did that come from?" he managed, and turned to face her.

"I never got to tell you properly, earlier."

"That's okay; I know the score, beaut." He walked over to her and pushed some of her hair back out of her face, and stroked her cheek. He put both his hands on her face, and drew it in close to his. Placing his rough lips on her soft, dry ones, he kissed her once. He ran one hand through her hair and massaged the base of her small skull. He pushed her softly away.

"What did you tell Jeff?"

"That I needed to see you – he's not stupid, Ollie."

He smiled.

They went to the bed and lay down.

Roxie ran her hands down his body as their clothed legs intertwined in knots of love. They kissed each other, softly at first – then more rushed, frenzied. Ollie put his hands to her body, and felt her breasts through her clothes; she groaned slightly.

She stopped his hands, and pulled her top and bra free.

She snuggled back into him, and kissed him some more. He pulled away, and gently nuzzled at the side of her neck, kissing and teasing, before going to her breasts. He felt her hands at the waistband of his jeans, tugging the belt open and lowering the zip. She slipped them down his legs to his knees, and he did the rest using his feet. Ollie then helped Roxie out of her trousers.

This feels wrong, Roxie thought, but she needed him, wanted him. She felt that their love had been parted somewhat over the past few days; that whatever was happening to the world was crushing everything. Normal life would never be the same again. And, although they told each other every day that they loved one another, they were only words. She wanted to *feel* it. Much like she knew Ollie needed to feel it. Death scared Ollie, she knew that. Because death was the only thing that was ever going to keep them apart, forever. And that scared the hell out of him. Eternal loneliness shared only with darkness.

She turned onto her side and felt Ollie enter her. She pressed her back to his chest, and let him thrust back and forth without moving her own body or hips. He put his arms around her body, pressing her closer to him. His hand went back to her breasts, and he began massaging them again – teasing the nipples.

He pulled out of her, and Roxie rolled onto her back. Ollie got on top, and thrust into her again, slowly pumping in and out as they looked each other in the eyes, and kissed.

"I love you," Ollie said.

"I love you, too," Roxie said.

His climax was hard, and he had to bury his face into Roxie's neck area to stop himself from shouting out. Roxie muffled her face with the blanket. They both lay there, burnt out, Ollie holding her tight.

"Ollie?"

"Yes, beaut?"

"Do you think we will ever have children of our own?"

He faced her.

"I'd like to think so," he said.

"Would you give up the road, start up a family with me?"

"Of course I would, beaut, in a heartbeat."

She smiled. "You're a good man, Ollie."

"That's a laugh," he said. "What about the things I have done? The people I have hurt for the gang?"

"You haven't been that man for years, Ollie. Not since I have been with you."

He shook his head, "Maybe you're right." He sighed. "I know I don't want that life ever again. I want to live normal, like. You know what I mean?"

"Of course I do."

"When we get out of this bloody mess, maybe we can start a family?" he said.

"I'd like that, Ollie," she said, kissing him.

"And Amy. We will have to take care of her now."

"Yes, I'd like that too," Roxie said.

He gave her kiss before getting up and putting his clothes on.

"Best we go back downstairs, beaut," he said.

She didn't answer, just smiled and nodded before dressing. For the first time since the outbreak started, she felt things were going to be fine, that they were all going to pull through this mess as long as they had each other.

Ollie walked out the door, and was struck across the back of the head by a sharp blow.

*

Ollie was dreaming; dreaming of drowning. In the dream he was a young boy of about ten, and he was out in the middle of a lake. He'd swum out there to meet his friend who was no longer there. He'd been fooled. And now he was alone and scared. The wood that encircled the lake was dense. Empty. Only blackness looked out at him as he struggled to try and keep afloat; the sun began to set as he flayed his arms in the icy water. He tried calling for someone, anyone, to come and help him. But nobody came or called back.

Then he was under the water, engulfed by the chilly liquid which stabbed at his body. It felt like there were a million icicles trying to penetrate his flesh. His feet become entangled in reeds and seaweed, and nothing could be seen above but darkness. His lungs were almost at bursting point. Water started to find its way into Ollie's mouth…

He woke up screaming, his lungs aching. He could still feel the cold water running down his face, finding its way into his mouth. Then he realised he was awake, and that the water on his face was real. So was the gun pointing at him, with a grinning Dylan behind it.

"Good morning, *shithead*. I hope you're ready to meet your maker," Dylan said, throwing the empty cup to one side.

Chapter 9

Panic seized Ollie as he went for Dylan, but he couldn't move. He looked down and discovered he was chained to one of the chairs from out the back. He thrashed in the seat, but it was no use. The chain was padlocked behind his back.

"Ha-ha! That's it tough guy, keep it up," Dylan said. "You won't be going anywhere, butty."

"Urggghh," Ollie grunted, and looked up at the man: he had a sort of clean-cut image that had been spoilt by a few days of growth on his chin – a killer with a smile. His teeth were perfect; his hair neat and almost girlish, but greasy. He didn't cut much of a threatening pose, even standing over Ollie, despite his stocky build.

Dylan clipped Ollie over the head with the Browning pistol in an attempt to calm him down.

"Keep still or I'll blow your fucking brains out," Dylan said, forcing the muzzle of the gun into Ollie's forehead; digging the cold steel into Ollie's skin as hard as he could, hoping it was hurting.

"Not so tough now, are you, action man? Maybe I should stuff the barrel of this gun up your arse and pull the trigger?" He let out a silent cracking laugh.

Ollie started to rage in his seat again; the veins in his arms protruded as he flexed and strained against the steel. He sweated profuse in his attempt to be free, then relaxed, exhausted. All the time Dylan laughed as he watched the man writhe.

"You fucking *cunt*!" Ollie shouted.

"Ha-ha! This is fun. Let's see how you react to this." He stepped aside to reveal Roxie and Amy. They, too, were bound to chairs – backs to one another – with rope. Amy was crying. Roxie appeared to be out cold. Ollie completely lost it.

"Let me out of this fucking chair, you bastard!" he yelled. The plastic chair Ollie was tied to creaked under his lunatic movements. "I get out of this seat, boy, and you're a dead man."

"Tough words coming from a man who's chained up with a gun on him. You really ain't scared to die, are you? Quite the hero."

Dylan smacked Ollie across the face, this time with the gun, causing a tooth to surf out of Ollie's mouth on strings of bloody saliva. Ollie's head rolled on its plinth, and his eyes flickered as he fought to stay conscious. Where the hell were Jeff and Maria while this was going on?

Then a harsh hand slapped Ollie around the chops, almost bringing his focus back. Then another slap, a third, fourth, fifth. He shook his head, and the hand was gone.

"Don't you fucking faint on me, boy," Dylan said. "I want you awake for the main event." He smiled down at Ollie, and turned away from him. Ollie saw that Dylan had one of the machine-guns shouldered, and Ollie's knife sheathed at the hip. Dylan holstered the Browning behind his back and picked up the other SA80. Its bayonet was sticky with dried blood. Jeff's gun.

"Not a bad old machine-gun, if you ask me," Dylan said. "Not quite sure what our boys have been complaining about out in Afghanistan." He drew the cocking mechanism back, and let it go. The loud *snick-snack* noise brought Roxie around. Amy continued to weep silently.

"It'll be okay," Ollie said to the young girl.

Dylan scoffed, "Huh, they all say that."

"Urrghhh," Roxie mumbled. "W…w…w…" She trailed off, and her head dropped back down, her chin touching her chest.

Ollie looked about him, and saw Jeff and Maria lying on the floor – untied. Jeff had blood spilling from his forehead, and Maria wasn't moving. Dead? No, she couldn't be. Then he saw the pipe Dylan had been cuffed to; it had been pulled from the wall. As he looked at Maria again, Ollie saw her stomach moving. Thank God for…The butt of the SA80 was planted into Ollie's gut. He gagged for air as he listened to Dylan laugh.

Ollie's scalp burned. He yelled out as his head was pulled back. His neck clicked as he stared up at Dylan.

"Don't you fucking pass out on me," Dylan said, and spat on Ollie's face. "This is what you get for killing another man's brother."

"Leave him alone, you bloody freak," Amy cried out. "He ain't done anything to you."

Dylan let Ollie's hair go, and walked over to Amy. He bent down in front of the child, so that he was eye level, and grabbed her by the cheeks as hard as he could, causing the young girl to scream out.

"Not done anything, you say? He killed my brother, you little bitch." He let her face go, roughly, and stood up straight. He picked up the machine-gun and pointed it at her face. She screamed and screamed. Tears rolled down her face, and Dylan grinned.

"Shut up. Stop that fucking noise," he told her. Amy wriggled in her seat, but she couldn't move. Then she realised the bayonet of the gun moving closer to her. She whimpered and sat back as far as she could in her chair.

"Ever wondered what a popped eyeball would look like, bitch? Or the pain of feeling cold steel slide its way into the mushy texture of your eye? Hmm?" He stopped the tip of the blade just shy of Amy's left eyeball, teased her with gentle thrusts.

"Get away from her. She's just a child, mun," Ollie managed. "Come back over here and pick on me some more."

"I do love your appetite for pain, Ollie, boy." He put the machine-gun down, and drew the knife at his hip. Standing in front of Ollie, he jabbed the knife's point underneath Ollie's chin, digging it in softly. Blood formed and a thin stream seeped down the knife's edge, and pattered onto the floor.

Ollie scrunched his face up tight, and absorbed the pain. He felt like the knife was going to punch through his throat. Then it was gone, and gliding across his chest in zigzag movements, cutting shallow lines. Searing heat scolded his whole body, and he whimpered in the grip of it. A fierce left hook came from nowhere, and threw his head to one side. Blood pumped out of his sagging mouth. He spat another tooth free.

"Is that all you got?" he said, and laughed. "Your child-touching brother was tougher—" A second punch, followed by a third stopped Ollie chatting.

"Don't you fucking talk about him," Dylan screamed. "Don't you fucking dare, you *motherfucker*!"

"Ha-ha. You're fucking pathetic," Ollie said.

135

"Shh, Ollie, you're making him worse," Amy said.

Dylan turned to look at her over his shoulder. "Another word out of you, bitch, and I'll come over there and slice your tongue out."

He turned back to Ollie, and ran his fingers across the glaring slit on the big man's chest. Ollie pulled his lips back and shouted through his clenched teeth. "Aarrgggh." He opened his eyes to see Dylan lick the blood from his fingers.

"Delicious, mun."

"You sick fuck," Ollie said.

"Ha-ha! Yeah, I guess you could say that."

"And I'm guessing it was you who killed Amy's parents?"

"Hmm, right again."

"You—"

"Now, now. If you keep behaving like that, you won't get to hear what I *did* to them," he said, and smiled

"I'm sure you're going to tell me anyway."

He punched Ollie in the guts. "Shut up."

Ollie coughed out blood, and wheezed for air.

Dylan looked over at Roxie; she was still out. So were Jeff and Maria.

"See, the thing is: me and my brother escaped from an army research facility not far from here. The place is isolated in a field on the border of Twsc."

As he spoke he circled Ollie with the knife, all the time keeping his eye on Amy and Roxie, and occasionally checking the two on the floor.

"Me and my brother, Eddie, were sent there from Broadmoor prison. We were lifers, you see, not much chance of getting out. And we were not the only ones, oh no, they had scores of us, all lifers, from different prisons across the fucking U.K."

Ollie felt for where the chains were clasped behind him, and found a rusted lock which held the chains together. He twisted the padlock, which did nothing, but he kept doing it. Bits of corroded steel filings came off in his attempts, and snowed onto the floor. Ollie continued to work away at it as he listened to Dylan speak.

"They were running some kind of fancy experiment there, injecting us with different kinds of shitty fluids, like. And as I said, me and Eddie got free. I think we managed to infect the whole town by bathing in the lake, the one the town gets their water supply from."

Dylan circled Ollie once more, heading over to the main window of the cottage. He peeked out. It was daylight. He could see none of *them* outside. They had gone. Or maybe there just weren't any left in the area.

"I mean, we had to wash when we escaped. We crawled through the sewage system to get out of the place, and Eddie cut himself in the process. His blood must have got into the water. Fuck that's funny. Ah well, bollocks to it."

"So if you are pumped full of some military experiment shit," Ollie said, "why aren't you sick?"

"Good question and one I can't answer. Me and Eddie seemed immune to any kind of reaction," he smiled. "I think Jeff and you might have done a bloody good job last night, boy. Mowed them all down. Great. It will make my escape with Jeff much easier." Ollie looked at him intently. "What? What you looking at me like that for? You didn't think I was going to take you all with me, did you? Especially *you* Ollie? You have a debt owing to me."

Dylan walked over to Ollie; his footfalls reverberated through the walls of the cottage.

"The thing is Ollie, you killed my brother, and the penalty for that is death. But not before I finish telling you my story."

"Go to fucking hell, pig," Ollie said, and tried to head-butt Dylan's face, which was almost close enough. Dylan stepped back, and holstered the knife.

"Fuck me you're one tough nut to crack," Dylan said, and laid into Ollie's stomach with more punches, combining lefts with rights, leaving Ollie breathless.

"As I was saying. Me and Eddie were transported from Broadmoor prison to this research facility, see.

Yeah, they had the finest collection of nut jobs going. All locked up in one lab."

"Is this how this thing all started? This outbreak or whatever the hell it is?" He could see Amy looking over at Dylan too. She had stopped crying.

"If you close your mouth for a minute, I'll get around to telling you. Now keep it closed or I'll nail it shut.

"From what I could make out, they were looking for some kind of new weapon to use on enemy troops. They never told us, of course; I just managed to get hold of snippets here and there. Fuck, whatever they were pumping into us made some of the cons go fucking nuts. Again, I didn't see much, just caught wind of stuff."

Dylan walked back to the window, and looked out again. The sun was so bright in the sky; it was drenching the ground in gold. It was one of the nicest days he had seen since the epidemic. Dylan went to talk again, but something very odd caught his eye. There was someone standing under one of the trees by the wood. Just standing there, facing the cottage.

Strange. Can't be one of them. It's daylight. Dylan walked over to the door, opened it, climbed into the truck's cab, and out the other side. The person by the tree had gone. What the fuck, he thought. Where in the hell did they go to? He didn't fancy going over there to take a look, and instead went back inside the cottage where it was safe.

All the time he was outside Ollie worked at the lock behind his back. He'd heard the thing groan a few times, but it had not yet yielded to his pressure. He'd also tried to reassure Amy whilst Dylan had been out of the room. Ollie had wanted to shout to Jeff and Maria, to try and get them to come around. But Ollie had not wanted to get Dylan riled again.

"Strange," Dylan said, with a confused look on his face.

Ollie held his breath, thinking Dylan had caught him trying to pry the lock free.

"I think one of them just stood out there in the fucking sun. I know it was under a tree, which would've shaded it a bit, but it's just too bright out there for them. What the hell is going on?"

Ollie was going to tell him about the things getting smarter over the past couple of days. That maybe they were starting to think again. That they could work together in packs, and were even able to communicate with each other. Maybe not through direct speech, but by grunts or growls. But they couldn't prove it. Besides, Ollie thought, let Dylan work it out for himself. He smiled.

"What the fuck you finding so funny? Huh?" Dylan marched over to Ollie and punched him on the nose. The bones crunched under the solid blow, and sent Ollie's head flying back. "You ain't smiling now, are you?"

Ollie picked his head up, his nose a bloody, streaming mass, and looked Dylan in the eyes. "I am going to kill you. Just like I did Eddie."

Dylan went to lay more blows into Ollie, but Roxie started moving. He looked over at her, she was coming round – "It's time," Dylan said.

"Kill me, will you, boy?" Dylan went over to Roxie, and yanked her head back by her long hair. She screamed as torrid pain tore through her scalp. Ollie roared and bucked.

"Stop it you bastard, you're fucking hurting her."

"You haven't seen anything yet, boyo."

Dylan clamped his teeth on Roxie's nose, biting as hard as he could. Roxie began screeching and flaying madly in her seat. Amy shrieked and cried. Ollie shouted at Jeff and Maria, but they were still out cold. Streams of blood spilt down Roxie's face and found its way into her month. Ollie heard the bone crush in the vice-like squeeze that Dylan was applying to her nose with his teeth. Then he was off her.

The tears running down Ollie's face sent chills through Dylan's back. "Fancy a guy like you crying over a slut like this? She's only a woman."

Roxie screamed and cried in agonising pain.

"Please, don't hurt her any more. She…she's all…all…"

"She's what? Precious to you? The love of your life?"

"All I have left, please, don't…I…" Ollie sniffled.

"Shut up, will you. You're making me sick."

Dylan unsheathed the knife, and brandished it in front of Roxie's face, before showing the gleaming steel to Ollie. Dylan then turned back to Roxie, who yelled and spat at him. He took the knife and circled her breasts with it, before slicing her top open down the middle, revealing her bra. He cut through that too, exposing her breasts.

"Whoop, look at them. What a great set. A bit tiny for my liking, but perky as fuck. You're a lucky guy, Ollie, butty."

Roxie cried for Ollie, and he tried telling her that it would be all right. Dylan scoffed at their pathetic pleas, and began circling her left nipple with the icy steel until it was erect.

"Nice," he uttered, more to himself than anyone else. He bent over and started sucking at the nipple, flicking it with his tongue. Then he bit. Not too hard; just hard enough to make her howl out and for blood to form and trickle down to her navel. Dylan poked his tongue into her bellybutton and licked, clearing it of blood, before running his tongue all the way up the crimson trail, stopping at her breast before continuing up to her lips, kissing her.

Roxie struggled and somehow managed to work her right foot free from the binding. She planted it hard in his crotch. The air wheezed out of him, and blew into her mouth. As he doubled, her knee met his chin, and his mouth snapped shut. Dylan collapsed to the floor, grabbing his balls as he cursed the bitch dead.

Roxie tried frantically to work her other foot out of the knots before Dylan could recover. Ollie found hope, and applied all the strength he could to the lock, yelling out to Jeff, who appeared to be stirring on the floor. Dylan could see that the upper hand was slipping away from him. He needed to get up, but he couldn't. Tingling hurt kept him to the floor, and every time he went to move, a bolt of throbbing torture shot straight to his head, making him nauseous.

"Come on Jeff, get up. Please," Ollie shouted.

Roxie's other leg was free, but her hands were tied too tight. As much as she tried to rattle herself free, her bindings wouldn't move. Jeff slowly gathered himself into a kneeling position. He was breathing heavy. Dylan had also managed to compose himself, and got back to his feet. Roxie tried kicking him in the face, to try to do more damage, but he was out of

143

range and staggering towards Jeff. He booted the man in the ribs time and time again, until Jeff started coughing up blood. Jeff collapsed back to the floor, and Dylan rolled him over.

"Can't have you running out on me, plane boy. I'm going to need you. You're my ticket out of here."

"I'd rather die, than help you."

Jeff screamed out a torturous yell as Dylan punched the knife into his thigh, and twisted it.

"Now, now, Jeff. No need to be like that," he said, smiling. "You will help me, I am sure of that." He pulled the knife free and marched angrily back to Roxie. "Nice try bitch," he said. "But that's just cost you your life."

He sliced one of her exposed nipples off; her mouth flew open in shock, yet no sound came from her. Grabbing her by the hair, pulling her head back, he ripped the blade across her throat. Blood sprayed right across Dylan's face; he opened his mouth to try and catch some. Ollie screamed in his chair and cried floods of tears. He could hear Roxie gargling his name; flecks of blood spit out of the slash at her throat.

"How'd you like that, then, boy?" Dylan said. He gripped the hysterical Amy by the hair, and placed the knife to her throat. "This bitch is ne—"

He was cut off as the sound of Ollie's lock breaking echoed in the room. Dylan looked at Ollie, his face pasty at the sight of all the chains falling off Ollie's body. He stood up, just as Ollie came rushing at him, tackling him to the floor. Ollie's weight on top of him was crushing. Dylan tried rolling Ollie off him, but Ollie was too heavy. Then Dylan felt teeth at the side of his neck, and had no time to try and stop Ollie ripping his gullet open. As Dylan lay dying, Ollie rained blow upon blow, upon him, breaking his nose, cheek bones and jaw before finally digging his thumbs into the man's eyeballs, and gouging them inwards, turning them to mush. With each blow he yelled, shouted and cursed until he was breathless. He rolled off Dylan, and suddenly felt a wave of pain as he discovered his own knife poking out of his stomach.

Ollie tried to get up, but couldn't move. He wanted to be by Roxie. So he crawled. Crawled until he got to her, and had her hand in his. But they were bound at her sides, and in his struggle to set one of her hands free, the last ounce of breath was taken from him.

Chapter 10

When Jeff came around, he immediately clutched at his ribs. None of them felt broken. He got onto his back, and stared up at the ceiling. He stayed like that, unable to move, for a little bit. When he found enough ability in his body, he moved. His eyes firstly fell on Amy. She had her eyes closed tightly. Tears rolled down from the closed lids.

"Amy," Jeff coughed out. "Amy, Amy!" Her eyes remained closed. Then he saw Ollie on the floor. Dead. Roxie, too, was unmoving. A large pool of blood had formed under her seat.

"No, oh Jesus, no. Not them. Please no. God, no," he cried out. He got to his knees and turned to Maria. She was still, but with no sign of visible injury. As he shuffled over to her, pain ripped through him from the wound in his leg. He stopped, and put his hand to the wound. It was leaking blood, and by the looks of the floor, he had lost a fair bit of the stuff.

He shambled over to their table and whipped the small, dirty cloth from it. He tore it to shreds, and tied some around his leg. He then moved back to Maria, and put his fingers to her neck. He felt a slight pulse there. She was alive. Jeff struggled over to Amy, and shook her slightly.

"Amy, please. Amy! Please, come on, snap out of it, please," he said. He could taste his tears in his mouth. "We have to get out of here, now."

Amy's eyes opened, and she looked into Jeff's. "He killed them both," she blurted.

Jeff put his arms around the child, and hugged her close to him. "Shh," he cooed. "It'll be alright, I promise. But please, we have to get out of here." He used Amy to help him to his feet, where he untied her. He looked down at Dylan. The man's face was almost beyond recognition. His eyes were so swollen the eyelids could not be seen, his jaw hung loose in a shattered state, and a dent could be made out in his forehead.

Jeff pulled his gaze from the dead man, and proceeded to try to untie the child, but the knots were too tight.

"Please hurry," she said, pitifully.

"Okay, I'm trying."

He looked around for the knife, and saw it jutting out of Ollie's gut. Jeff didn't want to pull it free, so instead dug into his pocket, and pulled out a lighter he had picked up while shopping yesterday. He scorched the ropes binding the girls to the chairs just enough to make them fray, then snap. Amy sprung out of the seat and into Jeff's arms. He looked over the girl's shoulder, and saw Roxie slide out of her chair, and land on the floor next to Ollie.

Jeff pushed Amy from him, and looked her in the eye.

"Stand right here, and don't move. Don't look at the others, okay?"

She nodded and put her hands to her eyes to wipe her tears away.

"I need to wake Maria up. We need to get out of here as soon as we can," Jeff said.

Jeff left Amy and moved over to where Maria lay unconscious. He shook her roughly by the shoulder; his leg and head burst with agony. The cloth he had wrapped around his thigh was soaked through with his blood. He could feel the wound throb and pump.

"Maria, Maria," he shouted at her. "Please, wake up. We need to get out of here."

He continued to shake her, and she finally stirred after a few minutes of trying. "Thank God."

"Mmmm, my head," she said, as she rolled onto her back, lazily. "What happened? How long have I been out?"

"I don't have time to explain right now, Maria, but Ollie, Roxie and Dylan are all dead. The…"

She shot upright, intense shockwaves of hurt cutting through her brain, causing her to put her hands to the side of her head. "Jesus Christ, my head."

"Maria, come on, we have to get out of here," Jeff insisted, and pulled at her arm to get her moving."

She slowly managed to get herself standing, and saw the state of Jeff's leg.

"What the hell happened to your leg, Jeff?"

"I had a run in with Dylan."

"Here," she said, handing him one of the machine-guns to lean on.

"Let's gather what we need, and get to the jeep."

"Oh my God," Maria shouted, and began sobbing.

Jeff caught hold of her by the shoulders, and shook her.

"Listen to me, will you. Get what we need."

"But…Ollie, Rox…We can't just…"

"We've got to try and keep it together, not just for our sake, but for Amy," he said, raising his voice slightly.

They both looked at the young girl. Her head was bowed; her body shook with uncontrolled sobbing.

"Okay," Maria said.

"That's it. Come on," Jeff said. "Amy, love, we just need to get a few things together, and we'll be going. Just stay brave. You can do that, can't you?"

Again the child nodded.

Maria helped Jeff over to the table, and sat him down.

"Let me have a look at that wound."

"We—"

"We have enough time. If you get hurt too badly, then Amy and I will be stranded."

He reluctantly sat down, as she fetched more of the shredded cloth.

"Amy love, come here, please," Maria said. "Come and sit by us." Amy sat down, and stared at the wall. Maria stroked her hair, and tried to soothe her. "We'll be fine, I promise."

"He killed my mam and dad, he did," Amy said. "Just like he killed Ollie and Roxie."

"Dylan?" Maria asked her.

She nodded.

"He was telling me and Ollie how he and his brother escaped from some lab around her."

"Who's Dylan's brother?" Maria asked.

"The man that's dead upstairs with my sister."

Maria and Jeff looked at the girl, mouths agog.

"Shh now," Maria said, stroking the child's arms.

"I heard him mention a lab too," Jeff said. "I was semi-conscious at that point. Apparently there is some sort of army barracks in the area."

Maria turned to Jeff and slowly unwound the drenched cloth. The blood was still flowing badly.

Maria mopped some of it away, and used a fresh piece of cloth. This one she tied very tight. Jeff screamed.

"Sorry, I know it hurts, but once we get to the jeep, you can take some painkillers," Maria said.

He nodded.

"So what were Dylan and his brother doing at this lab, or army camp?" Maria said.

"I'm not totally sure, I didn't catch…" Jeff started.

"He told Ollie that they were being used by the army to test some new weapon or something," Amy said. "It involved viruses and things that were put into them." Her lip began to tremble.

"Hey, it's okay," Maria said. "Come on, it'll be fine. I just have to finish dressing Jeff's leg then we can go." She tickled Amy under the chin, and smiled at her.

She took a second strip of cloth, and did the same with that one as the first.

"I guess we will never know the full story," Jeff said. "But my guess is that Dylan and his brother walked that virus, or whatever the hell it is, out of that facility." He winced as the second bit of cloth was pulled tight, and knotted.

"It sounds that way," Maria agreed.

"They did come out of the place with the virus," Amy said. "That's what he said to Ollie anyway. That they infected the town's water."

"*Jesus,*" Maria said. "So they started this mess. We better get the hell out of here, right now. Stay put, Jeff. I'm just going to pack up the things we used last night."

"Okay, okay," he sighed, holding his leg. "But hurry."

Jeff took the time to check the magazine in the gun – it was half empty. He would need to get some more out of the crates before leaving. The Browning was nowhere to be seen, and the shotgun was out of shells. Roxie had used the last of them in the previous night's attack.

Jeff cast his eye over Ollie, and the other two, then onto the knife. It would be handy to have, he thought. Jeff couldn't see anything else amongst the dead that would be of any use to them.

Maria hurriedly gathered the stove up, and the radio, popping them into one of the holdalls. There didn't seem to be anything else worth taking.

"Right Jeff, that's all of it. Le—"

"Ammo; we need more of it."

"Right, okay."

"Is there room left in that bag?"

"Yes."

"Put as many clips in there as you can."

Maria stepped over to the ammunition crates, and lifted the lid on one of them. The sun was shining through the gaps in the big window, splashing the planks of the cottage with yellow beams. The heat that was rising in the place intensified the smell: blood, death and gun oil wafted around inside.

She took out a couple of clips at a time, and placed them in the bag, all the while trying not to look at the dead. She felt sick. Her heart sank at the thought of Ollie and Roxie dead. *I wonder…*Her thoughts were derailed as the sound of rapping on the front door interrupted her. It grew louder, and louder – *tap, tap, tap, tap, tap…*

Maria looked over at Jeff, his face ashen.

He cocked the gun.

She moved over to the door.

"Amy, hide," Jeff said. "Open the door," he told Maria.

"No…Jeff…I—"

"It's okay, just slowly open it."

Amy pressed herself to Jeff's back.

"What if…if…it's one of *them*?" Maria said.

"It might be a survivor, like us; *they* can't come out in the day," Jeff said.

She gulped, and her heart thundered as she went for the key. As soon as her fingers touched it – the knocking stopped.

"They can't knock doors, either," Jeff said, pointing the gun at the door. His hands shaking, his forehead bathed in sweat, Jeff started panting.

The locking mechanism on the door *clacked* as the bolts disengaged.

"Are you ready?" Jeff asked.

"Yes…"

The door burst open, flattening Maria against the wall behind her. Jeff fired – his shot found the thing's shoulder, which did nothing to slow it down, let alone stop it. It got close, and jumped at Jeff.

Jeff held the gun out in front of him, and skewered the thing on the bayonet. It tried to claw at Jeff as he held it at arm's length, which caused the strength in Jeff's arms to weaken and buckle, bringing the thing closer to his face.

Maria closed and bolted the door, ran over to Ollie, and tugged the knife from his guts. His blood sprayed up into her face. She got behind the thing on Jeff, and plunged the knife into the kidney area, again and again. It screeched out in agony, before relaxing and slumping onto Jeff, who pushed the body off him. Amy was hiding under the table.

"Shit, shit, shit, shit, shit…" Jeff repeated. "How the hell can it be out in the sun? I thought they couldn't come out during the day?"

Maria just stood there, unmoving.

"And another thing, she must have opened the door to the truck and climbed through. Jesus, they are getting smart."

Maria was unblinking.

"If this one was out in the day – then that means there are…" he trailed off, scared of what he was about to say next. "We have to go – now!"

Maria looked at him, and blinked.

"We have to."

She closed her eyes slowly and swallowed hard. Then nodded, and spoke. "Okay."

*

Jeff had reloaded both the machine-guns, and handed one to Maria. He had the holdall on his back, and was now climbing through the cab of the army truck. He'd told Maria to stay behind with Amy until he knew it was clear.

The heat inside the cab was extreme; the leather seats scorching. The field ahead of him was clear. The wood seemed quiet too. He checked the top of the wagon and found no-one lurking up there. Could it have been just a fluke? One of them just got brave and tried coming out in the daylight? Jeff thought. He called to Maria, telling her that the coast appeared to be clear.

Maria sent Amy through the cab first, and followed close behind. On the other side, Jeff helped

Amy down, then Maria. She had Ollie's knife tucked into the waistband of her jeans. Her machine-gun shouldered. In her left hand she held the pitchfork Ollie and Jeff had found out in the shed the previous night.

"Let's get the hell out of here," he said.

Jeff hobbled as fast as he could across the field, with Amy and Maria tight at his sides. He swept the area time and time again, making sure that there were no more of them. At the top of the hill, they looked down onto Twsc – nothing had changed; except the cars that had been burning were burnt out; so too were the buildings. They were in time to see one of *them* collapse into a dusty, smouldering pile.

"Jesus," was all Jeff could say.

"Jeff!" Amy shouted.

He turned in time to see another thing running towards the three of them.

"Save your bullets," Maria said.

Maria hunched low as the thing drew near. She held the fork out in front of her, hoping to spear it. But stopping just shy of the prongs, it grinned at her, before ripping the fork out of her hands and turning it on Maria.

Jeff rattled off half a dozen rounds, taking the thing to the floor instantly. Maria picked the fork back up, and they all headed down into town.

"It grinned at me," Maria said. "It bloody grinned at me, for God's sake, Jeff. How? It knew what it was doing. It knew what I was doing, too!""

"I'm scared," Amy said.

"Come here," Maria said, and held the girl's hand. "You're not the only one."

"We have to assume now that they can survive in the daylight, and that they are definitely starting to think like humans again," Jeff said.

"Maybe only a handful of them can do this at the moment?" Maria said.

"If that's right, then we should be okay for the time being."

"I hope so."

They got to the jeep and Maria jumped in behind the wheel, knowing Jeff would have difficulties operating the pedals. Nothing had come at them between the hill and the jeep, and the town appeared nothing more than a ruin.

Jeff got in the passenger's side, as Amy climbed into the back. Jeff threw the holdall onto the back seat next to Amy. Once they were all in, Maria engaged the locks. She bent down and fumbled with the wires under the steering column. Ollie had to undo them yesterday to prevent the jeep from running.

"Shit," she muttered.

"What's wrong?" Jeff asked

"The light in here is poor. I can't see what the hell I'm doing."

Amy screamed as a dustbin ricocheted off the windshield of the Toyota, causing a thin split to develop in the glass. The thing that threw it was a fat, bald man with glasses; his body naked; his flesh covered in boils and erupting blisters, which pissed yellow fluid. He bent down to pick up the rubbish bin again, but the jeep kicked to life and Maria pushed the pedal to the floor. The back wheels spun, throwing up grey smoke. Maria ploughed straight through the tubby guy, who landed on the bonnet. His face smashed into the thick glass, and his skull disintegrated; chunks of brain and gobs of blood splashed onto the roof. When Maria took the corner out of the street they were parked in, the body slid off, tumbling into a parked car.

"Get the map out of the holdall, please, Amy, and give it to Jeff, there's a good girl," Maria said.

She heard the girl rustling around in the bag, looking for the map which was buried under the stove, radio and ammunition.

"I have it," she said, and handed it to Jeff.

"Great," Jeff said.

"See if you can find the first aid box in one of the bags behind you, Amy," Maria asked her.

Amy turned in her seat, and got to her knees. She looked over the back seat and saw another holdall there. She unclipped the hood on the bag, and pulled at the cords. Inside she found clothes, food, knives, a hatchet, and the first aid kit. She snatched it out, and climbed back over the seat, giving the small green box to Jeff.

"Got it," she said.

Jeff opened it and took out a small bottle of pills marked *Paracetamol.* He uncapped the lid, and plucked out two small pills – he swallowed them dry. He then picked out some dressing, a bottle of antiseptic, gauze, a swab and scissors.

Maria slowed the Toyota so that Jeff could work on his leg. He undid the soaked cloth on his thigh, and cut the leg of his trousers open. The wound itself wasn't really that deep, but Dylan had ripped the knife downwards, causing a nasty gash in Jeff's flesh. He swabbed the area first, then soaked the wound in antiseptic; gritting his teeth as the alcohol-based substance absorbed into his skin. Jeff gripped the dashboard and dug his fingers into the plastic, trying his best to fight the urge to scream.

Once the burning sensation had gone, he applied the gauze to the area followed by an abundance of dressing.

"This will have to do for now," Jeff said. "First chance I get, I'll sew it."

They drove through Twsc slowly, hoping a survivor would see them, and come running to them for help. But nobody did. The Asda Jeff and Roxie had gone to yesterday was nothing more than a burnt-out shell now. They are definitely getting smart, Jeff thought; and *definitely* evolving.

They took all the B-roads on the map, which were nice and quiet, as they headed to the hangar. Jeff had worried that some of them would be blocked up with abandoned cars – but there was very little in the narrow, lane-like roads.

The fields were empty on either sides of the road; no cows, sheep or wildlife existed. No birds in the sky, only the sun. Jeff lowered his head. Life would never be the same again. Then he thought about Ollie and Roxie. He shook his head.

"What's the matter," Maria asked?

"I was just thinking about the other two."

"Ollie and Roxie?"

"Yes."

"I know. I miss them already."

"Me too," Jeff said.

"What happened last night, Jeff?"

"I don't really know; Dylan beat me pretty bad. I was unconscious."

"But before he beat you?" Maria pushed.

"He managed to work himself free from the pipe he was cuffed to – pulled it off the wall."

"Where were you at the time?"

"Out in the kitchen. And as I entered the living room to go back by the window, he jumped me. That's pretty much all I remember."

"I'm surprised Ollie didn't wake," Maria said.

"He was upstairs with Roxie."

"Upstairs? Both of them? But why?"

Jeff looked over at her, but said nothing.

"Oh, I see," Maria said. "I suppose, in a way, it was nice that they got to be with each other one final time."

"When I woke up, I was tied to Roxie," Amy said. "I saw him drag Ollie down the stairs."

"Is that all you saw?" Jeff asked.

"No, I saw Dylan hurt Ollie. He was hitting him, telling him about the lab."

Nobody spoke much after that as they got off the B-road and took another. This one was the same: dead. No sign of life from man or beast. There were, however, a few abandoned cars dotted here and there. Maria didn't stop at any of them, just in case there were infected in the area. Her thinking was that if anyone was alive, they would flag Maria and Jeff to a stop.

161

"Where are all the animals, Jeff?" Maria said.

"I have no idea. But I'm guessing wherever they are they must be sick – just like the dogs that came at Ollie and me last night."

Maria didn't have to manoeuvre around the deserted cars much, as most of them were off to the side, tight to the hedges. Then a two car pileup came into view around the next bend. The driver of the one vehicle was stretched out through the windshield, arms extended, touching the grill; the face was plastered to the crumpled bonnet with blood, its skull sliced wide open. The passenger was also dead; throat slit, eyes missing. As Maria drove closer, she could see that that person had been scalped. Nobody appeared to be in the other car, which smoked and hissed.

"Looks like this happened recently," Jeff said – darting his eyes around the scene as Maria crept the Toyota past the carnage. "I don't think we should take our time. Put your foot dow—"

Something heavy hit the roof of the jeep, causing them all to scream. The back window blew in, and Amy wailed as she was pulled back by her hair. Jeff turned in his seat, and tried to get in the back, but he was held in his seat by his belt. He fumbled for the release button.

"Shit, shit, I can't bloody mo…Hang on Amy…"

The child cried as she was pulled closer to the broken glass. The thing that had her was half in the car, and half out. It was almost free of sores on the face and arms. Only slight signs gave it away as being infected. A small island of yellow, orange spots had formed at the side of the thing's left nostril; its hair patchy – as though it had alopecia; the eyes pearl-white. It snapped its teeth like a ravenous alligator.

Amy wound her foot around one of the belts and anchored herself. Maria brought the 4x4 to a complete halt as Jeff finally managed to work his way out of his belt. He grabbed the pitchfork Maria had brought, and punched the rust-decayed prongs through the thing's face, snapping the handle of the garden tool with the driving force. One tine punctured its left eye, which popped and blew blood onto a side back window. The other three points dug into its mushy flesh, penetrating a cheek, the nose and the mouth. The thing squealed and fell away, taking the fork with it.

"Go," Jeff yelled. "For Christ's sake, go, Maria!"

Chapter 11

Somewhere inside the research facility at Twsc Army and Scientific Barracks...

"It's not SIV – or 'swine flu' as the media has dubbed it – I'd just like to make that clear from the off. What we are dealing with here is a new strain, a strain created by a team of highly trained researchers and scientists, put together by myself." He put the Dictaphone on pause and put it down by his side. The floor he sat on was a bloody mess, with broken glass strewn about the place like confetti. He picked up the bottle of Grouse from his side and took a couple of deep swigs before replacing the bottle back by his side. He wiped his lips dry of the fiery liquid. Picking the Dictaphone back up, he proceeded to tape once again, "Before I go on to talk about this new strain, and what I have unleashed on the world, I would like to give my full name, rank and number. Plus I want to explain a few things." He cleared his drying throat before speaking again. "My name is Jaime Hill, my rank is Colonel and Science Lab Technician of this research facility at Twsc, South Wales; my number is 722665.

"Seven days ago the influenza that we created – known as "defector virus", with the aid of six top researchers from around the country – got free. I am not totally sure how, but I think that Sarah Llewelyn, a member of my team who I did not manage to kill, may have contracted the strain from one of our many 'volunteers', and walked it out of here? That is the only explanation I can think of because Sarah left in a rush last Thursday, the 8th of June. Come the following Monday there was panic everywhere on our streets – the 12th of June, 2009. Hell, this whole facility came away at the seams; funny how the world can fall apart so quickly.

"Anyway, how it may or may not have got free isn't the real issue. What does matter is the fact that it's loose and causing carnage. I'm not sure the world can survive this threat, but if it does, I hope that this tape will be found, and that it will clear up a lot of unanswered questions.

"Defector virus, or virus-d as it is known by the team and myself, is an influenza made up of other deadly strains, created to do two things – to immobilize enemy troops, then have them turn on one another before finally succumbing to the flu-like disease forty-eight hours afterward. That was our intention, but the bug got smart. It was able to mutate beyond our imagination, and it got free before we could tame it, before we could bring it back under our control. I hate to think what it is totally capable of once it starts to infect people."

Jamie took another pause, and again downed a few more swallows of whisky before returning to the tape recorder.

"The main elements for virus-d were/are – swine influenza virus, bovine spongiform encephalopathy and FMD – commonly known as foot and mouth disease. We did test other viruses and diseases such as zoonosis, rift valley fever, human immunodeficiency virus, various cancers, leprosy, smallpox, tuberculosis and meningitis. But we found that swine influenza, bovine spongiform encephalopathy and FMD worked really well together – better than we'd thought possible. Although zoonosis did offer us some good qualities; like swine influenza, it is an infectious animal disease that can be transmitted to humans. Some of the 150 or so diseases are: anthrax, brucellosis, bovine tuberculosis and of course, rift valley fever. This is interesting for the record, because other researchers and scientists (hell, even the government) in this country were led to believe that RVT was only found in Saharan Africa, which caused a widespread outbreak in Egypt in the late 70's killing thousands. 'They' think it only causes a great threat to the people of the Middle East these days, but believe

166

me – we had it in this very lab to use at our disposal, that and many others alike."

His gaze fell upon Andrew O'Hara. He'd been the first to die, shot in the face three times by Jaime. One of the bullets must have exited the man's cranium, because most of the skull was missing. Jaime could see the damage the slug had caused the brain; it was like looking into an egg with its top cut off. Blood and brain had oozed onto the carpet; the dead man stared up at the ceiling with vacant eyes, his tongue lolling to one side of his open mouth. "He used to have such a great smile," Jamie said aloud. "I executed my team when I found out that virus-d had escaped. I was in fear that maybe one of the others would go to the press with what we were doing here, and blow the lid off everything. The backers to this project would have been most upset with me. I won't disclose who my financiers are just yet, because I want to finish telling about the virus-d."

"As I said, the strain created by my team and myself was meant to immobilize and defect enemy troops. The virus would have been put into bombs with the intention of dropping them down on enemy camps. On impact, a gas would release from the explosion – infecting enemy troops within a couple of miles radius, which would eventually peter out. When contaminated with the germ, the host will show signs

167

of swine flu such as fever, coughing, sore throat, body aches, headaches, chills, fatigue, diarrhoea and vomiting. This intertwined well with the FMD virus which causes fever and vomiting, but can also cause malaise, red ulcerative lesions of the oral tissue, and sometimes blisters on the skin.

"When these were combined with bovine spongiform encephalopathy and injected straight into a 'volunteer subject', tests showed at first they developed signs of weakness, exhaustion and incapability of eating. Hours after the first signs of a flu taking effect on our subjects, the vomiting and diarrhoea came on fast, bringing with it chills and headaches. By the time the blistering of the skin had come along, the host was mildly volatile towards my team and me. On destroying a female partaker, and giving her an autopsy, we could see that the BSE had totally shut the brain down with the aid of the other two viruses, causing explosive hallucinations. This had a knock on effect, causing the patient to strike out with hot-blooded aggression.

"We thought we'd cracked it after four years of trying, and all that was left to do was tweak what we had. But we were wrong. Our subjects become more and more aggressive. They developed the power to be able to heave acid liquid that disintegrated human skin. Their acidic vomit could even melt through the chains that harnessed them, making it harder for us to be able to keep them alive while we did tests on them. This was not necessarily a bad thing, until I lost a team member – Captain Howard Ford, my second in command. A male patient managed to get free, and on cornering Howard, unleashed that God awful sick onto his face, which melted its way down to the bones.

"Not long after this, we learned that virus-d had escaped our lab. At first the news coverage was casting it off as 'swine flu', but I knew different, so did my team. That's when I decided to take action – by firstly killing all our remaining test subjects, then locking my team and myself in one of our test labs. I executed them one by one."

He stopped talking and let his eyes drift around the room, from Andrew O'Hara to Tina Jones, who was slumped down dead in a swivel chair – half of her face missing. The once white lab coat she wore had absorbed most of the blood.

"You were such a pretty thing." Jaime let his stare linger on Tina for a moment, before finally moving on to Joe Hargreaves, who was sprawled on top of a table, his arms hanging over either side and his feet barely touching the ground; he had two craters in his chest. Samantha Kidd was lying on the floor by Joe's left arm. Bloody bullet holes graced her back. "Guess you won't be fucking each other anymore, kids." A wry smile spread across his lips. "I know I'm losing it, that's what being locked in a room for five days, with nothing but dead bodies to keep you company does to one's mind. After I've finished recording all I have to say, I'll be taking my own life. A small price to pay for the work I played a hand in."

He wiped tears from the corners of his eyes, and knocked the tape recorder off for the time being. Jaime guzzled some more whisky and tried to compose himself. He looked up at the ceiling, "When did the bombing stop?"

He was sure that he'd heard fighter planes overhead only hours ago; they had been almost constant from the outset of the virus attack.

"The army must have lost the war against the infected. That does not surprise me. If others had witnessed what we had seen the virus do in this very lab, then they would not have bothered trying to fight it, just run for the hills and tried to wait it out. God only knows what stage of transformation virus-d is currently in."

He clicked the Dictaphone back on, and began to speak in a trembling tone.

"I'm not entirely sure who our money men were. I know the order came from pretty high up in the army. Hell it may have been handed straight down from someone in the government. All I know is that I was reporting our findings back to a superior officer by the name of Weathers, Major General Weathers. I was picked out for the project because of my long service in the army, plus my immaculate record and knowledge of chemical warfare. I was told to handpick a team of extremely creditable scientist to aid me in creating this weapon, and that expense was no object. I was also told that my team and myself were to keep what we were doing quiet, that we should tell no-one. I thought that would have gone without saying? Having said that, you'll be wondering why I'm telling all now? The answer to that question is simple – guilt.

"Somewhere on this tape I said that virus-d got smart. When we first put defector virus together, it was weak under our control, so to speak. We knew it had weaknesses. But the more and more we tried this on one of the subjects that had been infected with the virus for well over three to four weeks, we found they became adapted to the light. This was not the only change in the host we noticed. The longer this virus festers away in someone's body and mind, the more and more it will evolve. It will turn the old and very young into vigorous killing machines. The weak of mind will also be infected in the same way. People who already have warped minds will become even more disturbed. We also observed their intelligence, and found that they could work together through basic language, such as grunts and snarls. Not only that, but some test subjects became intelligent quickly, evolved in a matter of hours after becoming injected. Virus-d is totally unstable – it's capable of anything once inside someone. My God, what have I helped release on the world."

He switched off the tape recorder, and the tears came. His body shook violently as he bowed his head and pinched the corners of his eyes to try and hold the tears back. Jaime remained like this for a few minutes, before finally getting to his feet and walking over the broken glass to an unoccupied table. He placed the tape from out of the recorder – 'my confession' written on it in pencil – on the table's top, next to an envelope marked *To My Darling Katrina*. He picked it up, kissed it once and spoke softly, "I hope you managed to escape it all." He turned to face his dead team. "I'm sorry."

He drew his Browning 9mm pistol from the holster at his hip, and placed the muzzle to his temple. The gun clicked on an empty chamber, and a second, and a third – *click, click, click*. Jaime threw the handgun to one side, scanned the other dead bodies for a gun. Nothing. Then his eyes fell on the near empty bottle of whisky. He ambled over to it on shaky legs, scooped it from the floor, guzzled the remaining amount of liquid and broke the bottle on the edge of a cabinet. He looked at the jagged end, and knew that he had to do it. He could hear the infected out in the corridors, all around him, beating at the door to the lab. Almost seven days he had put up with that; seven days of being walled in, surrounded by their ghastly moans and snarls. He rammed the jagged end of the bottle into his neck, retracted, stabbed, twisted. His body gave an aggressive spasm. Jaime collapsed against a wall, and let the blood squirt and flow freely without trying to well it. He spewed the words, "I'm sorry, I'm sorry," over and over again as he sat there dying, drooling stringy bloody-saliva onto his chest and lap.

Chapter 12

Jeff had swapped seats with Amy, letting the child sit up front with Maria for the rest of the journey, so that he could rest his leg on the back seat. They were now outside "Wings Flying Club". A few cars were parked in the clubhouse's car park. The windows to the small, pub-like building were a shattered mess – upstairs and down. A couple of dead bodies lay on the gravelled floor at the entrance to the place. Jeff recognised one of them as the owner. Derek Copper.

"The place looks deserted, Jeff," Maria said.

"We can't risk getting out. If you drive around back, you'll see a mesh fence circling the entire perimeter of the airfield."

"Then what?"

"We drive through it."

Maria went to speak again, but something caught her eye. In the darkness of one of the bottom windows of the clubhouse, she saw a face. It was coming closer out of the gloom.

"Jeff…Over there. Inside."

"Shit. Get us round back."

Then Jeff saw the muzzle flash and crackle of gunfire before the bullets started pelting the framework of the Toyota – *ting-ting-ting-ting-ting-ting-ting*.

"Down!" Jeff yelled

The windshield caved in; the grill hissed; the bonnet whined in peppered agony. Jeff could smell singed metal. Then he heard one of the front tyres rupture.

"Drive, drive, drive," he shouted.

Maria, with her head ducked behind the wheel, drove half-blind. Amy was hunched in the well. Bullets tapped at the passenger door as Maria veered the jeep to the left of the building, and went around the back. Then the firing stopped. They were out of the gunman's sight. Maria ploughed the 4x4 through the mesh fence, taking it with them for part of the route over the airfield before finally leaving it behind.

The tyre that had been shot out now ripped, and both Jeff and Maria heard it tear completely off the alloy. They were going to have to make it to Jeff's hangar on the rim, cutting their speed by more than half. This gave the shooter time to get out of the building, and back on their heels. Soon enough, bullets tore away at the arse of the Toyota: the backlights disintegrated under a pebble-dashing of hot lead; the dials on the dashboard burst and exploded.

"Brake," Jeff said. "And keep down."

Jeff grabbed the SA80 and waited for the gunman to run dry of ammo.

Maria felt like a sitting duck as bullets continued to whizz and whine into the jeep. When the firing ceased, Jeff wasted no time in springing from his position. The man with the gun was less than thirty feet away, reloading; Jeff unloaded the entire magazine of his machine-gun into the attacker. Riddling the man's chest, gut, legs, arms and face before he finally collapsed to the floor. "Got you," Jeff hissed. "Head over to that hangar on the right. My plane is in there."

Maria rolled the crippled 4x4 over to the huge, white hangar. The roof was ark-shaped, with a massive roller door gracing its front, and a small, standard sized door in its centre.

"Once I get that door open, reverse the jeep close to it so that we can unload," Jeff said. He dug the bunch of keys from his pocket, and fumbled with them, trying to find the right one for the little door. "Got it," he said, more to himself than Maria.

Jeff checked to see if the area was clear, and got out. Volts of pain skipped up his leg, almost taking him to the floor. He composed himself and hobbled over to the door.

Once it was open, he signalled Maria, who reversed. Jeff got the boot open, and took everything out as fast as he could, dumping it just inside. Amy climbed over the seats, got out and ran into the hangar.

"I've finished. Move the jeep out of the way of the shutter door. I'll cover you when you get out."

"Okay, Jeff."

He shut the boot, and Maria pulled off to the left and stopped. Satisfied that the Toyota was not in the way, she got out. Jeff was stood by the hangar, sweeping the gun from side to side – the airfield was quiet.

One large plane stood out in the middle of the runway, with a couple of smaller planes here and there. There was also a truck which looked like it could have been a fuel tanker; it was nothing more than a burnt-out wreck. Towards the end of the runway was another smoking ruin, which looked much larger than the fuel tanker – maybe a plane? Jeff thought, unable to work it out.

Maria ran for the hangar, and she and Jeff got in. Jeff closed and locked the door – they were finally safe. Jeff put his head to the cool, metal door and sighed.

"Nothing will get in here. Nothing," Jeff said.

Light from Perspex windows in the ceiling lit the hangar, but it was still pretty dim. Maria couldn't see to the back. Only Jeff's small plane was inside, which was white, with British Airways markings on its fin, wings and nose. The letters G-EGLL SUNRISE were etched on its side. Maria could see eight seats inside, and was shocked at how big the plane was. She could smell oil and petrol in the hangar, and there were small slicks on the floor.

"How could that thing out there have been using a gun?" Maria said. "They can't be evolving that fast, surely?"

"I'm not so sure it was an infected person," Jeff said.

"You mean…"

"He was wearing military colours," Jeff said. "And we did pass that army barracks on our way out here."

"You think it was a soldier? Maybe he had lost his mind?"

"Either that, or he thought we were like them."

Maria made an O shape with her mouth, and said nothing.

"Can we go now, please," Amy said.

Jeff turned, and smiled at the youngster, "of course we can."

"Not so fast," a voice shouted out.

Maria shrieked and clung on to Amy.

Jeff turned to where the voice emanated from, and readied his gun.

"Don't bother, matey, I'm in the dark with my own gun – you'll lose! Now put your weapon on the ground, I'm not going to hurt you. Just had to make sure."

Sweat stung Jeff's eyes as he frantically squinted into the dark, trying to find his target. He couldn't just put his gun down, no way. What if it was another psycho like Dylan? Or that soldier out on the airfield? Then the person came out of the shadows. Followed by a second, who was much smaller. A teenager?

As the pair stepped closer, Jeff could make out that the first person was a male, and he was clutching at his left side, where blood seemed to be trickling from a wound. The second was a teenage boy of about seventeen, and he was the one holding the gun.

"We really don't want to hurt you," he said. *He has a Cardiff twang in his accent*, Jeff thought. The boy had beads of sweat running down his face, and his grip on the bolt-action rifle seemed slippery. "Please, just put your gun down," the man agonised.

"Jeff, maybe we should," Maria said. "He seems badly hurt."

"And what if he is like Dylan?"

"Put your fucking gun down, pal," the boy shouted, edging closer to Jeff, who in return turned his gun on the teen.

"No," the man yelled, and stepped in front of the boy playing at being a man. "Put the gun down,

179

Dafydd," the man said. "These people aren't going to do us any harm, are you?" he asked Jeff.

"We don't want trouble, but it keeps on finding us for some reason. I want to trust you, but I'm worried it will get us killed," Jeff said, still keeping his gun on Dafydd.

"Look, I'm hurt here, matey, and not capable of much. And unless I get some urgent help at a hospital, I'm not going to make it through another few hours." The man gritted his teeth as the intense pain in his side shot through his body; his knees buckled and he collapsed against the side of Jeff's plane.

"Dad!" Dafydd shouted, and dropped the gun to aid his father.

Jeff lowered his gun to help the falling man, and felt foolish, for now he had let his guard down, giving the man and his boy an opportunity to rush them – but they didn't. The father was telling the truth; he was in a serious condition. A large chunk of flesh was missing from the man's side, exposing some ribs. And now that he had moved his hand, the wound pumped blood.

"Press your hand tight to his side," Maria stressed, searching through the equipment they had. She got the first aid kit out of the satchel, along with some bottled water. "Here, Jeff," she said.

Jeff took the first aid kit and started opening it, but the man pushed it out of the way.

"Don't bother wasting your time and resources. I'm a goner," he said, and smiled.

"Dad, please, let—"

"Shh, boy. I'll be more use to you like this, you'll see," he said, then turned to Jeff. "Can you fly this can with wings?"

"Yes," Jeff said.

"But—" Dafydd started.

"It's going to be okay, I promise you," he told Dafydd. Then he turned to Jeff. "I'll help you fly out of here by opening the doors, and taking the blocks from under the wheels of the plane, but you have to promise me one thing?"

"What?" Jeff asked.

"Take my boy with you, and look after him. I told him that I would, but I've obviously failed him there," he said, a wry smile on his face.

Dafydd buried his face into his father's neck and cried.

"Of course we'll look after him...Jesus!" Jeff yelled, as the roller door came under attack from outside. The metal door dented and shook on its runners as kicks and punches were issued to it.

"We're running out of time here," Maria said. "Those things are trying to get in."

"Dafydd, Dafydd, boy. Look at me, will you?" The teen looked his father in the eyes. "You have to go with these people, and help them as much as you can."

"Come with us, Dad, please!"

"Look at me, son. I'll be dead before we leave the tarmac."

"We'll leave you two to it," Jeff interrupted. "We have to load the plane."

The man nodded.

Jeff rallied the girls and got them to help him. He climbed inside the plane and started it up. He was happy to see the fuel gauge up near the full mark, meaning it would be enough to get them to Scotland. He switched on his CB radio, knowing that when he was in range, he could try to contact his sister, as she always had hers on.

Amy and Maria loaded their stuff into the belly of the plane, which acted as the cargo area. Once finished, Amy climbed aboard, leaving Maria to go to Dafydd and his father.

"Are you sure you won't come with us?" Maria said, putting her hand to the father's shoulder.

He looked up at her with wet eyes, "Yes, love, pretty sure."

She could just about hear his whispered response over the assault on the roller door. His face ashen; his lips turning a blue-purple colour.

"Go on, son, go with her."

"Dad, please, let me stay with you!"

"No, now go, please, Dafydd."

"Come on," Maria cooed.

"Get your damn hands off me, bitch!" Dafydd yelled.

"Dafydd!" he shouted, "that's no way to speak to a woman – I'm shocked at you. That's not how mam and me brought you up, now is it?" The boy lowered his head. "Please, go with her. You'll be safe. I may have let you down, but I will not break my promise to mam."

"Okay, I'm sorry, Dad." He stood, helping his father up, who held his hand out for support while clutching his side.

"Now go, the pair of you."

Maria got in, while Dafydd picked up his gun and a hold-all of his own before climbing on.

Dafydd's father hobbled under the plane and released the blocks. He then went to the roller shutter, and signalled up to Jeff to throw the key down. Jeff opened the little side window in the cockpit, and threw down the necessary key.

The sound of the propellers inside the hangar were deafening as it reverberated off the tin-like walls. Dafydd's father unlocked the door, and rolled it skyward. A pack of *them* had formed outside – ten, maybe fifteen of them flooded inside.

They were soon on Dafydd's father, pulling him to the ground and ripping at his guts, throats, eyes, arms, legs...pulling him in all directions. Dafydd couldn't see this, as he was sat at the back. Jeff moved the plane forward, slowly nudging them out of the way like bowling pins. The left engine whined in agony as Jeff saw a body being sucked in to it. Jeff heard the thing's bones crunch and splinter upon impact with the wooden rotor blade.

Once Jeff was free of the hangar, he sauntered the plane down to the end of the runway. He could see the trail of dead bodies he'd left behind him as he powered down the strip, and took the small plane into the air. The few who had managed to work their way onto the plane now faced an agonising drop to the ground as Jeff soared higher and higher.

As Jeff kept climbing, he looked out of his side window, and saw Cardiff city centre nearby: buildings had been reduced to smouldering rubble; traffic jams of burnt out cars and buses; charred bodies and hordes and hordes of the infected shuffled along the streets in broad daylight, searching for more victims.

184

When he came to straighten the plane out, the horrific scene below could not be made out – only bodies like ants. Maria sat next to Jeff in the cockpit; Dafydd and Amy sat in the back of the plane. The door to the cockpit was open, so Jeff and Maria were able to keep an eye on the youngsters. They communicated through their headsets, their voices crackled.

"Do you think I should go back there and have a chat with him?"

"You could do," Jeff said. "I'm not sure I like leaving Amy alone with that boy."

"Why?"

"You saw how hostile he was?"

"But come on, Jeff. The boy was about to lose his dad."

"I know, I know. I'm just worried, that's all."

"I know you are, Jeff."

"We have to be careful. We can't afford any more slip-ups."

"You're thinking about them again?"

"Aren't you?"

"Of course, but we can't mistrust everyone we come across," Maria said.

"I just feel like it was my fault, you know?"

"How can you say such a stupid thing, Jeff?"

"I was meant to be guarding us all."

"You weren't to know that psychotic freak would break loose and jump you."

"But I should have been paying more attention, Maria."

"And Ollie and Roxie should have stayed where they were, and not gone upstairs like a pair of teenage lovers."

"Hmm, it still doesn't make me feel less responsible for what happened to them."

"But nobody is to blame."

"I should have listened to Ollie, and thrown Dylan out."

"But you weren't to know, none of us were! We could have listened to Ollie and ended up throwing an innocent man to his death!"

"Yeah, I guess so."

"No guess so about it, come on, Jeff." She rubbed his arm. "I'm sure Ollie wouldn't blame you for it."

"Ha-ha, I'm not so sure about that," he said, wiping a tear from his eye. "We can't save everyone. We got Amy out of there, didn't we? And now Dafydd?"

"That's true."

"You're a good man, Jeff. And Ollie and Roxie knew that. I'm pretty sure they would've wanted to see us escape this madness."

"Yeah, I know you're right. They had a lot of time for Amy, too," Jeff said.

"Ollie told me he was glad he'd saved her. He felt a great deal for the child," Maria said, choking back a sob. "I think he would have treated her like his own, as would Roxie."

"Do you fancy having a check on them?" Jeff asked. "Dafydd must be very upset after what happened back at the hangar."

"Okay, I'll be back in a bit."

Maria took off her headset and put it on her seat. She patted Jeff on the shoulder as she made her way to the rear of the plane. Dafydd was screwed up into a ball in his seat behind Amy, who was sat looking out the window. Maria sat in the seat beside Amy, and buckled her belt.

"Hey, love, how you holding up?"

Amy turned to face Maria, her eyes wet. "I miss my mam."

"Aww, sweetie, I know you do. I miss my mam, too."

"How did you lose yours, then?" Amy asked.

"Because of what's happened."

Dafydd moved into a sitting position behind – Maria knew her plan was working, that going directly to the boy and talking to him would not work – she needed to earn his trust.

187

"Aw, I see."

"I never had a sister like you though," Maria said. "I always wanted one."

"We could be sisters now," Amy said, a half smile on her lips.

"I'd like that very much," Maria said.

"Will it take us days to get to Scotland?" Amy asked.

Maria smiled, "No, sweetie, not that long. About forty to fifty minutes."

"Aw, cool."

"Can you see much down there?" Maria asked, looking out the window.

"Not really, everything is too far away, like."

"Where are we going to go when we get to Scotland, Maria?"

"Jeff has a sister there, who lives on a farm miles from big cities and towns."

"Does she have animals?"

Maria smiled, "I don't think she does, love."

"That's a shame, I love horses."

Maria leant over to Amy, and held her hand. "Me too."

The plane dipped viciously then rattled. Amy squealed, and Dafydd gripped hold of the arms on his seat.

"What's going on, Jeff?" Maria called.

"Little bit of turbulence. Can you come and join me up front for a little while, please? Just until we get past it."

Maria slipped out of her seatbelt and headed back to the cockpit. She used the seats and walls of the plane to help her, as the force of the rocking was threatening to knock her off her feet. Once back at Jeff's side, she slid into her seat and replaced the headset.

"What can I do?"

"Just hold the steering as steady and solid as you can, because when we hit another air pocket the controls can slip out of your grasp."

"Okay," Maria said, concentrating.

Jeff swept his eyes over the gages and dials to make sure everything was in order. Another air pocket dragged the plane down, causing Jeff and Maria to leave their seats slightly.

"It's okay," Jeff said. "There's no need to panic. The skies ahead look clear. Another few moments and we should be out of this." The plane bounced again, just as violently, and again and again, receding into calmer jolts each time until nothing. "That's it," Jeff said. "All over with. You can go back to the others now, if you want, Maria."

"I'll stay for a little while, just in case we hit some more."

"Well, you can if you want, but I really don't think we are in danger of any more turbulence."

"How far off Scotland are we?"

"I'd say another twenty to twenty-five minutes before we land."

"Have you tried your sister on the CB yet?"

"No, not yet. I'll give it another ten minutes or so. I'm going to have to take us down a good few feet to make sure I can get a decent reception."

"I see. Have you tried any of the radio bands?"

"Yes, nothing but dead air out there for miles around us. It's creepy, you know. It's like we are the last four left in Britain." That thought made goose pimples engulf Jeff's flesh, and shrink his scrotum, as his words bounced off the walls around his brain – *the last four left in Britain!* And why stop there? Has it started wiping out Europe? This could be it, the human race over with as we know it.

"Jeff?"

"Sorry, I was lost in my own little world then. What did you say?"

"Will we be able to land somewhere close to your sister's house?"

He shook his head, clearing the thoughts. "Yes, we can land in a field right behind her house. She has acres of land."

"No close neighbours?"

"Not really, no. Closest one has to be at least half-a-mile away."

"Bloody hell, no wonder you knew your sister would be okay. It's a hell of a plan you had worked out."

"Yeah, well. I just hope it all *goes* to plan. How are they back there?"

"I sat with Amy and spoke with her – she's pretty upset about her mother."

"Did you speak with Dafydd?"

"No, not yet. I was hoping my chat with Amy would bring him around to speaking to me."

"Didn't work?"

"It was starting to, but then we had all that turbulence. I'll go back and have another go. You seem to be okay up here."

Maria got back into the seat beside Amy, and smiled at her.

"Did Jeff tell you how far from Scotland we are?" Amy asked.

"About twenty minutes," Maria told Amy. "Would you two like something to drink?"

"Yes please," Amy said.

Dafydd nodded.

"What would you like? I took some pop out of the bags. I think we have coke, would you both like coke?"

Amy nodded, so did Dafydd.

Maria got up, and took a bottle down from the overhead rack above her. She uncapped the bottle, and took a swig. She offered the pop to Amy, who also had a large drink.

"Would you like some, Dafydd?" Amy said.

"Yes," he said sharply, a scowl on his face.

"Here you go then," Amy said, and passed him the coke. Amy and Maria watched as Dafydd drank from the bottle with long gulps; emptying more than half the contents before stopping for breath, and belching. Amy giggled, "Ugh, what a piggy."

The teen looked at her coldly, before smiling.

"Got anything to eat, then?" he asked. "I'm bloody starving, I am."

"Only in the hold of the plane, I'm sorry," Maria said. "Shouldn't be long before we land though, and then I can get you something."

The boy looked very unclean – grubby. His face was black, as though he'd been down a mine; his hair long, and unkempt; his fingernails long, with dirt underneath them. His clothes were ragged. Maria felt only sorrow for him. He'd clearly lost all of his family due to this mess. She was about to speak to him, when Amy beat her to it, as if the child sensed it.

"I'm sorry about your daddy, Dafydd," Amy said. "My mammy and daddy are dead too."

The lad looked up at both women, tears streaming down his face, and tried to speak.

"I…I…felt," he sniffled and wiped his nose. "Helpless. I stood and watched my mother try to kill my father."

"Oh, that is bad," Maria said. "Do you want to talk about it?"

The boy shook his head, "No, I never want to talk about it, ever."

Maria left it at that, not wanting to push Dafydd anymore.

"Even if we had got back in time, it wouldn't have made a difference – my mother was already infected. It's just Dad and me never knew it, like," Dafydd said, looking out his window.

Chapter 13

They arrived at the Coal2u merchants just after midnight. The drive from Bangor to Chesterfield, Derbyshire, had been an easy one for Gwyn – the motorways had been practically empty at that time of night, and having Dafydd for company helped.

Gwyn had been in the haulage business for almost thirty years, and this was the first time he had been contracted to pick up coal. Him being Welsh, he found it rather funny and ironic that this should be the first time.

Gwyn and Dafydd stood by their lorry, waiting for the foreman to come to them with the details of their load. The forecourt of the mill was lit up by huge floodlights, like those at football grounds. JCB's powered back and forth, ploughing coal into the large warehouse-style buildings, ready to be sacked then shipped out across the U.K. Workers rushed about the place, and Dafydd could see the mounds and mounds of coal in the factory being worked by a masked workforce.

The intense power of the lights on the courtyard picked up a scant, black mist caused by the dust off the coal. It snaked in the air like some unwanted python, Gwyn thought. A chill slid down his back.

"Mr. Llewelyn?" a voice called from behind Gwyn, the accent mild English. Dafydd smiled at the way the man pronounced Llewelyn – saying the surname as though it only had the one L.

"Aye," Gwyn said, "that's me," and turned to face the man, who was much shorter than him, and stuck his hand out. The other man did the same.

"Hi, I'm Chris," he said. "I'm the foreman here at Coal2u."

The both men shook hands. Chris' looked rough and chapped due to years of coal shovelling. Chris' chest was barrelled, and a thick tuft of hair sprouted from the top of the unbuttoned shirt.

"Nice to meet you, Chris," Gwyn said.

"And you are?" Chris said to Dafydd.

"Oh, that's my boy, Dafydd. I took him on as my helper a year back, see."

"So a father and son haulage company? That's nice."

"Your boy not in the merchant trade then, Chris?"

"Yes, but he is off sick at the moment," Chris said, a mournful look in his eye. "Well, never mind that, we've got to get you fellas back on the road."

"Sorry to hear that. Nothing serious, I hope."

"No, just the sniffles. So, I have it down that you're here to pick up five-hundred sacks of coal, is that right?"

"Yes, that's right, Chris."

"Good-good," he said, and scribbled something down on the paper attached to his clipboard.

"Can I ask you something, Chris?"

Chris nodded.

"Why do you need me and my boy here to deliver this order for you? Surely you have your own transport wagons, a company this size?"

Chris stopped writing, and looked up at Gwyn, his face ashen.

"Yes, we do have our own transport, but most of our drivers are off, have been for the past couple of days or so. And it's not just the drivers that have been ill, but also most of our work team. We've had to bring in every casual and part-time worker we have on our books. Christ, we even have students here making a fast buck; our team has been decimated."

"Bloody hell. Sounds like you have a bug or something going around up here," Gwyn said. "Been the same in Cardiff, it has. Even my poor wife is laid up in bed."

"A bug in the air, no doubt," Chris said, smiling at them both. "We tried a few hauling companies, but you quoted us an unbeatable price for the shipment."

196

"We aim to please," Gwyn said.

"Great. But we do have one problem."

"What's that then?"

"We're going to have to handball the sacks onto your lorry, Gwyn," Chris said. "I am sorry about any inconvenience this may cause you."

"Oh, right, I see. That's okay. We going to do it Buster-style, is it?" Gwyn said, and laughed at his joke."

"Buster? Ah, I get it – Great Train Robbery?"

Gwyn nodded, still chuckling.

"Well," Chris said, "I'll see how many men I can muster up to help us get the load on, but I can't see it being many."

"Duw, you lot really are struggling."

"Right, why don't you two go and grab yourselves a cup of coffee in our staff canteen. I'll come and get you when we're ready to start loading up, okay?"

"Yeah, okay," Gwyn said, and he and his son followed Chris to the canteen.

Gwyn fed the Klix vending machine with all his loose silver, which was enough for a hot chocolate for Dafydd, and mocha for himself. Most of the canteen sat in darkness, except for a small light in the corner that had been left on. A fridge-freezer buzzed somewhere behind the food counter and an eerie blue light spilt out from the kitchen fly zappers.

All the tables had their chairs on them where the cleaners had moved them to mop the floors ready for the morning team. An area at the back of the restroom was carpeted, and had soft padded chairs to be used. A small TV clung to one of the walls.

"Come on, boy, we'll sit back by there, see what's going on in the world, hey?"

Dafydd didn't answer, just nodded.

They took their drinks to the 'plush' area, and Dafydd plonked himself down. Gwyn headed for the TV, and switched it on. The screen filled with scenes of violence; smoking wrecks, explosions, people engaging in fights, buildings collapsing into dusty remains, causing the reporter to keep looking over his shoulder in apprehension. Armed police on horseback and foot met with the rioters head-on; the ones on foot were beating their shields with their truncheons to try and strike fear into their enemies' heart. The sound was down on the television set, so Gwyn couldn't make out what the man was saying. He turned the volume up.

"These scenes of ghoulish carnage started only hours ago on the streets of Cardiff…"

"Bloody hell, Dafydd, they're talking about Cardiff on the news, boy."

"…Local police reports show that an emergency call is being taken every two minutes…"

"Maybe you should ring mam, Dad?"

"Yeah, good idea."

Dafydd kept listening to the news to see what was being said while Gwyn tried his wife.

"…*Sources tell me that the first calls taken were from a town just outside of Cardiff by the name of Twsc. They appeared to be just routine calls to begin with, which escalated into more serious ones that have now spilt out onto the streets of Cardiff…*"

"There's no dial tone coming from the house phone, Dafydd. Just a women telling me that there is a fault with the line."

"Let's try her mobile?"

"Okay. Quick."

The phone the other end started ringing, and Dafydd's heart jumped. It rang a dozen times before…

"Hello?"

His mother's voice sounded croaky from sleep.

"Hello, who is this, mun?!"

"Mam, it's me, Dafydd."

"Oh, is there something the matter?"

Before Dafydd could answer, Gwyn took the phone out of his son's hand.

"Sarah? Are you okay, love?"

"Yes, but—"

"Have a look out the window there and tell me what you can see."

"But—"

"Please, there is no time for questions."

The line went quiet, and Gwyn turned to Dafydd.

"What have they said on the news, bach?"

"It's everywhere, Dad…"

Gwyn looked into his son's eyes, and saw fear staring out at him.

"Everywhere?"

"Yeah, they seem to think Britain is in the grip of swine flu, causing the infected to turn on people that aren't. I'm scared, Dad. What are we going to do?"

"We…"

"The streets are quiet, Gwyn. Not a cat moving out there."

Gwyn relaxed and breathed out.

"Now what's this all about, dragging me from my sick bed at this hour, mun?" Gwyn could hear a laugh in his wife's throat.

"Put the TV on."

"But—"

"Please, Sarah, just listen to me."

"I *am* listening to you, Gwyn, but you are starting to scare me."

"Just put the TV on, and all will be explained."

"Okay, hang on. I'm taking you to the TV with me."

Gwyn heard the women he'd been married to for twenty years make her way to the living room, and switch on the television. Gwyn could just about hear the reporter on the set…

"*The people of South Wales are being advised to stay behind locked doors tonight due to the recent reports of violence that seems to be sweeping the nation. These acts of violence appear to be caused by people who have become sick. Some say that swine flu is the cause…*"

"Oh my God, Gwyn, what the hell is going on? People are killing one another in this area."

"Yeah, Dafydd and I just heard the news up here. We wanted to know that you were okay there."

"What shall I do, Gwyn?"

"What's it telling people to do on the news?"

"Hang on. I'll turn it up…"

"*Reports indicate that an emergency call is being taken every thirty seconds around the country. Hundreds have been killed, with thousands receiving treatment for injuries and blood loss. Safe houses are being set up in various boroughs across Wales and the U.K – lists of these safe houses will be broadcast within the hour.*"

"God, Gwyn, this is serious, love."

"Barricade yourself in. Dafydd and me are coming home, right now."

"Okay, but try and hurry. The roads might be hard to pass with this going on."

"We'll be there as soon as we can. I know lots of back roads I can take to cut the time of the journey down, beaut. Has it said anything about other parts of the U.K, such as Derby?" Gwyn said.

"No, I have the local news on. I'll keep you posted on what's going on out on the roads."

"Okay, speak to you soon. I love you, beaut."

"I love you too, Gwyn."

Gwyn snapped the phone shut.

"Come on, we have to go."

*

The coverage on the news in the canteen didn't say anything about Derby, or the surrounding cities. Gwyn and Dafydd didn't bother looking for Chris to explain – they just jumped into their lorry and headed home.

Gwyn powered the lorry out of the Mill, and onto Mill Lane. He then turned left. When he got to a roundabout, he took the road signposted A61 – Derby Road, before coming to the A617 heading to Chesterfield/Matlock.

The roads appeared just as quiet as they did on the way up. Gwyn had expected the roads to be jammed up with people trying to get home, or to safety. But there was nothing apart from the odd car here and there; not even flocks of police cars or helicopters in the sky.

This gave Gwyn the incentive to drive much faster than the sixty-five mile per hour speed limit when he got onto the M1; he didn't even slow for the cameras. As they headed down to the next junction, Gwyn turned the radio on to see if there were any more reports; perhaps which roads to avoid.

"...*The Bull Ring market area is flooded with jammed cars and rioters. The armed response units have been called in to try to stamp out the violence that is quickly spreading over into Solihull and Coventry...*"

"It doesn't seem to have come up this far, bach," Gwyn said. "But Birmingham sounds like it's going to be hard work to get past."

"We should be okay, as long as it doesn't spread out onto the motorways, Dad."

They continued on the A42, and saw the next sign they needed – M1/Nottingham.

The radio station they had been listening to began to break up, eventually becoming nothing more than a nasty static. Gwyn merged onto the M42, and exited at the A4097/Kingsbury/A446 – soon they would be in Birmingham.

"Try and get something on the radio, Dafydd."

Gwyn's phone burst to life, making him jump. He picked up his mobile, and saw Sarah's name and

203

number scroll across the flashing, green screen. He flipped it open.

"Hello?"

"Gwyn, love, where are you?"

"We'll be coming up on Birmingham shortly."

"Try to avoid the place the best you can, love."

"What's going on there? We've heard a little bit on the news, like, but not much."

"The place is in chaos. Not only that, but the government have ordered the release of the army."

"Jesus, what is going on? How is it there with you? Is Toni okay?"

"Yeah, she's fine. I've let her sleep. I just popped up to check on her before I rang you."

"Okay, good. Have you looked outside at all?"

"Yeah, the street is deserted."

"Have you barricaded the door?"

"Yes."

"My gun is out in the shed; you know how to use it."

"Where's the key to the cabinet? I would have got the shotgun sooner, but I'm not sure where you keep the key."

"It's in my drawer by the side of the bed."

"As soon as I hang-up, I'll go and get it," Sarah said.

"Good girl. I think Dafydd wants to speak to you."

Gwyn handed the phone over to his son, and tried getting a radio station.

"Hiya, Mam. You both okay there?"

"Yeah, Dafydd, your sister and I are both fine. You just make sure you get home nice and safe."

"*...Scientist of germ warfare, Howell Davies, had this to say earlier.*"

"*Half, or maybe more, of the country's population have become sick. Many avenues are being looked into, but swine flu does seem to be the culprit behind this breakout. We are advising people to stay at home, and not to let anyone in, not even people that you know and trust. This influenza is highly contagious, and can jump from human to human by a simple scratch or bite, or from infected fluid getting into your mouth, eyes or ears...*"

Dafydd heard the report clearly over the phone.

"Are you there, Dafydd? Dafydd?!"

"Yeah, yes, I am. Sorry, I was listening to what was being said on the TV your end."

"They think it's swine flu," Sarah said. "You know, I've not been feeling too well myself."

"You've only had a case of the sniffles, Mam," Dafydd said, trying not to let his mother worry.

"Yes, I know, you're right. It was going around at work."

"There you go then. No need to worry, is there?"

"You don't think it started there, do you, Dafydd?"

"Where?"

"Where I work?"

"Don't be silly, Mam, it's an army barracks—"

"But they do have a research lab there?" Sarah said.

"You're worrying over nothing now, Mam."

"I love you, Dafydd," she said, and hung up the phone.

Dafydd sat there with the phone to his ear, too numb with fear to close the phone.

"Everything okay, bach?" Gwyn asked.

"Yeah, Mam was just telling me how much she loves us both, and to make it home soon." He didn't have the heart to tell his father what his mother had really said.

*

They wouldn't need to go through Birmingham, just skirt around it. As they got closer to the city on the M4, massive blazes could be seen rising from its core.

Lots of cars filled the opposite lane heading out of the city, but nothing seemed to be heading into the city. Gwyn didn't slow down. He wasn't going to stop for anyone. But as he started getting away from Birmingham, his lane started to fill with cars, trying to get away from Birmingham. This almost brought the lorry to a complete halt.

"Bloody hell, we'll never get home if this lot don't get moving," Gwyn said.

"It looks like it could be like this all the way, Dad."

Dafydd fiddled with the radio, trying to pick up something. He swept the needle the full length of the bands, AM, FM, Shortwave and Long, nothing.

"My God, if it wasn't for all these people in their cars, the radio would suggest we were the last people on earth."

"Maybe the power is just down, Dad?"

"Yeah, maybe."

Up ahead the cars came to a stop, as did Gwyn.

"No, no, damn it."

"It's okay, Dad. We'll be fine."

Gwyn tried Sarah, but couldn't get an answer.

"Where the hell could she be, Dafydd?"

Dafydd looked over at his father, and wondered whether or not he should tell him what his mother had said.

"Maybe she's with Toni," he offered, knowing it was a poor excuse.

"But she would have taken her phone with her, surely, boy?"

"You know mam; she doesn't remember to take her mobile everywhere. You know what she's like, mun. How many times have you argued with her over it in the past?"

"Hmm, I guess. But you'd think she'd carry it about with her in this case?"

Gwyn flipped the phone apart again, and dialled his wife's number, but still she didn't pick up.

"Nothing?" Dafydd asked.

"No," Gwyn replied. "Nothing."

"Like I said, Dad, you know what she's like…"

Gwyn's phone rang; it was Sarah's number. He picked it up.

"Hello, Sarah," he demanded.

"Yes, it's me, beaut, what's wrong?"

"Duw, mun, Sarah, I thought something was wrong."

"I was in the toilet I—"

"Why didn't you have the phone with you? How many times—"

"There is no need to shout, Gwyn. I forgot it, that's all."

"I'm sorry, it's just—"

"It's okay, I know."

"Did you get the gun?"

"Yes."

"Is Toni ok?"

"She is still sleeping."

"Good."

"Where are you both?" Sarah said.

"Stuck in Birmingham at the moment; the traffic is heavy."

"Are you moving?"

"No."

"How much longer will you be?"

"Once we get out of this, it shouldn't take us more than an hour and a half."

"That's good. I'm missing you both."

"Have you had any trouble there?" Gwyn asked.

"Erm, no, not really."

"What, what is it? Tell me."

"There was kicking at the door about thirty-minutes ago, but it went away."

"Jesus, but nothing else?"

"No."

"Have you tried calling people? Friends and family?"

"Yes, but I couldn't get an answer with my dad, or your parents, sorry, Gwyn."

"It's ok, don't be sorry. Keep trying. Try the neighbours, and our friends. Alert who you can."

"Okay, okay, I will. I better go," Sarah said. "The battery is dying on my phone, and I need to get it charged."

"Okay, beaut. I'll give you a ring later on, make sure you're ok."

"Okay, I love you, and tell Dafydd I love him too."

"We love you and all. Bye," Gwyn said, and the phone was hung up the other end.

"Did she tell you," Dafydd asked?

"Hmm?"

The bottleneck of traffic was moving out of Birmingham slowly, and soon they would be at their next junction. Gwyn looked over at Dafydd.

"I guess she didn't then,"

"Tell me what, bach?"

Dafydd breathed out loudly, and ran his fingers through his hair. How was he going to tell his father?

"Please, boy, tell me!"

"Mam thinks she might have this flu, Dad."

"What?"

"She seems to think that she may have picked it up at the lab."

"No, don't be silly. It's just a cold, nothing more."

"Hmm, that's what I told her. I wish I hadn't said anything now."

"It's okay, you did the right thing, bach."

"She actually sounded better on the phone just now, Dad, than she has done in the past few days."

"You thought that too…"

Gwyn's door suddenly flew open, and a girl jumped at him. A hand flew at Gwyn's throat and began to choke the life out him. Dafydd shot back against his door and watched his father struggle with the youngster. He yelled.

"Dafyyyy...." Gwyn struggled out. "H...elp...under the seeeat...."

Dafydd sat frozen, staring at the child's face, which looked to be ravished by boils and welts. Yellowy fluid ran down her brow, getting into her eyes and mouth, which she snarled back out. She tried biting Gwyn, but he managed to keep her back with one hand pressed against her chest.

A loud thump from behind Dafydd brought him out of his trance-like state. He turned around and looked out the window. There he could see another sick person, about his own age, dragging an aged woman from her car by the hair. The elderly woman screamed as Dafydd watched the youngster bite into her throat.

"Aarrrgh, fucking hell," Dafydd shouted.

Gwyn managed to get the better of the girl – he rammed her head against the framework of the door, once, twice, three times, but still she clung on, even though her head was flowing with blood. She snapped her jaws and rattled her whole body, aching to be free. Dafydd reached under his seat and lifted his arm. He caught the girl full on in her mouth with a heavy wrench he'd found, cracking her jaw and busting some teeth. She slumped down, unconscious. Gwyn pulled her head back by her scruff, and threw her out through the door.

"Fuck! What the hell took you so long, boy?"

"Sorry, Dad...I...I..."

Gwyn put his hand on his son's leg, "It's okay. It's okay, we just need to calm down. Lock your door."

"I already have, Dad."

"No sodding flu I know of would make people do this to one another," Gwyn said.

"Maybe it's that legionnaires disease that's been on the news recently, Dad?"

"No way, boy. *Look* at these people."

Dafydd thought he was going to piss himself at the sight outside. He whimpered and cowered away from his door.

"You'll be fine with me, boy. Keep that wrench on you."

All around them cars were being invaded by people spewing out of Birmingham city centre. Men, women and children were ripped from their seats and killed. Some were even killed inside their cars. The screaming was unbearable.

A large male managed to climb the piping hot grill on Gwyn's lorry, slithering across the bonnet to the windshield, where he beat his fists on the glass.

"*Shit*, what are we going to do, Dad?"

"Our exit is not that far away, it's just up ahead. I bet we could push our way up the middle of these cars."

"Well we can't stay here, for fuck's sake."

Gwyn put the lorry into gear, and steered right. The sound of crunching metal made Dafydd grit his teeth as his father bumped car after car out of their path. The thing on their bonnet lost its grip and fell under the wheels; his body caught in the rear tyres which caused him to be dragged along for a short while.

The lorry grumbled through everything in its path – taking doors and wing mirrors off cars and squashing the sick, and possibly some that weren't; Gwyn had passed the point of caring. Dafydd covered his ears to try and block out the awful sounds.

Soon they were at their junction: 4A. Gwyn stayed on that road for the next ten minutes, before leaving again, and joining the M5, which was rather quiet. *But for how long?* Gwyn thought.

After another hour or so, Gwyn left the M5, taking the exit onto the M4. Twenty minutes after that they were on the outskirts of Newport, and in ten minutes they would be driving down their home street in Cardiff.

In between Newport and Cardiff Gwyn tried calling his wife, but she hadn't answered. He'd also tried his parents, to no avail there either. Maybe Sarah had managed to contact them?

After five more attempts at trying to get in touch with Sarah, he started to panic, even though Dafydd tried playing the fact that his mother never took her phone places with her.

When Gwyn turned the truck onto King's Avenue, where they lived, he was shocked to be stopped by a tank, and two army trucks blocking the entrance to the street. He stomped on the brakes and the grill to the lorry stopped just short of hitting one of the trucks. No military personnel could be seen.

One of the army jeep's front lights was flashing, splashing the tank every so often with an eerie orange colour. Gwyn and Dafydd sat looking at the scene before them.

"Now what, Dad?"

"Hmm, I'm not sure."

"You're not going to be able to drive up there."

Gwyn wound his window down and switched off the truck's engine, which grumbled to a hissing stop. Over the cooling system's noises, Gwyn could hear distant screams and shouts; crackling gunfire and explosions. His flesh itched as goose pimples invaded his skin. He wound the window back up.

"What's the matter, Dad?"

"It sounds like a warzone out there, Dafydd, bach."

"We have to get to mam, now."

Gwyn nodded his head, picked up his phone, and tried his wife again. On the fourth ring, Sarah picked up.

"Gwyn, where are you?" she said, panic in her voice, which threw Gwyn.

"Err, erm…I'm at the end of the street, love."

"Hurry, please…"

"What's wrong?"

"Sarah? Are you there?" Gwyn said. "Hello."

Only dead air hissed through Gwyn's mobile. He tried ringing again, but only got an engaged tone.

"What's wrong, Dad? Was mam Okay?"

"I…I…I don't know. I didn't get much…We better get up there."

Dafydd went to get out of the truck, but was pulled back by his father.

"Wait."

"What, mun, Dad?" he said, and scowled.

"Look under your seat. There should be a crowbar and a flashlight."

Dafydd rummaged about under the passenger seat and came up with the objects. He kept the wrench he had used in Birmingham for himself, and gave the torch and crowbar to his father.

215

"Here," he said.

"Thanks, bach. And don't worry; we'll get to mam and Toni."

Dafydd looked at his father, and half-smiled.

"Right, when I get out, you follow me close, you hear, boy? I want you safe behind me. So get out of the truck my side."

"Okay, Dad."

Gwyn checked the wing mirrors, making sure nobody lurked behind them. He took another look in front, and to the side of his door, and found nothing. He took the keys out of the truck's ignition, and got out slowly. Dafydd shuffled over the seat, and got out behind his dad.

"Let's make this fast, Dafydd."

The pair managed to squeeze between the two haphazardly parked jeeps to get into their street. Nothing moved, but there was plenty of noise from neighbouring roads.

"This is bad."

"It's okay; we'll be home soon, and safe," Gwyn said.

They scanned their sides, keeping a look out for danger. The place seemed normal apart from the obvious. Gwyn quickly moved up the street to their house, with Dafydd in tow.

When they reached their house, Gwyn opened the little steel gate, and went up the path to the front door. He knocked lightly.

"Sarah, it's us, Gwyn and Dafydd. Open up?"

Dafydd stood with his back to his father, making sure nobody was creeping up on them, but the street was quiet. It seemed that the violence had not yet spread this far.

"Come on, Sarah, open the bloody door, mun." Gwyn thumped the door harder.

"Where in the hell has she got to now, mun?" Gwyn said.

The door flew open, and Sarah rushed to Gwyn, putting her arms around him in relief. He gave her a quick kiss, then bundled her and Dafydd inside. Once in, he bolted the door with the key which was already in the lock.

"I thought you said you'd barricaded the door, love?"

She flushed.

"Sarah?"

"Well, I was going to, but I couldn't find anything to—"

"For God's sake, woman, you could've been killed," Gwyn said.

"Sorry, I just…I didn't have the strength to move anything."

"Are you still feeling sick, Mam?" Dafydd asked.

Sarah nodded.

"Ok, let's get you to bed," Gwyn said.

"No, I want to be with you two."

"Where is Toni, Mam?"

"Still sleeping, love."

"Okay, first thing's first; get the kettle on, beaut," Gwyn said, smiling.

"Okay," Sarah said, and went out to the kitchen.

"She's not looking too good, Dad."

"I know, boy. Help me find something to put against the door."

They went into the living room, which was rich with trinkets and photos lining the sideboard and mantelpiece.

"The sideboard," Gwyn said.

Dafydd put the wrench down on the sofa and began clearing the wooden furniture of its clutter, ready to be lifted. Once finished, they carried the heavy sideboard out of the room and rammed it tight against the front door, rendering the door handle useless, as now it could not be pushed downwards.

"That should keep the bastards out," Gwyn said.

"What about the front window, then, Dad?"

"No need to protect that, bach – the glass is doubled-glazed," Gwyn said, confidently.

Gwyn went over to the TV, where there was a reporter on the screen, and turned the sound up. Gwyn's bolt-action shotgun was resting against the audio set; he checked its chamber, and found a bullet loaded there. Dafydd sat by his father, and watched the news.

Sarah came into the room with their tea, and smiled.

"Here you go then," she said.

"Thanks, love," Gwyn said.

"Yeah, thanks, Mam."

She smiled, and left to go upstairs.

"I think I'll just check on Toni. Won't be long."

Gwyn touched her arm, "Wait, before you go, beaut…Dafydd told me that you think you may have…swine flu?" he said, and gulped.

"No, just a cold, mun. No need to worry, Gwyn."

"What kind of work were they doing at Twsc barracks?" Gwyn asked. Dafydd looked at his mother, then at his father. Beads of sweat formed on the youngster's forehead.

"You told your father?" Sarah said.

"I—"

"Don't go blaming him; he did the right thing in telling me."

She sighed. "You know I'm not supposed to divulge what goes on there, Gwyn. It's…"

He stood up, and gripped her by both her arms, drawing her toward him, "I think we are beyond the point of worrying who knows what, Sarah, bach. People are killing each other on the streets, and they think it may have started in Twsc."

She glanced down, unable to look Gwyn in the eye.

"I'm not part of the medical personnel at the barracks like I told you...I'm a highly trained germ warfare technician drafted in by a superior officer to help build a new weapon."

Gwyn let go of his wife's arms, and collapsed back onto the sofa.

"I wanted to tell you, but I couldn't..."

"How long, then?"

"Gwyn, please."

"How long, Sarah, please?"

"All my career."

Gwyn looked up at her, his face twisted into shock. "You've been lying all this time?!"

"You knew when we got together that I couldn't disclose my job to you."

"Are you telling me that you *created* this mess?"

"Not just me, but others too. A small team of us in fact, but nobody knows for sure it's—"

"Oh, please, enough already. Did you know this was going to happen?"

"Not to this extent, no – we had the germ in the lab for almost five years without any trouble. We never thought it would get out."

"Why the hell didn't you warn us? We could have left, gone far away."

"I was scared, Gwyn."

"Of what?"

"Of what they would do to me if they knew I was still alive."

"What?"

"I need to go and check on Toni. I'll be back down to talk to you."

"No, we need to talk now."

"Please, Gwyn, let me just check on our daughter."

"No, tell us, Mam," Dafydd said, sounding just as annoyed as his father. Sarah looked at her son in shock. "Please, Mam."

"I don't know all the details, because the others and I were kept in the dark about why we were creating this weapon."

"Oh, dear God, mun."

"It's not as bad as it sounds, Gwyn. Honest. We get asked to design different things all the time."

He shook his head as she sat down beside him, putting her arms around him. "We'll be okay, I promise you."

"How can you say that, Sarah, bach? The bloody army have been drafted in, in some parts of the country."

She let go of Gwyn, and wiped the tears from her eyes, "I have to go and check on Toni."

Gwyn didn't say anything, neither did Dafydd.

"Gwyn? Please, say something."

"I can't believe what I've been hearing. I'm hurt and disappointed that you, of all people, can land us in hot water as deep as this."

"Please, I was only doing what I was told to do – it was my job!"

"Your job may have cost us our lives here, Sarah."

She stood up, and walked out of the room - "I'm going to check on our daughter."

*

She straightened and glanced down into the toilet. There was definitely blood in her bile. She flushed, put the seat down and sat on the toilet. Sarah put her head in her hands, and wept. She knew she was dying, or even transforming. She should have killed herself hours ago, but she hadn't. She'd needed to see her husband and son one last time, to tell them the truth about the lab. She'd also wanted to make sure that it was virus-d, and not a common cold.

But she now knew that it was virus-d; she'd seen the effects of it many times in the past. Sarah thought she had got out of the research facility in time, before the virus had escaped via the two test subjects.

She started coughing violently, and stood up. She went to the bathroom cabinet and looked in the mirror; a cluster of boils had gathered on her forehead – one popped and yellow-brown pus leaked down her face. Blood spouted out of her right eye and joined the murky trail already running down her cheeks.

Sarah sobbed as she opened the cabinet. She took out all the bottles of pills she could find, and uncapped them. She filled the small glass by the sink with water, and started shooting tablets down her throat, one after the other, taking sips of water now and then.

*

"Where the hell is your mother?" Gwyn said.

"She went up to see Toni, didn't she?" Dafydd said.

"It's almost been forty minutes, mun."

Dafydd shrugged.

Gwyn didn't say anything; just looked at his son, then at the television with horror on his face. The guy on screen was reporting live from the Rhondda Valleys, as he and his crew were attacked by a group of infected people. All Gwyn and Dafydd could do was watch on in alarm. The cameraman dropped his camera, which kept running even after it hit the floor, displaying a gore scene of the presenter being pulled to pieces by the sick. Before Gwyn could react in any way, the screen went blank and a blood-freezing scream from upstairs chilled Gwyn.

"Jesus, Mam!" Dafydd shouted, picking up the wrench and heading for the stairs.

"Wait!" Gwyn called after him.

Dafydd saw the bathroom door standing open, and blood streaks on the linoleum flooring.

"Mam?" he called. "Mam!"

Gwyn ran up the stairs behind him, gasping at the sight of blood.

Dafydd eased over to the bathroom door, and looked in. The glass in the cabinet mirror was smashed and resting in the sink. Small plastic bottles littered the floor; there were pills everywhere. Some of the pink tiles were smudged with blood, so too was the shower curtain.

"Let me see, Bach," Gwyn said gently.

Dafydd turned out of the room, and faced the door of his sister's room. Bloody prints could be seen on the door's handle. His heart smashed against his ribs, and pelted at a terrific rate.

Gwyn came out of the bathroom and joined Dafydd on the landing. Nothing could be heard in the house.

"Sarah, are you in there, beaut?" Gwyn called.

Dafydd put his hand to the door handle, plunging it downwards. He kicked the door wide, and bounced backwards.

Sarah was stood over her six-year old daughter, a blooded shard of glass in one hand, and the child's scalp in the other. The bed was soaked in blood, which dripped off the sheets and onto the carpet, where it was slowly seeping into the floorboards.

"Oh, my God," Gwyn said, covering his mouth.

Sarah shot her head towards them, staring for a second before charging at the two men.

Dafydd stepped out of his mother's way, leaving her to slam into his father. Sarah took Gwyn through the banister, and they crashed to the hallway. Gwyn couldn't move – his rib appeared to have snapped in the fall, and now pierced his right side. Sarah got onto her back, and looked straight up at Dafydd, who was staring down at them both. She snarled and gnashed her teeth at him, before rolling over onto Gwyn.

He screamed as the women he loved pulled at his exposed rib – digging her fingers into the wound. Strings of blood hung from her drooping lower lip. Gwyn squeezed her throat and pushed her back, trying to fling her off. He shut his eyes and closed his mouth, not wanting any of her infected blood to get into him.

She stopped digging at his wound, and instead clawed at it. Gwyn shouted out as burning hot pain raked his body. His arm lost its grip and buckled. Sarah's head fell forward, where she managed to bite into her husband's injury. Again he wailed as he felt his side being chewed and ripped open. Then all of a sudden she was off him.

Dafydd stood over his mother, wrench in hand. Her mouth lay open, her tongue flopped to one side. She was out cold.

"Get the gun," Gwyn said. "We have to get out of here."

Dafydd rushed into the living room, picked up the gun and headed back to his father.

"Go upstairs and look in my wardrobe. On the shelf above, you'll find boxes of bullets. Go and get them," Gwyn managed.

Dafydd nodded, taking the wrench and leaving the gun. He ran upstairs, and into his parents' room. It smelt of his mother's perfume. The bed was a mess, and the curtains were drawn.

"Hurry, boy. We haven't got much time."

Dafydd routed through the large wardrobe and pulled out a rucksack. Then he found the bullets, and his father's hunting knife. He threw everything into the bag. When he got back to the top of the stairs, he was just in time to see his father shoot his mother.

*

They went out into the street, which was still quiet, and headed down to Gwyn's truck. Gwyn got in behind the wheel, and started it up.

"Where the hell are we going to go, Dad?"

"The airport."

"Why?"

"They said on the news that they were running flights out of Cardiff all night."

"But your side?"

"It's only a small bite, bach."

"I can't believe mam…is…is…She almost *killed* you, Dad," Dafydd said.

"Shh, come on now. We both know mam would never hurt either of us."

"But…"

"That was not your mother back there, Dafydd. She was sick."

He looked at his father, glassy eyed. "She killed Toni. Cut her," he cried.

Gwyn tried to gulp the bow in his throat down. His wife and young daughter were dead.

"I know," was all he could say.

Gwyn put the truck into reverse, and headed out to Cardiff airport.

The roads between their house and the airport were manic. Gwyn stuck to the quieter B-roads and

227

lanes, trying to stay clear of built-up areas. When they were close, the pain in Gwyn's side became unbearable. He pulled into a lay-by to inspect the wound.

He put the interior light on and lifted his shirt. The chunk of rib jutting out had snapped, and was just hanging there. Gwyn held his breath as he pulled the dangling bit of bone free.

"Pass me the first aid box, Dafydd, please."

Dafydd opened the glove box, took the large, plastic container out, and gave it to his father.

"Will you be okay, Dad?"

"Yes, yes, fine, bach."

Gwyn wrapped the injured area well with bandages after cleaning, and put gauze on it. He gave the box back to Dafydd, and continued with their journey. As they passed a chain-link fence with barbed wire on its top, which was part of the airport's perimeter, Gwyn and Dafydd could see that the place had come under siege, it was a place of death and carnage; a refuelling truck out on the tarmac was on fire – its driver running around ablaze; a Boeing jet that appeared to have not long taken off could be seen plummeting out of the sky a few miles away, before hitting the ground and exploding into flames.

Hordes of sick people were on the runway, attacking those trying to board another Boeing. A hangar erupted in flames and the noise from the blast caused the glass to shatter in the terminal windows.

"Jesus," Gwyn said.

"Is there much point in staying, Dad?"

"We have to try something, Dafydd. Look, over there," Gwyn said, pointing to a handful of survivors, being led by what looked like pilots and cabin crew into a distant hangar.

Gwyn drove through the fence, which uprooted and tangled in the semi's big wheels, and headed over to the hangar. They both jumped out of the truck, Dafydd with the gun and rucksack, and Gwyn with the crowbar. They ran to the big roller door and hammered on it, pleading to be let in, but nothing came from the other side.

"Dad!" Dafydd shouted, and Gwyn turned in time to see a pack of the infected running at them.

"Shit! We'll never make it back to the lorry in time."

"Look, there," Dafydd said, pointing to a bit of upturned metal in an opposite hangar.

Dafydd managed to squeeze in. Once on the other side, he pushed at the opening to help his father in. They sat in the darkness for a while, listening to *them* outside, scrabbling at the walls.

"We'll just rest for a while, get our breath back."

"What are we going to do after that?"

"It'll be light shortly. I say we wait until then, and then try to get back to the truck."

Gwyn and Dafydd huddled against each other, and fell asleep for a couple of hours – until Gwyn woke in complete agony, shouting and screaming that the pain in his side was burning. Dafydd settled his father and undid his soaked bandages. The veins surrounding the bite mark were protruding through his father's skin. The torn flesh wept pus that smelt rancid.

"I need to get your wound clean, Dad."

Gwyn was barely conscious, and slipped back into sleep. Dafydd left his father's side and scurried over to the hole in the side of the hangar – taking the rifle with him. He stuck his head out slowly and found the surrounding area clear. He scrambled through the opening some more until he could see more of the area outside – nothing.

He got to the lorry and found the medical kit in the glove compartment, along with a bottle of water on the floor. He rushed back to his ailing father, who was still passed out from the pain. Dafydd cleaned his father up, and reapplied fresh dressing.

"Dad," he tried, shaking Gwyn softly by the shoulder. "Dad, mun. The coast is clear outside – if we go now we could make it to safety."

Gwyn didn't respond, and so Dafydd settled back down by his dad's side, knowing they wouldn't be able to go anywhere until his father was fit enough.

Chapter 14

"**M**aria," Jeff called. "Can you come back up here, please?"

Maria excused herself from Dafydd and Amy, who were now chatting, and left them to it. When she got to the cockpit, Jeff had the handle to the CB radio in one hand, and was speaking into it.

"Welshlady, Welshlady, come in please," Jeff said.

Maria took up the co-pilot's seat once again, and put on the headset. She could feel the plane descending. The CB radio cracked and hissed as Jeff took his finger off the handle's button. He was waiting for a reply.

"Welshlady?" Maria asked.

"Yeah, it's her handle name."

"Handle name?"

"That's a name people give themselves on a CB radio."

"Ah, right, got you."

"You've never seen Convoy?" Jeff said.

"Erm, can't say I have."

"You should look into it. It's a classic with Kris Kristofferson."

"Hmm, I'm more of a Burt Reynolds fan myself," she said, smiling.

"Burt Reynolds? How old are you again?"

"Ha-ha! I know. He was a passion of my dad's – he loved the Cannonball Run films."

"So it's influence off your dad?"

"Yep."

Jeff laughed, then put the handle back to his mouth and pushed down on the talk button. "Welshlady, Welshlady do you read me? Welshlady, Welshlady, come in please." Jeff took his finger off the talk button, and hung it back on the CB.

"Maybe we need to drop down a bit more first?" Maria suggested.

"Yeah, I think you're right. How's Dafydd doing?"

"He seems okay; won't tell me what happened though."

"Poor boy."

"Amy was chatting to him as I left them."

"Once we get to my sister's place, we should be safe."

Maria nodded and looked out the window. She could see the ground now, but they were still pretty high up.

"Where are we?" she asked.

"We just flew over Glasgow and the Clyde Valley. Another fifteen-minutes or so, and we should be close to landing," Jeff said, frowning.

"What's the matter?"

"I'm just worried because I can't get hold of my sister."

"What's her name?"

"June, named after her birth month."

"I like names like that," Maria said. "I had an Auntie May, who died when I was young. I've just realised something, Jeff."

"What's that?"

"We've spent three days together now, and I don't know anything about you."

"What would you like to know?"

"Tell me about your parents. You know about mine."

"Ok, well, my father was a lawyer, my mother a therapist."

"Are they still alive?"

"No, my dad died when June was young, and our mother passed away two years ago."

"I'm sorry."

"In a way I'm glad they are not here to see this mess."

"So how long has your sister been living in Scotland?"

"She moved away when mam died – married James; a fisherman from Milford Haven."

"I see. That would explain the fish farm. Is June younger?"

"Yes, but only by three years."

"I guess you miss her?"

"Very much so. We didn't spend much time apart as children. We were always seen together – she was, and *is*, my best mate."

"I can see why you're so worried you haven't heard from her," Maria rubbed his arm. "She'll be fine, I'm sure of it."

Jeff took the plane down some more as they headed over Loch Lomond. The ground neared and Maria's ears started popping.

"I'm just going to go back and check on Amy and Dafydd," she said.

Jeff nodded, and picked up the CB handle.

As Maria headed into the passenger area of the plane, she heard Jeff try his sister again.

"Welshlady, come in, Welshlady, come in. This is Valley's Boy, come in Welshlady, over and out."

Jeff took his finger off the talk button and waited. Nothing but air crackled violently back at him. He hung up the handle, and waited for a reply.

*

"Do you know how to play slapsies, Dafydd?" Amy asked.

"I don't feel like playing games."

Amy's mouth screwed up into a pout.

"But it'll be fun," she pushed.

"Huh," Dafydd sighed. "Okay, how do you play it, then?"

Amy clapped her hands together and smiled.

"Okay," she said. "Put your hands together, like this," she showed him by placing her palms together and holding them out in front of him. "You have to try and slap my hand, either side, before I move them. If you miss, I get a free turn at slapping your hand."

"That's it? Not much of a game, is it?" he said, mockingly.

"Come on, mun, it'll be fun, I promise."

"Okay," he said, reluctantly, holding his hands out in front of himself. "Who gets to go first, then? You, I suppose?"

"Yeah," Amy said, giggling.

Dafydd smiled at her giggling, and stifled a laugh of his own.

"Right, fire away, then," he said.

Amy faked a hand movement, but Dafydd didn't flinch. She tried another dummy movement, and again he didn't move. Then she went for it with her left hand, trying to connect with his right, but he moved and she missed.

"I guess it's my turn now?" he asked.

"Hmm," Amy said, and scrunched her face up. "I guess so."

She put her hands out to be slapped, and closed her eyes.

"Are you ready?" Dafydd asked.

"I guess, just make it fast, please."

He slapped her left hand, gently, not wanting to hurt her too much. Amy pulled away from the slap and blew on her reddening hand.

"Ow," she mocked. "You got me pretty good there."

"Get your hands back down then," he said.

"Are you two having fun?" Maria asked from behind them.

Amy jumped, and looked around at her; Dafydd sat back in his seat and looked out the window.

"Are we almost there, yet?"

"Close. I came in to make sure you two are wearing your seatbelts."

"Oooh, I took mine off to have a game with Dafydd, sorry."

"It's ok," Maria said, smiling. "Just put it on now, because we will be landing shortly. You too, Dafydd."

"It's already on," he said, shortly.

"Okay, good," she said, ignoring his tone. She turned around and headed back to the cockpit.

*

"Welshlady, come in, Welshlady, this is Valley's Boy, do you read me?" Jeff said. A couple of minutes had passed since he'd last tried.

"Still no luck?" Maria asked as she nestled back down into her seat.

"Nothing, not a damn thing. And what worries me most is that we just entered the Highlands. We're less than five minutes from landing, and I can't get her. The signal should be more than ample now. I mean, look how close we are to the ground."

"Hmm. Well, we can always go and check on her house, see…"

"This is Welshlady, come in, Valley's Boy, over."

Jeff thumped the steering, and shouted, "Yes!"

He picked up the handle from the CB, and spoke to his sister.

"This is Valley's Boy, we are five-minutes from landing. Do you read me?"

"I read you loud and clear, Valley's Boy. It's good to hear your voice, Jeff. I thought you were never coming, over."

"I got caught up in Cardiff, picked up some company on the way, hope that's okay, over."

"You Samaritan, you. God, yes, it's more than fine; have plenty of room here, over."

"Is it quiet where you are? Will we have much trouble getting from the plane to your house? Over."

"*Very quiet around here, not much trouble at all. I'll meet you out on the field, over.*"

"Okay, over and out."

"Gosh, she sounds just like you, Jeff."

"Hmm? Oh, yeah, very much so."

"Sounds pretty trouble free where she is."

"I knew it would be. She's very much on her own where she is."

"And it's a fish farm?"

"Yes."

"Any workers there?"

"No. When I last spoke to her she told me she had sent them all home to their families when the outbreak occurred."

"So just her and James?"

"Yes. Oh, and Gyps. If she managed to survive the virus."

"Gyps?"

"Gypsy's their dog. Lovely old thing."

"I can't wait to meet them. They sound like such a nice people."

*

The plane skimmed over fields and houses as Jeff came close to landing. Soon they were in a massive grassland area, with huge concrete pools dotted here

239

and there, which would have been used for the fish. A single house lay off in the distance – June and James' house.

After clearing all the pools, Jeff took the plane to ground and kept moving until the house was much closer. A woman could be seen waving them to a stop. By her side sat Gypsy.

When the plane stopped, Jeff switched off the engines and rushed out of his seat as quick as his leg would allow. He went through to the passenger sectiont of the plane, and flung open the door. His sister stood the other side, waiting for him to come out. She rushed to him, and threw her arms around him.

"I thought you weren't coming, Jeff," she said, squeezing him tighter. Gypsy barked.

"It's so good to see you, too, sis. I've missed you so much. And you too, Gyps."

They stood there like that for a few moments, while the others disembarked.

"Right," Jeff said, beaming at his sister. "I'd like you to meet the people I've brought with me. This is Maria." Maria stepped forward and shook June's hand. "And these two are Amy and Dafydd." Amy stepped forward and gave June a hug. Dafydd just stood there, hands in his pocket.

"It's lovely to meet you all. What happened to your leg, Jeff?" June asked, anxiously.

"Aw, it's nothing that can't wait. Where's James?"

"Inside, but...*Kathryn?*" June said gravely.

Jeff seemed to reel backward at the question, then dropped his head and shook it.

"Aww, Jeff," June said, and gave him another hug. A much tighter one. "She was like a sister to me," she whispered in Jeff's ear.

"Is this your dog?" Amy interrupted, bending down to stroke the salt and pepper sheepdog, which licked the child's hands in return.

"Yep, she's mine all right. Had her since she was a pup. Her name is Gypsy."

"I see you've got yourself well protected," Jeff said, motioning to the shotgun slung across his sister's shoulder. He wiped tears from the corners of his eyes.

"Yeah, well, I only ever used to use it for hunting. We get some nice game around here. Never planned on killing people with it," she scoffed.

"Seen much action up here?" Maria asked.

"Not really, no. MacDouglas came around here the day the outbreak started, just to check on me and James. Told us he was going to hole up with his family. Not seen him since."

"MacDouglas?" Maria asked.

"He owns the farm about a mile over there," June said, pointing beyond her house.

As they walked the length of the field to the house, Jeff could see dead bodies scattered in the grass. Most had bullet wounds.

"I thought you said you hadn't seen any action around here?" Jeff asked, gesturing to the dead bodies.

"These are about the only ones we've had," June said.

As they got closer to the house, Jeff could see his sister and brother-in-law had done a good job of keeping themselves safe. All the windows were boarded up on the outside; a sheet of steel covered the front door, making it impenetrable. The two chimneys smoked on either side of the slate roof.

On the inside, more boards covered the windows, and candles were being used instead of the lights. June explained that she didn't use the electricity, said the noise of the generator attracted the sick. She found that when she knocked it off, none came.

Once they were inside, June closed and locked the heavy door and called her husband. The house was rather dark, but the light from the candles was enough to get by. There was enough heat circulating from a big open fire in the kitchen, where a tin teapot hung.

Jeff, Maria, Dafydd and Amy put all their gear down on the kitchen floor, thinking they might need a few things for the stay. Gypsy went over to her basket, where it was warm, and licked at her paws.

Just then, James entered the room. He was a large man with thick, scraggly dark hair. A bushy beard covered half of his weather-chapped face. His nose was bulbous and throbbing red.

"Good to see you, Jeff," he said, heartily. They shook hands and hugged. James clapped a hand to Jeff's back. "Where's Kathryn?"

June looked at her husband, giving him that 'look'.

"Aww, right, I…I…erm…"

"It's okay," Jeff told him. "Really." He smiled lamely.

"Well, let's not stand around jawing," June said. "I thought you might like to have something to drink when you got here, so I put the pot on the fire before coming out to meet you."

"That would be great, thanks," Maria said.

"I'll have one, too," Jeff said, working his way out of James' bear hug.

"I think we should sort that leg of yours out first, Jeff," June said.

"It's fine for the time being. The bleeding has stopped. I don't think it was as bad as I first thought."

243

"I'll have some pop," Amy said, rummaging through one of the holdalls.

"And you, erm, Dafydd, what would you like?" June asked.

The boy blushed and avoided eye contact.

"Well? I'm not going to bite your—"

"Coffee, please."

It was the first time Jeff had heard the youngster speak politely in his company. Maybe it was James' presence that had done it, Jeff thought, and smiled. He looked over at Gypsy, and something struck him.

"Gyps is the first living animal I have seen in days," Jeff said.

"Aye, wee Gypsy has managed to survive it, but the fish didn't; rose to the top of the water within days," James said.

"Bloody hell," Maria said.

"Poor Mr. MacDouglas," June cut in. "He lost his entire stock of cattle, too."

"Jesus," Jeff muttered.

"Is he married?" Maria asked.

"Yes, with four boys, too," James said

"They're safe over there?" Jeff asked.

"Why aye, lad. I've known Andrew for three years now. He'd do anything to keep his family safe. He got his house all boarded up like ours," James said.

Nobody spoke as June made her way over to the pot hanging above the fire. She put on an oven glove to take it down. Mugs were set on the table, and June told everyone to take a seat. She placed the teapot at the table's centre.

"Watch it, it's red-hot," she warned.

Maria and Jeff took up chairs next to each other. June and James sat opposite them.

"Why don't you wee ones go in the back room there, and take Gypsy with you while we have a chat out here?" James said.

"That's a good idea," Maria said. There were certain things that she didn't really want Amy to hear.

"Do we have to?" Dafydd said.

"Yes," Jeff said. "Take our bags in there, and unpack things you think we may need."

"Can I at least take my coffee with me?" Dafydd asked.

"Of course you can, lad," James said.

"Thanks."

The adults waited until the children had moved all the bags out of the kitchen and into the living room before they started talking about their situation. June took a look at Jeff's leg, deciding that the wound needed a change.

"Well we have my plane," Jeff stated.

"But what good does that do us, man?" James asked.

"We could refuel it. Fly it to a remote island off Britain," Jeff said.

"Hmm," James said, running a hand through his thick beard.

"Why don't we just stay right here?" June said. "We're well stocked, and safe."

"I've tried staying locked up in a house twice now, and both times people have died," Jeff said.

"I'm sorry about your Kathryn," James said.

"Me, too," June said.

"Others have lost their lives staying holed up too," Jeff said. "Maria and I lost friends in Cardiff."

"Friends?" June asked.

Jeff proceeded to tell June and her husband about Ollie and Roxie – how they had been killed by Dylan, and how Amy had escaped rape and death at the hands of Dylan's brother.

"And you seem to think that these two men are responsible for this disease being set free?" June asked.

"Yeah," Maria said. "Amy heard Dylan confess to Ollie before he killed him."

"Jesus," James said.

"What a mess. That poor child has been through some awful times," June said.

"And Dafydd?" James asked. "What's that wee lad been through?"

"We don't really know much about him," Maria confessed. "I did try asking him, but he wouldn't open up to me."

"All we do know is that his father's dead," Jeff added.

"He told me on the plane that he saw his mother try to kill his father."

"My God, poor child," June said.

"This is why I don't think it is safe to stay in Britain," Jeff said. "It's not just the sick we have to worry about; there are degenerates out there too."

"But it has been dead quiet up here. Excuse the pun," James said.

"It can't have been that quiet – you have dead bodies strewn everywhere on your land, James."

"Aye, that is true. But that's all we've had," he protested.

"He's right you know, Jeff. They are all the trouble we've had."

"They're getting smarter, too," Jeff added.

"Smarter?" June said.

"Yes," Maria said. "They are showing signs of intelligence. They are evolving into something much more dangerous."

"Ha-ha!" James scoffed. "How do you know this, lass? Were they on an episode of Countdown? Ha-ha!" James' bellowing laughter filled the kitchen, and brought a titter from June.

Jeff really liked James, had done from the first time he'd met him – but the man could be pig-headed at times.

"Huh," Jeff sighed. "We have witnessed them working as units to try and get at us."

"Ach, what you saying, Jeff? Are you going mad, too?" June asked.

"It's the *truth*," Maria said. "We were locked up in a cottage with an army truck parked across the window and door. At first we were safe, but after a day, they got wise – they appeared to work together to move the truck away from the cottage, enabling them to get at us."

"Is this true, Jeff?" James asked.

"Yes, I'm afraid it is. And that's not the only thing, either."

"Go on," James said.

Jeff took a drink of his tea, before telling his sister and James about how the sick immobilised their vehicles by cutting tyres. He told them they may or may not have intentionally blacked out the petrol station Maria had been in.

"And you saw all this?" James asked.

"Yes, well, I can vouch for the moving of the truck, and the slashed tyres. Maria told me about the petrol station, and I have no reason not to believe her."

"Then I guess we haven't either, lad" James said.

"Good. Because there is more."

"More?"

"Yes. We've both seen them perform acts that only a functioning human could."

"Such as?" June pressed.

"Waving, winking and smiling – as though they know how to…"

"Taunt," Maria said.

"Taunt?" James said, puzzled.

"Yes," Jeff said. "Maria is right. They seem to know how to strike fear into us. They know how to…scare us." June and James looked at each other, unsure what to say. Their skin crawled. "And I'm scared that if we don't move from here, and we get cornered by more than ten, say, then we could be in big trouble. God knows what they will be capable of in another twenty-four, or forty-eight hours."

"But they are at a disadvantage, Jeff. They can't come out in the light," James said.

"I hate to have to tell you this, but they can. Seems like daylight doesn't affect them anymore," Jeff said.

"Oh, that's just bloody great," June said. "This means they *are* evolving then."

"All I can suggest is that we keep moving. Head off Britain to a small, unoccupied island. There must be one or two surrounding the Orkney?"

"Aye," James said. "There's a few, like. But what do we do once we get there?"

"Stay there until this mess sorts itself out," Jeff said. "We could stock the plane up with as much stuff as we can, and get the hell out of here. We could come back and forth now and then to get supplies. We could even fly to different countries for supplies," Jeff stressed.

Nobody said anything, just drank their tea in silence until June spoke.

"You two must be tired," she said. "I'll go and make up the spare bed for you, Maria. Do you mind the sofa, Jeff?"

"No, not at all. But what about the children? Where will they sleep tonight?"

"Well Amy can share with Maria, that's if she doesn't mind?" June suggested.

"That's fine," Maria said.

"Good," June said. "Dafydd could sleep in the living room with you, Jeff. We have a recliner one of you could use."

Jeff nodded. "I'll be able to keep my ear out for any trouble in the night."

"I don't think there will be much need for that, but if it makes you feel better..." June said – then excused herself to go and tend to the spare room, and get the blankets and pillows that Jeff and Dafydd would need for their night's sleep.

Chapter 15

Jeff placed the SA80 by the side of the reclining chair, so it was in easy reach in case of any trouble, and got back into the chair. He leant back, tilting the recliner backwards, clicking it into place.

He stretched his leg out, which was ringing in pain. June had stitched the wound before turning in for the night, giving Jeff painkillers to help ease it. They had worn off, leaving him in agony. But it was better that it was done.

Opposite him, Dafydd lay stretched out on the sofa. Jeff could just about make out the lad's features in the dim light.

Jeff sat there listening to the boy's rhythmic breathing, and was glad that Dafydd was asleep, for he didn't know what to say to the youngster. Everyone had gone to bed over an hour ago, but Jeff could not sleep. In that hour he had got up and paced the living room over and over. He'd even gone out to the kitchen, and peered through the gaps in the boards over the windows – he was paranoid.

Now, lying in the chair again, he tried to sleep. But all he could think about was how dark it was around the house. The night had moved in fast, even though it was the summer. By eight o'clock the sun had gone, and the night had set in. Nothing across his sister's farmland could be seen, and that had worried Jeff. He could picture the infected, skulking behind the fish tanks or hiding in the numerous barns and sheds. Would the plane make it to the morning? He got up.

Jeff grabbed the gun and headed back out to the kitchen on tiptoes, not wanting to disturb Dafydd. What was he hoping to see outside anyway? Jeff put his face to the boards on the kitchen window, and looked out: the moon was out from behind a cluster of clouds that were in the sky earlier, and Jeff could see an array of flickering stars. A scant mist had moved in from the sea, and now covered the farm and plane. The light bulb in the sky gave an eerie, milky glow to the thin mist.

Jeff could just picture the infected moving through the haze right now, like zombies marching through a fog banked graveyard. He squinted, thinking he saw something moving out by the plane. A man. A man with a long hilted weapon. No. No, Can't be. It's nothing – just my imagination running wild with me, Jeff thought. Then, in the denseness of the night, the figure turned toward him, and pointed a long, bony finger at Jeff, which made him shiver, and coy away from the window.

"Can't be," he said. "How could it have seen me?"

He looked again; the thing was still there, pointing its finger, before disappearing into the night. Jeff's back found a wall, and he almost screamed out.

"Just like the one with the baseball bat in Twsc," he said. "They know…they can…sense us."

"Jeff?" a voice whispered.

Jeff turned his gun on James, who recoiled out of the way.

"Oh, Jesus. Jesus, God," Jeff said.

"What the hell you doing, man?"

"I…" He didn't want to tell James about his new discovery, just in case the man scoffed again. "I thought I heard movement outside, that's all. What are you doing up anyway, James?"

"I heard you, I'm guessing. Unless we both heard the same noise?"

Jeff had lied about hearing a noise, so he knew that James had heard him.

"Sorry, I didn't mean to wake anyone. I guess I'm just edgy with what I've been through."

"Ach, don't worry your wee self, Jeff. Kind of jumpy myself."

James' mix of Welsh and Scottish lingo made him smile, and relaxed him somewhat. Jeff had noticed that his sister had also adapted some Scottishisms too.

"Come," he said, leading Jeff to the kitchen table. "Sit yourself down."

Jeff was reluctant to go anywhere near the window, but allowed himself to sit.

"Got a nice bottle of Welsh whisky here," James said, and laughed under his breath. "Shipped up from Hirwaun's distillery."

He got two small glasses down from a shelf above the kitchen sink. Old bone china plates and cups lined the shelf down, and glass jars with old-fashioned prints on them indicating which Tea, Coffee and Sugar were in.

The tumblers clattered together as James placed them on the table. The cork made a hollow *popping* noise as it was pulled from the bottle. The strong smell filled Jeff's nose, and brought tears to his eyes. He wasn't much of a drinker, but he felt the time called for one. James gave good measures to both glasses, before returning the cork back to the bottle.

"I'm glad you're awake, to be honest," James said. "The leg okay?"

"A little bit of pain, but I'm sure the whisky will help. What's on your mind?" Jeff said.

"Yes, well, I've been thinking long and hard about what you said earlier. About the infected getting smarter."

"Okay."

James took a slug of his whisky, half emptying the glass. Jeff followed suit, and pulled his lips back due to the brute strength of the fiery liquid.

"Ha! Good stuff, hey?"

"You could say that," Jeff wheezed.

"Right, taking into account what you said earlier, maybe leaving the U.K would be a sensible move."

"I think it is our only option, to be fair," Jeff said.

"Maybe, but I think it is our safest. I would have stayed here, locked up nice and tight, but your stories about them getting smart rattled me, got me thinking about your wee plane out there."

"About flying to an island?"

"Yeah. Out to the Orkney."

"Do you know the small islands?" Jeff asked.

"Yes, some better than others. But I have one in mind in particular."

"Which one?"

"North Ronaldsay."

"North Ronaldsay? That's miles out. It's the most northern of the Orkney isle."

"That's right, Jeff, lad. And not only miles out, but also the smallest of the islands out there."

Jeff thought about this for a moment, and liked the idea.

"Is there any property there?"

"I used to fish with the farmer who lives out there," James said. "He's the lighthouse keeper there."

"That's great," Jeff said.

"We could head out there first thing tomorrow. Pack up everything we can take from here, and go."

"Sounds like a good plan," Jeff said. "But we could give it a couple of days before leaving."

James looked at him puzzled. "Why would we want to do that, Jeff? You were all for rushing away from here earlier."

"I know, but I just thought we could prepare ourselves first. I'd like to give you and June some basic flying lessons, because if anything should happen to me, you lot would be stranded."

"Hmm, good thinking, Jeff. I never thought about that. Having someone else capable of flying would be handy."

"So we are agreed that you and June will learn to fly first, before we leave?" Jeff asked.

"Agreed," James said and swallowed his whisky, as did Jeff. "Another?"

"Yeah, okay, why not? It's definitely helping with the pain in my leg." James filled the glasses half full again, and smiled over at Jeff. Jeff knew the whisky would help his mind to switch off, and was glad of the big measures. "What about your neighbours, the MacDouglases?"

"I never thought about them. Would there be enough room to take them, too?"

"How many of them? June did say earlier."

"Six of them: Andrew and his wife, Siobhan, and their four boys – Clyde, the oldest. Kai and Ramzi the twins, and Angus, who's only three."

"That shouldn't be a problem. Do you think they would want to come with us?"

"I can't see why not. Andrew would only keep them all locked away if there was no means of escape."

"Okay. We'll go over there tomorrow and speak with him?"

James nodded as he drank his drink.

"Right, I best try and get some sleep," Jeff said.

"Me too," James said.

Both men got up from the table, and Jeff waited while James put the glasses into the sink and the whisky in the pantry. As they headed into the living room, they saw Dafydd, who was sitting up on the sofa, sobbing.

"What's the matter, son?" James asked.

"It's okay, James," Jeff said. "I'll take it from here. You get yourself to bed now, and I'll see you in the morning."

"Are you sure, Jeff?"

"Yeah, I'm perfectly fine. Now go on, get yourself off to bed."

"Okay then. Night both."

"Night," Jeff said – Dafydd said nothing. Jeff went back to the recliner, and lay down. "Want to talk about it?"

"Not really, like," Dafydd said.

"I know what you are going through, Dafydd."

"Do you?"

"Of course I do, most of us in this house do."

The youngster sniffled and snorted.

"It's not my dad I'm upset about; it's my mam, like."

Jeff got up, and went over to the boy. He knew he was taking a chance, but he sat down next to him, and put his arm around Dafydd's shoulders.

"Hey, it's okay. We're all here for each other, but you have to let us help. You have to put your emotional barrier down, and let us in. I'm not going to hurt you. None of us are, Dafydd."

"My mother was a germ warfare scientist at Twsc army barracks." Dafydd felt Jeff's back go rigid. "What is it?" Dafydd asked.

"Your mother worked at that place?"

259

"Yeah. She hid the fact from me and my dad," he said, wiping the tears from his eyes using his jumper's sleeve.

"Why should she want to do that?"

"She had to, like. She weren't allowed to say anything about what was going on over there."

"She told you this?"

"Yes."

"Bloody hell. Did she tell you what was going on over there?"

"She said was they were building a new weapon."

"And that's all she said?"

"No, she said more. She told us that this weapon they were working on involved a virus or something, and it escaped the lab."

"Jesus, God."

Dafydd shrugged out of Jeff's grip, and looked the older man in the eyes. "It's not her bloody fault that it got free, like. She was only doing her job!"

"Hey, hey, it's okay. I'm sure your mother had nothing to do with it," Jeff said, trying to calm the teenager.

"Sorry. And I'm sorry for the way I acted and spoke to you and Maria earlier – I know you're only trying to help me."

This made Jeff smile; he felt he was finally getting through to the youth.

"So what happened to your mother?"

"I don't want to talk about it."

Jeff decided not to push the issue.

"You any good with that thing?" Jeff asked, referring to Dafydd's bolt-action.

"Yeah, not bad, see. My dad loved that 410 shotgun. It was the first gun he ever bought. He always used to say he would give it to me one day."

Jeff put his arm back round the boy's shoulders, and pulled him in.

"I lost my wife, and I'm awfully scared I'm going to lose my sister," Jeff said. "That scares me more than anything in this world."

"She has you here now, Jeff. And her husband. Nothing bad can happen to her."

"I hope you're right about that," Jeff said.

"What was James talking to you about in the kitchen, then?"

"Oh, nothing really. We were just wondering whether to make for one of the Orkney Islands."

"I think maybe that would be a good idea."

"Yeah?" Jeff asked.

"Yep. Not going to be many people on them islands. We would be safe."

"Nice to know you're on board with the plan, Dafydd."

"I heard James talk about that family, too."

261

"The MacDouglas family?"

"Yeah, that's the ones. Them."

"James seems to think they will come with us if they know we have a plane."

"Will it take all of us?" Dafydd asked.

"It should do. We may be a bit weighed down, but that just means it will take us a bit longer to get over to the Orkney Islands."

"Can you teach me how to fly?"

"You heard that too, did you?"

Dafydd blushed, and couldn't maintain eye contact with Jeff.

"It's okay," Jeff said. "I'll give you some lesson, but first I want James and June to learn, okay?"

He beamed, "Okay. Deal."

"Deal," Jeff said. "Right, now let's get some sleep, or we won't be good for anything in the morning."

Jeff got up, and went over to the candle to blow it out. He returned to the recliner, the pain in his leg minor, and slumped down in it, covering his clothed body with a thick duvet his sister had given to him.

"Nighty-night, Jeff," Dafydd whispered in the darkness.

"Night," Jeff said, closing his eyes and letting sleep take him.

*

Dafydd woke up the next morning to voices coming from the kitchen. He recognised one speaker as Maria. He looked over to the recliner, and saw that Jeff's duvet was now folded and sitting in a neat bundle on the seat.

Dafydd stretched his arms, yawned and settled back down. He could now hear Amy speaking, but he couldn't make out what they were talking about. His nose filled with the smell of frying bacon, and the noise of pans and china clicking tuned his ears.

He didn't want to move from the warmth of his blanket, and instead lay there letting the smells from the kitchen fill him, making his mouth water.

Dafydd thought about the conversation he'd had with Jeff last night. He felt guilty again about how he had spoken and reacted to them all at the hangar. Then his bladder forced all thoughts from his head – it was time to get up.

Throwing the duvet to one side, he practically jumped from his lying position to a standing one. He arched his back, yawned again and ruffled his shaggy hair. He walked out of the living room. There was a rumble coming from somewhere in the building, and he realised it must be the generator – June had told them that she put in on from time to time to get some things done, like bathing and cooking food.

Dafydd entered the kitchen and saw Maria standing by the oven, keeping an eye on the sausages that were browning nicely. The bacon was stacked on a plate with black pudding and mushrooms. Amy was sitting at the table, and Gypsy was in her basket.

"Morning, Dafydd," Maria said.

Amy followed suit – "Morning."

"Hey," he said. "Breakfast smells lush. Where's everyone else, then?"

"Jeff took June and James out for flying lesson. They shouldn't be much longer; they went out early this morning."

"Sorry, I have to pee," he said, and darted off to the bathroom.

Amy giggled. "Boys!"

Maria smiled and turned back to the sausages that were ready to come out of the pan. She placed them all on the plate and put the plate in the oven to keep all the food warm. *They shouldn't be much longer*, Maria thought.

"How long before we can eat?" Amy asked Maria.

"Not much longer."

"I'm starving, I am."

Maria smiled, "I know you are."

The flush on the toilet startled Maria, and then she realised that it was just Dafydd.

"Duw, I needed that – I was bursting."

"Eww," Amy giggled out.

"Nice," Maria said.

Dafydd smiled and sat at the table opposite Amy. "Problem with that?" he said.

"Yeah, it's disgusting, like."

"That's boys for you," Maria said.

"Charming," Dafydd said, almost laughing now.

"Well you asked for it," Amy said, poking her tongue out at the boy.

"Watch a bwganbran don't come out of the fields and pull your tongue out," Dafydd said.

"A what?" Maria asked.

"A bwganbran – it means scarecrow in Welsh," Dafydd explained.

"I knew that," Amy said. "I went to a Welsh school too."

"Then you know how evil they are then, right?"

"Scarecrows are not evil. They are made of hay, like. What's so evil, and scary, about that?"

"Okay, don't believe me then."

Maria could see doubt starting to creep into Amy's eyes, and could sense her starting to get worried.

"Right, that's enough, Dafydd."

"Oh, come on, I almost had her then."

"Nah, you didn't," Amy said.

Dafydd shrugged his shoulders.

265

"Can you get the teapot off the fire for me please, Dafydd?" Maria asked.

"Yeah, sure thing. But didn't you just use the kettle this morning? They have the generator running."

"They don't have one," Maria informed him.

"Ha-ha," Dafydd laughed. "Us city folk ain't used to living like this, ma'am."

Amy sniggered.

So did Maria.

Then he got up, walked over to where the pot was hanging over the fire, and took it down. He put it in the centre of the table. Maria was busy getting mugs off the shelves. She handed them to Dafydd two at a time for him to place. Then Maria got cutlery out, and again handed them to the boy.

"Right, I don't think I'm forgetting anything, do you two?"

"No," Amy said.

Dafydd shook his head.

Then Maria heard the plane motors whirring out in the fields – they were back, and she could stop worrying about whether they would or not. She looked out the window and saw Jeff, June and James all running toward the house. Her heart started to pound.

The look on Jeff's face said it all – danger.

"What's wrong?" Amy asked. "Are *they* back, then?"

Maria didn't move, didn't speak – she couldn't take her eyes off Jeff's face.

"Maria?" This time Dafydd.

Amy and Dafydd got up from their seats and flanked Maria. They watched as the three outside rushed to the house, with Jeff getting there first. He burst through the door, almost out of breath.

"What's wrong?" Maria asked, terror in her voice. She had her arms around both Amy and Dafydd.

"We think…" He caught his breath. "We think we may have found survivors – lots of them."

Maria's eyes widened. "Where?"

"There's a safety point been set up on one of the Orkney Islands."

Maria's mouth went wide, and she whispered, "What?"

"Cool," Amy said.

Dafydd punched the air, "Yes."

"Don't get too excited, it might be nothing. We have to check"

"How do you know this?" Maria asked.

"I found a transmission broadcasting on the plane's radio."

June and James came through the door.

"Did he tell you?" June asked.

"Yes," Maria said.

"I'll crank up the old wireless, see if I can pick up the signal," James said.

They all followed James into the living room, and watched as he switched on the old radio. June shut and locked the door before joining the others. By then, James was easing his way through the radio bands, finding only dead, hissing air.

"Damn it," James said.

"Maybe it was because we were up high," Jeff said.

"Maybe," James agreed.

Then James went passed something that sounded like a voice far off in the distance, muffled by static. He turned the dial back slowly and found it. A voice became clearer, until eventually they could hear what was being said:

"This is not a recording. This is being broadcast today – the 19th of June. The time, 10.00 A.M. My name is Ray Ford, and I'm a Captain with the British army. I have set-up a small post on the Island of South Ronaldsay, just off the coast of Scotland. I have fifty men here under my command, including doctors and medical staff. We are well armed and stocked. We have word that the virus has spread from Britain, and has entered France, Spain and Germany. We are calling all survivors to come here. Many have already made it here, and are being treated. There are no infected in this camp. Everyone that makes it to this outpost will be checked for the disease.

Please, if you can hear this transmission, come to us. We will not harm you, I repeat, we will not harm you."

The radio went quiet; the Captain had stopped speaking.

"Well," Jeff said, turning to Maria. "What do you think?"

"I think we should head over there right now, we'd be stupid not to, right?"

"Aye, I agree, lassie," James said.

"But what if they *do* mean us harm?" June said.

"It's the army," Dafydd said.

The room fell quiet as they all thought about it. The silence was broken by Amy. "I saw them kill people in my street, and not just sick people."

"My God," June said.

"And there was that unhinged soldier at the airport," Jeff said.

"We don't know he was crazy," Maria said. "He could have been sick."

"What's that about a mad soldier?" James asked.

"We were attacked at Cardiff airport by a man wearing military clothes – he was using a gun, which made me believe he wasn't sick," Jeff explained.

"Bloody hell. If we can't trust the army, then who can we trust? I mean, killing innocent people?" James said.

"I think we need to trust them. What else are we going to do?" Maria asked.

The Captain's voice kicked back in: *"This is not a recording…"*

Chapter 16

Jeff was the first to finish his breakfast, putting his knife and fork down on his plate in an X shape.

"That was lovely, thanks, Maria," he said, burping but stifling it with a closed fist. "Pardon."

"That's okay, I'm glad you enjoyed it. It's been a while since I cooked an English breakfast."

Jeff looked over to June, who was feeding Gyps a few remaining scraps of her meal. His sister was looking older, he thought, much older than the last time he had seen her a few years back, when Kathryn and he had vacationed there. June's hair had grey creeping in at the sides; her face had adopted a multitude of lines and wrinkles.

"What do you think we should do, June?" Jeff asked.

June straightened from feeding Gypsy and looked over at Jeff, who was stretched out in his seat.

"I think wee Maria is right; we should make for Ronaldsay first thing tomorrow morning."

"It's a risk, though," Jeff said.

"A risk worth taking, I think," Maria said.

James nodded his head in agreement, his mouth full. But that didn't stop him from talking. "We could always go and check it out, see what's what there."

Jeff seemed to consider this for a moment.

"And if we don't like what we see, then we can take the plane and fly out of there, and do what we talked about last night, Jeff," James said.

"Okay," Jeff said. "What about your neighbours?"

"What about them?" James asked.

"Are we still going to take them?"

"Well, aye. You and I will go over there later, get them over here," James said.

"I think it's a bit late for that, James, dear," June said.

"Nonsense, woman," James said.

This made Dafydd and Amy smile.

"Okay, suit yourselves, then."

"Maybe she's right, James," Jeff said. "It is almost four."

"Ho-ho! I guess I can't take on siblings," James said, laughing loudly, his cheeks going red. "First light then."

"Okay," Jeff said. "I didn't think we'd be out flying so long."

"I'll pack up all the food we have here, plus whatever else we may need," June said.

"I'd better get that fuel in the plane," Jeff said. "We might not make it to the Orkneys on what's left in the tank."

"Andrew has fuel on his farm, if we need more," James said.

"Does he?" Jeff said.

"Yes, he keeps drums of the stuff for his tractors and machinery," James said.

"That'll be handy," Jeff said.

"Right, best get these dishes washed and put back out of the way," June said.

"I'll give you a hand," Maria said.

"Me too," Amy said.

"I'm off outside to chop us some wood for the fire," James said. "You men coming with?" he asked Jeff and Dafydd.

"Yes," Jeff said.

Dafydd nodded.

*

James led Jeff and Dafydd out to a field behind the house. Dafydd had his father's bolt-action with him, and Jeff had the SA80. But the area was quiet, and they had not seen a sick person since leaving Cardiff a day ago. It was literally 'dead' here.

Behind the house was a garden, where a great oak tree stood. It stretched wooden limbs over the chopping blocks, which were basically old tree stumps. An axe stood by the side of one of them. To the left, stacked against the wall making up the perimeter of the garden, was a pile of wood, all cut into chunky sections ready to be split.

273

"I'll go and get another axe. Why don't you make a start, Jeff?" James said.

"What am I going to do?" Dafydd wanted to know.

"Why, you have the most important job of all," James said. "You get to keep watch over us with your gun, lad."

"Great," Dafydd said, huffing.

"Hey, come on," Jeff said. "It's not all that bad. Would you prefer to be washing dishes with a load of giggling women?" Jeff asked.

"Now you put it like that, like, maybe it ain't that bad."

"I thought as much."

Jeff walked over to the axe, and took it in his hands.

"Right, just keeps your eyes peeled, okay, Dafydd?" Jeff said.

"Of course I will, mun," Dafydd said, taking the gun from his shoulder. "Not like we are going to get attacked, is it? It's bloody dead around here."

"Just keep your eyes peeled."

Dafydd saluted Jeff, "Aye-aye, Cap'n," he said, and they both laughed.

Jeff grabbed one of the lumps of wood, standing it upright on the stump before him, and cut it clean in half with the axe. James approached them with an axe of his own and joined Jeff in chopping the wood.

After twenty minutes of cutting, Jeff's shirt was saturated with sweat, and he was starting to breathe heavy. He leant the axe against the stump and took five minutes.

"You okay there, Jeff, mate?"

"Yeah, just a little out of wind."

"Maybe you should give the lad a wee go, and take a few minutes on guard duty?" James suggested.

Dafydd's eyes lit up. "Yeah, come on, Jeff. Come and have five minutes, you're not as young as you used to be." He smirked. James sniggered.

"You cheeky…I'm not that old!" Jeff protested.

"Yeah-yeah," Dafydd said.

"Hey, why don't you go and get us something to drink?" James suggested. "Just go and ask June, lad. Maybe we'll get lucky and she'll give us some of her famous ginger ale."

"That sounds good," Jeff said.

"Yeah, she keeps bottles of the stuff in the cellar. It should be ice-cold."

"I'll go now," Dafydd said.

"Okay," Jeff said, but then thought about it. "Maybe I should come with you, just in case anything happens."

275

"No, I'll be fine, honest. You two stay here, I won't be long."

They watched Dafydd as he headed toward the house, his gun ready for action.

"That's one brave young man," James said.

"I agree. Poor boy lost his father in Cardiff," Jeff said. He filled James in on the whole story. "He won't tell us the rest of his story, not sure he ever will."

"It's understandable. Poor lad. Never mind – he has us now."

"I guess so," Jeff said.

"We have to make it to Ronaldsay. I honest to God think we'll all be safe there, that this nightmare will be over, Jeff."

"I'd love to think that you're right, James, really I would."

"But?"

"But I've seen so many terrible things the past few days, unjust things. I'm not sure I entirely trust the army, especially knowing they are to blame for this bloody virus getting loose in the first place."

"True. But I don't see any other options, Jeff."

"I know, you're right, I know you are. And that's why I sided with you all earlier."

James placed a huge hand on Jeff's shoulder and said, "Good man."

Dafydd was on his way back, bottles of drink in his hands. He was smiling, and shouting something, but neither Jeff or James could make out what the youngster was trying to tell them.

Behind Dafydd, less than a hundred feet, was a gangly man wearing bib and braces. In his hands he held a shovel.

"Jesus," James said. "Dafydd, get over here, now!"

"Quick," Jeff screamed, his lungs burning.

Dafydd realised something was wrong. He turned around to see the infected man closing the gap between them. Dropping the bottles, he readied his bolt-action.

"No!" Jeff shouted. "Get over here, now!"

James ran to the boy, axe in hand.

Dafydd dropped the hammer on the rifle, which clicked. Jammed.

"Fuck," he said, turning to run. He ran directly into James, knocking himself backwards onto his arse.

"Get up, and get over to Jeff!" James yelled. "Now!"

As the infected ambled closer, James saw that it was Andrew MacDouglas from the farm across the way. Andrew had deep slashes across his face, which were pissing blood. Most of his hair had fallen out, and his hands were cut to ribbons. The handle to a pair of scissors jutted from his left shoulder, and

277

gunshot wounds were visible in his left thigh – the reason for his slow gait.

"Andrew?" James said. "Andrew?" he repeated.

Andrew responded by opening his mouth wide – pillars of saliva stretched from one side of his parted lips to the other. Strings of the stuff slid out of his gob, soaking into the material of his dungarees. He swung the shovel over his shoulder, ready to smash it into James' face.

"What the hell are you waiting for?" Jeff said. "Kill it!"

James couldn't do it – he'd known Andrew since moving up here, and so backed away, but not wuickly enough. He took the spade to the jaw, and it floored him.

Jeff rushed over to Andrew with his axe, but missed with his swing and took a hit from the shovel to the base of his skull. Jeff went to ground, but he was not out cold. He tried getting up, but repeated blows to the back from Andrew gave him little opportunity. James appeared to be out cold, and wouldn't be coming to the rescue.

Dafydd arrived at Andrew's side and smashed the butt of his gun into the man's temple. Andrew's knees buckled and he collapsed, giving Jeff and James time to recover. Jeff stood over the fallen Andrew. He drove his axe into the man's gut. Jeff kept his mouth

278

closed as blood sprayed across his face. He tried to pull his axe free, but it was stuck. James came to his side, now with little sympathy, and pounded Andrew in the chest with the axe, then again in the neck. Jeff finally managed to free the axe,, and made the final blow to the thing's face.

"If this has happened to Andrew, then God knows what he has done to his family," James said. "Or if they are even okay."

"We better get over there, now," Jeff said."

James agreed.

*

After taking Dafydd back to the house, and explaining to the women what had happened, James and Jeff headed out over to the MacDouglas place on foot, instead of taking James' car; it would have taken them longer as they would have had to drive miles to get there. This way they could just cut through the fields.

They crossed a large meadow between James' house and Andrew's place. Nothing seemed to move, apart from crows here and there. Some could be seen resting on a scarecrow, screeching and cawing as the two men passed by. A tractor stood motionless in the field, its driver slumped over the steering wheel – his face turned away from them. Crows had gathered on the farmer's hunched back and the bonnet of the tractor.

"Think we should check it out?" James asked.

"Maybe. Do you know him?"

"It could be one of the MacDouglas boys, and he could be hurt."

"Ok," Jeff said.

They walked over to the old, grey Ferguson tractor. Jeff had his gun out in front of him, while James had his wife's shotgun. Slowly they moved through the almost waist-high grass, their hearts slamming against their chests.

Jeff reached the man first, poking the muzzle of his gun into the guy's side, which disturbed the birds and sent them flying skyward. The farmer didn't move.

James went around to the man's other side, allowing him to see the unblinking eyes of the dead farmer. There were holes in his cheek, and most of his lips had been eaten away by the birds. Teeth and part of his tongue were visible through the pecked holes.

"Jesus. How long has he been here?" Jeff said.

"Not sure," James said, looking into the thing's milky eyes. "Days, I would have said."

"Wonder what killed him? I don't see a mortal wound of any sort, do you?" Jeff said.

"No," James said, moving his eyes over the body, before going back to the face and seeing the dead farmer's eyes. Shut.. "Huh!" was all James had time to say. He stumbled backwards, his legs tangling as he went.

The thing flew out of its seat on the tractor and jumped down onto James. Jeff heard James wail on the other side. He ran around the vehicle to find James holding the thing at bay with the shotgun: James had it pressed against the thing's throat as it clawed at the air, trying to scratch James' eyeballs out.

Jeff didn't hesitate. He pressed the muzzle of his gun to the side of the thing's skull. He fired a single shot. The bullet exited the other side of the thing's head, and it slumped down onto James.

James rolled the body off him and jumped to his feet.

"Did you see that, Jeff! Did you? For Christ's sake – it was playing possum. How could it do that? They can't!"

"Nothing shocks me anymore, nothing. I told you about the things I have seen *them* do; they're getting smarter all the time."

"How can you be so blasé?"

"I'm not, James. I've just accepted it now."

James huffed and let out a dry laugh.

"Did you know him?" Jeff said.

"It looked like one of Andrew's helpers. Not sure of the man's name."

Jeff nodded, and started moving.

*

Soon they were at Andrew's home, standing by a large barn. A chilling squeak was coming from within – a generator was running off in the background somewhere.

They entered the large wooden structure to check on the noise, with Jeff leading the way. In front of them, impaled on a hay hook and swinging from one of the beams making up the roof, was a teenage boy. His head hung low, causing his chin to touch his chest; his long hair covered the sides of his face.

"It's Kai MacDouglas," James said. "And he looks pretty dead to me."

"I guess," Jeff said, making his way over to the swinging body. Blood trickled out of the bottom of the boy's left trouser leg, spitting at the hay covered floor. "This happened pretty recently," Jeff said.

"It would seem that way," James agreed.

Jeff looked up at the boy's face – he was definitely dead. Jeff left the body and headed to the back of the barn. He'd spotted a pair of legs jutting out from a bundle of hay. Jeff waved James on to see what he had found.

"Jesus," James said. "It's Kai's twin brother – Ramzi; neither of them more than sixteen, seventeen."

The boy lying dead behind the hay had a hole in his chest – buckshot wounds peppered his guts. Jeff lowered his head.

"My God, it's slaughter," Jeff said.

He turned to leave, and saw the tears in James' eyes.

"I knew these boys. Watched them grow."

Jeff put a hand to James' shoulder.

"Let's check the rest of the place."

Leaving the barn behind, they headed over to the farmhouse. It was an older looking house to James and June's, made from brick and wood. A large wooden porch with a veranda graced the front, along with six large windows; three above, and three below, all of which were boarded up. Swinging baskets could be seen either side of the door, with blooming red flowers. Stencilled across the glass in the door was the family name – MacDouglas.

Jeff walked up the three steps to the porch, and rapped on the door with four stiff knocks.

"Siobhan," James called from behind Jeff. "Are you here?"

Jeff could hear the fear in James' voice, and feel it in his own legs as they trembled. He placed a sweaty

283

hand to the doorknob and turned. It squawked, just the once. Jeff threw the door wide; his gun's barrel led the way.

The long corridor led into what seemed to be a kitchen at the end. Jeff turned right, and was immediately looking into a large sitting room. A TV adorned the corner of the room. He poked his head into the large room, and found it empty. He called James on with his hand. Jeff eased himself and walked into the sitting room. Mounted above the television was a deer's head, its eyes forever fixed on the wall opposite. Jeff moved further into the room. A solid wooden dinner table stood in the middle, with eight chairs surrounding it. A plush rug lay in the centre of the room on top of the wooden flooring.

Jeff turned and went back out to the passageway where James was waiting.

"Anything?" he mouthed.

Jeff shook his head then signalled James to follow him. A room branched off to the left of the corridor – another sitting room, but much smaller. Books lined the walls, and there was no TV. A rocking chair, with a long shafted lamp standing over it, was in one corner of the room. A grandfather clock standing against one of the walls ticking heavily gave Jeff the creeps. He'd never liked those clocks, not since he was a child. Like the first living room, this one appeared undisturbed.

"Where are the rest of them?" James whispered.

Jeff shrugged, not wanting to tell James that he thought the whole family was dead – why else would the front door have been left unlocked?

Jeff walked the length of the passageway into the kitchen. He expected to see the kitchen dripping red with blood. Maybe the wife, Siobhan, lying dead on the floor with her remaining sons, but he was wrong. The room had a disinfectant smell to it. The floor seemed freshly mopped, the appliances gleaming. The windows were boarded up. Jeff lowered his gun and turned to James, who had the gun down by his side.

"Now what?" James asked.

"I…" Jeff started.

A low groan – like wood on wood – penetrated the ceiling. Something was upstairs.

Jeff faced James his face ashen. His jaw hung loose. He was about to say something, but stopped himself. He listened again to that awful noise – *creak, creak, creak, creak…*

Jeff looked at the ceiling; the sound was intensifying, "Best we check it out," he told James.

At the foot of the stairs heading to the second floor, James took the lead. His heavy boots made the bare steps groan as he climbed. Jeff stayed close behind. Neither man used the banister. At the top of the stairs they were faced with a short corridor with two closed doors off it, and one that stood ajar – they went to that one first, thinking the noise was coming from there. James stifled the need to call out.

The intended door had brightly coloured tiles on it, spelling out *Angus*. James halted Jeff and entered the room alone. Jeff waited on the landing, about to head over to one of the closed doors when James came back out of the room – his face ashen. He pinched either sides of his nose, trying to stop the tears that were now spilling down his cheeks.

"What…" Jeff began, walking over to where James stood. Over James' shoulder Jeff could see into the dusky room: the baby blue wallpaper behind the cot was mottled with a brown, yellow colour. The carousel too.

"Don't go in there," James whispered. "For God's sake, don't. He was so…so…little, just a baby."

"Jesus," Jeff said.

The creaking became louder now. Jeff headed over to one of the shut doors, leaving James to try and gather himself. He picked the closed door to the left, convinced the noise was coming from that room. He slowly pushed the handle down…*creak…creak…creak…*

With the door open, Jeff just stood and watched the scene before him: someone was sitting in a rocking chair – *creak, creak, creak*. Two heads peered over the top of the seat; one of the faces looked directly at Jeff, the eyes unblinking, dead. They reminded Jeff of the mounted head down in the living room. The other person in the chair appeared to be brushing the hair of the lifeless person.

As Jeff moved closer to the rocker, the living person began to sing. It was a female voice, and the song that came out was disjointed, as if the person was being throttled at the same time. It was a song Jeff knew only too well, as his mother used to sing it to him, "*Hush, little baby, don't say a word, Mama's going to buy you a mockingbird.*"

Jeff raised his weapon. The singing stopped, as did the rocking. Jeff swallowed hard. The person rose out of the seat, slowly. The sight of cords hanging from the stump of the decapitated head the person was holding made Jeff violently retch.

He dropped his gun and collapsed to his knees. Tears stung his eyes, and he could just about make out the person, coming closer…

Just then, James stepped into the room and was horrified at the sight of Siobhan's face, which seemed knotted with agony. Welts and sores decorated her once pretty face and cheeks. Her lower lip sagged, but her jaw seemed strong. Her eyes had lost their stunning emerald colour, and were now replaced by a pearl white.

James saw Jeff immobilized on the floor. A small pool of vomit had gathered under him. James raised his gun, and was about to shoot Siobhan when suddenly the door closed on him, pushing him sideways. His legs tangled with the bed. James flew over it, crashing to the floor the other side.

Before he could get up, Clyde was on him, scooping James' big frame up as if he were a doll. Clyde pinned him to the wall; James' feet dangled off the ground. He struggled like a fly caught in a spiderweb, but he couldn't break Clyde's grip. He'd dropped his gun.

James became dizzy as the hands around his throat tightened. He thrashed his legs and aimed for Clyde's groin with his foot. It connected once or twice, but nothing. There was only one thing left to do. James pushed his thumbs deep into Clyde's eyes, forcing them back into the brain. Clyde let go, and James fell to the floor. He reached for the shotgun as Clyde staggered around the room, crashing into things, holding his eyes as the agony coursed through him.

James looked over to Jeff to find Siobhan had somehow jumped on his back – her fingers were in

Jeff's mouth. The head she had been holding was nowhere to be seen.

James went right up close to Clyde, placed the barrel of his shotgun to the lad's chest, and pulled the trigger. Clyde screeched as he was blown backwards into the wardrobe. Blood spilled out of the wound and soaked his Clyde's checked shirt. He was dead.

James rushed over to Jeff, who was yelling and screaming for help, as he danced around the room with Siobhan on his back. She was screeching and snarling as Jeff tried shaking her free. But she stuck to Jeff as though she was glued to him. Her one flailing arm smacked James in the face, sending him backwards and causing his nose to bleed.

Jeff forced her back into the chest of drawers, which had a vanity mirror on it. The sound of the glass shattering was deafening; Siobhan screamed out in agony. Jeff tried to call out to James, but he couldn't get his words around her fingers, which had curled around his tongue, trying to rip the organ from his head. He resorted to biting down on her mushy digits, managing to bite one off completely. She fell off him, and Jeff spat the offending finger from his mouth.

He issued her a boot to the face, which snapped her head sideways.

James and Jeff stood over the unconscious woman, knowing they could not leave her alive.

"Who's he?" Jeff asked, pointing to Clyde.

"The eldest son," James said.

"So that's the whole family dead?" Jeff asked.

Siobhan started to stir on the floor.

"Yes. Do you want to do it?"

"Not really, but what choice do we have? One of us has to – we can't let her live."

Jeff picked up his gun, and took aim.

*

Neither of them said a word on their way across the fields to James' house. They were exhausted, not to mention horrified at what they had found over at Andrew's place. Jeff was glad to see his sister's farm come into view – he needed something stiff to drink. Tomorrow they had to leave Britain and never return. There was nothing left on this rock they called an island but the dead and the diseased. Life here was finished.

Chapter 17

Jeff was the one to tell June and Maria what had happened over at the MacDouglas farm – James would have been happy enough to have left it there, to have told the women nothing. Jeff, on the other hand, felt he had to relay his information. He couldn't just keep them out of the loop.

Jeff poured himself a shot of James' whisky with trembling hands. Downed it, and refilled. He did that three times before he could utter a syllable. June was mortified to learn about the MacDouglas boys and their mother – Maria not so much. Jeff told them everything at the kitchen table, without Dafydd and Amy present – they'd been sent to the living room again while the adults spoke.

"We need to leave first thing in the morning," Jeff said.

"But…but, we haven't had time to gather up everything here that we could use," June said.

"Then I suggest we all start getting it together now and loading the plane. First light I want us all out of here," Jeff said.

"And go to North Ronaldson?" James asked.

"No, South Ronaldson," Jeff said. "I think we should take our chances with the Captain and his dubious outpost."

"Dubious?" Maria said. "Then why the hell do you want to take us out there, Jeff?"

"What options do we have, Maria, hmm? Think about it? We're walled in, trapped."

"What about that wee island you were on about yesterday, Jeff?" June asked.

"I don't know if we can take that chance. We'd be all alone out there. What if something should happen? We have Amy and Dafydd to think about too," Jeff argued.

"But…" Maria tried.

"Besides, if the army do want harm us, we can always take the plane and leave," Jeff said. "Now, I think we should pack everything up, load the plane, and leave at first light."

James was keen on the plan, and was happy enough to support it. After all, Jeff had come this far, and not just on his own. He'd survived scores of attacks and had brought survivors with him. Maria and June also agreed it was a good idea to make for South Ronaldson at first light.

"While you pack up here," Jeff said, "I'm going to take the plane over to the MacDouglas farm, and fill it up with petrol. I should be able to land right by the tankers Andrew has over there"

"Wait," James said. "Are you mad? You can't go back over there, not after what happened earlier."

"I have to. We need that plane as full as we can get it. Do you have any empty petrol cans here I can take with me? I may as well get as much as I can."

"Yes I do," James said. "Why don't we leave it, Jeff?"

"You don't have to come with me, James. I'll be fine on my own."

"Then I'll come with you," Maria said.

Jeff turned to her, "Good. You can fill the cans as I fill the plane."

June lowered her head, scared for her brother's safety, and that of Maria. She knew she couldn't talk him out of going back over there.

"Just be careful," June said. "We'll have everything ready to load into the plane by the time you get back. Then I'll make us all something nice to eat." She smiled at her brother. James put an arm around his wife.

"I'll come if you want me to," James said.

"No, it's fine," Jeff said. "It would be great if you could show me to those petrol cans of yours, though, James."

"Of course," James said, and led Jeff and Maria out to the barn at the side of the house.

*

June and James watched the plane take off from their field – Jeff had promised that he and Maria would not be any longer than an hour, maximum. Once the plane was out of sight, June set about taking tinned food out of the cabinets and boxing it.

James went in to Dafydd and Amy, who were sitting in the living room talking. Gypsy was lying on Amy's lap.

"He went back there, didn't he?" Dafydd said.

James nodded.

Amy looked up from stroking Gyps.

"Why?"

"To get more fuel for the plane, boy."

"But we had some stored in the plane, like." Dafydd said.

"I know, but he wants to make sure we have enough."

"How come you never went with him, then?" Dafydd said, with a smirk on his face.

"Because Maria offered to go…"

"Maria?" Amy said, panic all over her innocent face.

"Yes, but it's going to be alright. There is nothing over there that can harm them."

"So why didn't you go with Jeff then, James?" Dafydd said again, cockiness in his tone.

"I told you, Maria offered to go with him, now leave it at that, boy." James said, sitting down beside Amy and stroking Gyps. "Good girl," he said. "Good girl."

"So what do we do now? Sit and wait for them to get back, is it?" Dafydd said. He could hear June out in the kitchen, opening and closing cupboards and drawers.

"Yes, well, no. We need to pack up all our stuff, and get it out into the kitchen before Jeff and Maria get back, so that we can just get everything we can onto the plane. We'll be leaving when it gets light."

"I don't want to go. I like it here," Amy said.

"But where we're going, lass, we'll be safe for good."

"How do you know that?"

"Because the army will look after us, and if they don't, we will leave for another island."

The child looked down at Gypsy, and the dog licked her cheek.

"Can Gypsy come too?"

James chuckled, then said, "Well, of course she can. We can't go leaving old Gyp behind, now can we?" He laughed some more.

*

June smiled upon hearing her husband laughing and chatting to the children in the other room. She went to the pantry and dug out four large cardboard boxes to pack away some canned goods. She tried not to think of her brother and Maria as she boxed stuff up.

She opened the doors to the cupboard above the sink and took down all the cans two by two until the left side was empty. On the right, she took all the dry food in packets.

Then she turned on the drawers under the sink, and looked for other things that would be of use to them. There was nothing but cutlery. And in the cupboards, only detergents and cleaning fluids. June looked to the cooking surface, where she spied the knife block. She withdrew the butcher knife from its slot and placed it on the work surface.

James, Amy and Dafydd all came into the kitchen and put their loaded bags down on the kitchen floor – ready for the plane.

"Can I take one of those boxes?" James asked June.

"What for?"

"I'm going to pack some bedding to take with us."

"But won't we need them for tonight?" June said.

"Damn, you're right. What if I take all the spare sheets and duvets from under the bed?"

"Good idea," June said. "Can you get the flashlight and batteries from the drawers in the cabinet in the living room, James?"

He nodded and turned to leave, but remembered something. "Have you packed Gyp's stuff?"

"No, I'll do that now."

As James headed back into the living room, he heard June instructing the children to go and take a look in the pantry to see if there was anything else in there that they could take with them, and to fetch out Gypsy's food.

James made his and June's bedroom and knelt at the side of their bed. He pulled out a long drawer that was built into the base of it. He saw that there wasn't much left, as most of it was already being used. He pulled everything out as neat as he could and took it to the kitchen.

June and the children were busy placing more stuff into another box when he entered. He didn't say anything, and went straight to one of the two boxes that had not yet been used. He placed all the bedding he had on the table and sifted through it, putting what was adequate in his box.

Before they were finished packing, they could hear a plane approaching. June smiled. Amy and Dafydd looked at each.

"They are back, mun," Dafydd said.

297

Amy put her hands to her mouth and giggled.

"Can we go out to them?" Amy asked June. "Please."

June looked at the child, then up to her husband, who simply shrugged his shoulders and smiled.

"Let's wait until they land?" June said.

"Okay," Amy said flatly.

June put her hand under the girl's chin, raising her face to look into the child's eyes. "Are you pouting?" June asked, grinning.

"No!" Amy said.

"What the..." James started.

June looked up to see James staring out the kitchen window. Amy and Dafydd joined them. Jeff was leaning against the plane, vomiting into the grass. Maria was standing behind him, rubbing his back.

"Ugh," Amy said.

"I'll go out to them," James said.

"Can we come?" Dafydd asked, indicating to Amy and himself.

"No," he said, a worried look on his face.

James headed out the kitchen door, taking the axe with him. June watched her husband go out to the two by the plane. The sun had started to set, and the sky was filled with a burning red. Shadows crept around the water pools filled with dead fish. The three figures were fast becoming silhouettes.

"We'll never be able to pack the plane now. It's gone too late," June said, shivering. Amy put her arm around June's midriff, and June put her arm around the girl's shoulders, drawing her in. "It will have to be in the morning now," she said, dreamily. They watched as James and Maria helped Jeff toward the house.

*

Jeff sat at the kitchen table, his hands on his wounded leg. "It just split open when I got out of the plane, and made me nauseous. I'll sew it back up," he said to June.

Dafydd and Amy had gone to bed, so had James. Tomorrow would be an early move for them all.

"Drink the *Andrew's*, Jeff. It should help settle your stomach," June said.

He picked up the glass of fizzing water and gulped it down without stopping. He pulled a face when he'd finished.

"Ugh. I never did like that stuff." He burped and put a hand to his mouth. He picked up the sewing kit June had fetched him.

"So did you get everything you needed from over there?"

"Yes, I filled the plane until it couldn't take any more. Then we filled all the cans we took over there, just to make sure we have plenty."

"Good, good."

"What time does it get light around here?"

"Well, it's summertime, so the sun should be up at around four-thirty, to five o'clock."

"Great. I think we should be up and gone within an hour of it getting light," Jeff said. "There is no point in hanging around." He began to stitch the wound.

June nodded. She looked sombre.

"What's the matter?" Jeff asked.

"Oh, it's nothing."

"Well, it must be something, June. Come on, tell me." He stopped tending to his leg, and placed a hand on her knee. He could see tears in her eyes.

She sniffed. "I'm leaving my home, Jeff, that's what. All my belongings, all my memories."

He sighed. "You'll be coming back, June. This won't be forever."

She laughed lightly, "How silly am I being?" she said. "Weeping over a bloody house and a few photos. I'm just glad I have you here, Jeff. I'm glad I haven't lost you too."

He put his forehead to hers and placed one hand on the back of her head. "Well, I'm not going to be leaving you. And when this is all over, I'm moving up here, to be closer to you and James. You're the only family I have left now, June." She put her arms

300

around him, and he the same. They held each other tightly. "I love you sis"

"I love you too, Jeff. How's the leg?"

"Getting there," he said, wincing as he threaded his skin.

*

James' phone alarm went off at five to four. He scrabbled around for it in the dark, found it, and hit the off button. He rapidly opened and closed his eyes, rubbing at them to shake the weariness from him. Once he was satisfied he would not drop back into sleep, he lay there and let his mind wander. June was snoring lightly by the side of him.

He thought about the poor MacDouglas family. How he'd never seen such horror in his life. He felt a bit ashamed of himself; he'd been too scared to go back with Jeff, and had been secretly relieved that Maria had spoken up. *God, how could I have let a woman go out into such danger?* he thought.

He rolled over onto his side and put his arm around June. She started stirring, and murmured something unintelligible.

"June," he whispered in the gloom. "June, love." She didn't answer. He rested his head against her back, snuggling in.

He drove the thoughts of being a coward away from his head. How could he be a coward when he had saved Jeff's life over at the house? But he couldn't shake the notion. *What must June think of me?* he thought.

James moved from her, and perched on the edge of the bed. He rolled his head around, clicking his neck several times. Then he arched his back and rose to his feet. He threw the curtains to one side and saw the sun rising. It would be light in twenty to thirty minutes.

Turning back to the bed he went over to June again, and shook her lightly by the shoulder, "June, love. June." he said, his voice raising.

"What is it?" she said, groggily.

"It's time we made a shift, love."

"What time is it, then?"

James picked his phone up and lit the screen. "It's almost twenty-past four."

She groaned and threw the covers off her.

"I'll go and call Jeff. I'll leave Maria and Amy to sleep for a bit – no need for them to be up so early."

"You could have left me sleeping too, matey," she said with a playful tone.

"But who would make the coffee?" he asked.

She threw a pillow at him. "Bloody cheek!" She gave him a look that said *I love you, you fool.*

"Do you think I'm a coward?"

She scoffed, and snorted a pig laugh. "What?"

302

"A *coward*, damn it! Do you?"

She could see that he was serious. His fists were balled at his sides. The way the sun shone through the bedroom window cast a golden light on his face. His bare chest hairs appeared blond as they fused with the natural light. She took his left hand in both of hers and pulled him over to the bed, where he sat.

"Don't be so soft, James. You are *not* a coward."

He gulped. "But I must be. I never went with your brother to get the fuel yesterday. I just couldn't do it."

"That does not make you a coward, James. You'd already been through hell once. And let's not forget – you did save my brother's life."

"I know, but I just can't help but…"

"Shh," she said, putting a finger to his lips. "You don't have to worry about anything. Nobody thinks any less of you, certainly not me. I think you're a brave and wonderful man, James." She kissed him.

"Thanks, love," he said, standing up and walking over to the long mirror in the corner of the room. He picked his jeans up and put them on, then took a plaid shirt from the chest of drawers.

June got out of bed behind him. He turned around and looked at her naked beauty as she dressed. Her breasts were firm and her skin supple for her age. She looked no different in James' eyes to the first day they had met.

303

"Are you staring, James?" she said.

"Not at all, beaut."

"Such a liar, you are," she said, jokingly.

"What a thing to say about your doting husband," he said grinning.

"Doting? Ha! I wish."

He looked over at her; she was trying to contain her laughter as she slipped her robe on. He went to her.

"Oh, so I'm not then, am I?"

"Nah."

He gently pushed her onto the bed, and straddled her. He pinned her arms down at her sides and nuzzled at the sides of her neck, snorting and grunting as he did so. June thrashed and bucked, laughing uncontrollably.

"Ha-ha – stop it! You'll wake everyone up!" she said.

"Well they need to get up."

"Okay, okay, I give up, I'm sorry, you *are* doting," she said, shrieking with laughter.

"Thank you," he said, as he climbed off. "I'm going to wake Jeff."

*

Jeff lay there listening to his sister and James laughing and joking in their bedroom. He knew he would have to get up pretty soon, and dreaded the fact. He'd

304

spent most of the night nursing his aching body and throbbing knee.

When he heard James coming from the bedroom he tried to sit, but felt lethargic from the lack of sleep. He just about managed to get to his elbows as James came through the door to the living room.

"Oh, you're awake, then," James said.

Jeff nodded.

"I think June is going to make us a cuppa while we get started, Jeff."

"Sounds good," he managed. "My leg is killing, and so is my side."

"Your ribs?"

"Yes."

"You want to put off the trip today, butty?"

"No, no, I'll be fine once I've got coffee and painkillers inside me," Jeff said.

"Well, okay, if you're sure."

"Yeah, I'm sure," Jeff said.

"Dafydd, you awake," James called. The youngster was breathing rhythmically. "We'll leave him, shall we?"

"Yeah, it should only really take you and me to load up. There isn't much stuff." Jeff managed to pull his laden body from the comfy chair, and stood.

"Hmm, I'll get you some painkillers," James said.

"Morning, Jeff," June said as she walked into the living room.

"Hey, morning, sis."

"Where is the Ibuprofen, June? Jeff's leg and ribs are playing him up."

"Still rotten, hey, Jeff?" June said. "They are in the cabinet above the kitchen sink."

"Afraid so, yes."

"Sure you'll be okay for flying today?"

"Good God, yes. I'll be fine to fly. Promise."

"Alright, if you say so," June said.

"Why don't we go and get the stuff packed onto the plane?" Jeff said to James.

"Yeah, that's fine by me."

"Okay, boys. I'm going to get the pot on for us. Make us all a nice cup of tea."

They followed June into the kitchen, where she started filling the teapot. James went to the door, unlocked it, and had a peek outside. Nothing was moving out there. The sun was almost high in the sky now, driving away the meandering morning fog and soaking up the dew on the glistening grass. James breathed in the fresh air.

"The coast is clear, Jeff, if you want to go out to the plane and open her open."

"Don't you men want a cuppa first, then?" June said.

"We'll have it when we come back, June, love," James said.

"Yeah, let's get loaded up, and ready for the off," Jeff said.

"Oh, okay," June said.

James grunted, indicating that he was ready.

Jeff shouldered his machine gun, and picked up one of the boxes, as James took the other SA80 on his back and picked up the holdalls. They made their way out to the plane. Even though the sun was out, the air felt nippy; goose pimples invaded Jeff's skin.

"It's a tad chilly," James said, as though he could read Jeff's mind.

"Yeah, but by the looks of the sky it is going to be a lovely day; especially for flying."

James got to the plane first, and put the holdalls down at the belly of the plane. "Shall I run back and get more while you put these in?"

"Good idea, I'll just make a start here. I need to check the engine too."

James gave him a thumbs-up and headed back to his house for the rest of the stuff. When he got there, he noticed Dafydd was up, drinking a mug of tea at the kitchen table.

"Need a hand, James?" he asked.

"No lad, but thanks for asking. You stay in here, and help June and the others get ready. We will be leaving shortly."

"Your tea and Jeff's coffee are ready," June said.

"Great, love. I'll take Jeff's out to him," James said, taking a large swallow of his tea, before replacing it on the table and picking up another box, along with Jeff's coffee.

"Ok, well I'm off to wake Maria and Amy," June said.

*

Jeff was happy with the condition of the engine, and was now sat in the cockpit about to start the plane to see if it was running smooth before the flight. He saw James approaching in the distance. The engine kicked to life; Jeff climbed back out of the plane and stood by the left propeller first, listening. It was fine. He went around to the other side, and was greeted by James. Jeff took the mug of coffee and Ibuprofen from him. "Thanks."

"No problem, Jeff. So, everything fine here?" he asked, placing the new box with the others.

"Yeah, the engines are all running perfectly. Not that I thought they wouldn't be."

Jeff downed a couple of pills and a swig of coffee before starting to pack their equipment away in the cargo area. James returned to the house to get what was left. As he lifted the second box to put it away, he felt a massive pull on his thigh, and his knees buckled under his weight. He collapsed against the side of the plane. His fingernails dug into the bodywork, scraping some of the paint away. His breathing became guttural as he tried to force the pain out of his body. Then searing heat tore through him. He forced himself into a standing position just as he saw James and Dafydd coming his way.

"You okay, Jeff, butty?" James asked, placing his hand on Jeff's back.

"Yeah," he said. "My leg gave way."

"Bloody hell," Dafydd said. "Are you sure you're okay, then?"

Jeff nodded. "I'll be fine in a minute. Are the girls ready to go?"

"Yes," Dafydd said. "They sent us on ahead with the rest of the things. June said she was going to lock up, then head over with Maria and Amy."

"Okay, in that case you may as well get in, Dafydd," Jeff told him.

"Me too," James said. "Everything is loaded."

Jeff watched as Dafydd and James got alighted. Then he helped escort June, Maria and Amy, who was carrying Gypsy, onto the plane. He requested June sit in the cockpit, as she could help fly the plane.

Once they were all in, Jeff climbed aboard, and got into his seat in the cockpit. He put his headset on, as did June. James closed and locked the door, and took a seat behind Maria and Amy. Dafydd was sat on his own in front of them.

Jeff turned the plane around and hurtled down the field until he had picked up enough speed to take off. Once in the sky, he banked, and headed back over his sister's farmhouse.

Chapter 18

Private Scott Rhoads drove as fast as the Land Rover would allow him. He had to make it to John O'Groats before it started getting dark, or he'd risk getting caught out in the middle of nowhere. He had a plan – he would take one of the boats at the harbour and sail to the outpost on South Ronaldsay. He would be safe there until this blew over.

Scott, and a squadron of three-hundred men, had been sent to the north of the English borders to set-up blockades, hoping that they could contain the outbreak to just Wales and England. They had failed.

Scott had been part of a platoon holding Carlisle and its surrounding areas. They'd been ordered to kill all infected on sight, and to dispose of the bodies by means of fire. They hadn't found many sick, only plenty of non-sick, who the military had managed to herd out just before the infected had reached the borders. Scott and the other soldiers hadn't stood a chance of stopping them.

They managed to hold their ground for a few a days. But then ammunition started running dry, and the airdrops had lessened as time passed, until there were none, leaving them to fend for their lives. As the barriers started to show cracks, Scott left his post for the nearest vehicle and decided to drive as far north as he could.

He'd driven as many hours as he could, before exhaustion took over and he had to stop and get his head down for a few hours. He found an abandoned Ibis hotel, out on a stretch of motorway between Fort William and Inverness. Most of the Scottish people had fled after word about the outbreak reached them. It had caused pandemonium.

*

After a few hours at the hotel Scott moved on. He was now about twenty miles away from John O'Groats. He'd never seen a motorway looking so dead. He came across a few crashed cars and smoking wrecks every so often. He didn't bother stopping – he had no intention of stopping for anything, even if there could be survivors.

He looked in his rear-view mirror just in time to watch an aircraft descending from the sky. His mouth sagged, forming an O-shape. His forehead burst into a sweat, and his palms became slippery on the steering wheel. He pushed the accelerator down as far as it would go. The plane got closer, until the nose was almost touching the back bumper.

Scott swerved, hoping to avoid a collision. But as he veered to the right, the plane's right wing clipped at his backend, and flipped the Land Rover over. The sound of crunching and scraping metal was the last thing Scott heard over his own screaming voice.

The Land Rover rolled and pivoted until it came to a stop on all fours against an overturned bus. Most of the bodywork had been ripped free, exposing the framework. The windshield was gone, and so was the passenger door. The whole front was missing, and the engine was now sitting on top of the bus.

Scott's face was submerged in the airbag. He groaned as he pulled his face out. His right shoulder stung from the tension the seatbelt had applied to pinning him in his seat. He rolled his head around, checking for whiplash. There appeared to be none. He opened his eyes, and could see the plane's tail-wing poking out over the top of the bus. It had come to a stop a little further down the motorway.

Scott undid his seatbelt and tried to open his door – it was jammed shut. He grabbed his gasmask and Browning 9mm and climbed out. He leant back against the 4x4, steadying himself, allowing time for his legs to regain some solidity. He slipped the gasmask on, holstered his weapon, and moved away from the now smoking and leaking jeep.

He looked about him as he moved closer to the plane – nothing appeared to be moving. He hated the gasmask; it restricted his viewing. But he needed it now – there was likely to be infected on board the plane.

Scott got closer to the door. He drew his gun and trained it on the plane door. It slowly opened, and a woman stepped out of the smoke. Scott could see a small fire behind her.

"Freeze!" Scott yelled, firing a safety shot into the air.

"Please…" the woman coughed. "Don't sh…shoot."

"Get down on the ground, now!"

She fell out of the plane. Scott could see that she was covered in blood. Her hair was matted to her skull, and the clothes she wore were torn to ribbons. Scott approached with caution. She wasn't dead; she was wheezing and coughing. He kept the gun trained on her.

"Have you got it?" he asked.

She didn't answer, just coughed.

"Have you got it, damn it?!" he yelled.

"There's more inside – help them! Before he gets them!" she managed to scream.

Scott moved away – *I don't need this shit. I have to get out of here.* He scanned the area for another car. For *anything.* Anything that could get him away from this screeching woman and her problems. Then it came at him from the plane. An infected. He tried to aim his

314

gun, but was too slow. The mask was pulled from his face by the sick man, and Scott took in a sharp breath of air – *I'm dead*, he thought.

The thing took him to ground; there they wrestled until Scott managed to get his gun under the thing's throat and pulled the trigger. The bullet came whizzing out of its skull, splashing its brains all over the plane.

"Fuck, fuck, fuck!" he shouted. Still on the floor, he tried to scrabble away from the plane on his back. Just then, a young male emerged from it, carrying a small girl, followed by what appeared to be a yapping dog. He took her to safety, before returning to the plane and dragging the fallen woman out of harm's way. Seconds later, the plane erupted in a ball of flames.

"Jesus Christ!" Scott shouted, shielding his face from the wafting heat.

"You have to help me!" Dafydd yelled over the crackling of smoking metal and popping glass.

Scott looked over at the teen, who was holding the young girl close to his chest. There was blood leaking from her forehead. Scott scrambled to his shaky legs and ambled over to them. The other woman appeared to be out cold.

"Can you shut that dog up?" Scott said.

"The dog's owners just got blown to fucking bits! Now help me, you bastard!" Dafydd roared.

Scott recoiled, shocked by the younger man. "I—" he started.

"Please, come on!"

"What do you want me to do?"

"Get us out of here – you're the fucking *army*! Think of something."

Scott looked about him and saw a string of cars further down the motorway.

"Look, down there," he said, pointing to the vehicles. "Do you think you can carry her there?" he asked, gesturing to Amy.

Dafydd nodded, and turned to Maria. "Can you manage her?"

Scott looked at the woman – he knew he could, but he really didn't want to help. He wanted to run away from them. He didn't care for these people. He didn't *know* them.

"Yes," he said, reluctantly. "Let's move, then."

Dafydd got Amy off the ground and followed Scott, who carried Maria over one shoulder to the cars. He hoped that one of them would be open.

"Come on, Gyps," Dafydd called.

The dog whimpered, but followed.

They tried four of the five parked cars before finding a silver Ford Mondeo open. Dafydd piled into the back with Amy and Gypsy. Scott put Maria in the front passenger seat and put her belt on. He got in the driver's side and was relieved to find the keys in the ignition. The engine kicked into life after a few attempts. He turned the car around, and again his journey to John O'Groats was underway.

"Where are you taking us?" Dafydd wanted to know.

"John O'Groats."

"You know about Ronaldsay?"

So they too had heard the radio broadcast.

"Yes, I do."

"I guess you would have. You being in the army."

Scott eyed the lad in the rear-view mirror; his blood-spattered face caused Scott to feel something akin to compassion.

"What happened up there?" Scott asked.

"On the plane?"

"Yes."

"We didn't know Jeff had the virus. He seemed fine this morning before we left the house."

"Jeff?"

"The one you shot," Dafydd said.

"So what happened?" Scott repeated.

*

317

Jeff levelled the plane out and kept it steady. Once steady, he asked James to come up front. Then he winced as pain from his leg shot up his body.

"Something wrong, Jeff?" June asked.

"Hmm?" he said, turning to her.

"I said is there something wrong?" she asked again, looking worried.

"Oh, erm, no, not really. Just a bit of a throb in the old leg again."

"Maybe we should get James—"

He cut her off. "Would you mind closing the cabin door, sis?"

She looked at him intently – something was wrong. His manner was off. So was his tone.

"Of course not. Why?"

"There's a chill coming from back there; it's irritating my leg."

June got up from her seat and closed the door.

"Thanks," he said. "That's much better already."

June smiled and got back into her seat. She looked out of her side window – they were not that far off the ground.

"Where are we exactly, Jeff? It can't be that much of a flight to John O'Groats?"

When he didn't answer, June turned around to see Jeff just sitting there, transfixed. Strings of saliva hung from his listless lower lip like thick ropes. June saw a red colour creep up her brother's neck as his nose started bleeding.

"Jesus, Jeff! You're bleeding."

He didn't move, didn't flinch. Just kept staring out of the window, hands on the steering of the plane. As June watched on in horror, Jeff's whole face turned crimson, started to smoke. Even his hands. His skin blistered and bubbled until parts popped with a yellow mucus. June screamed for James, as the realisation that her brother was infected hit her.

Jeff heard James outside the cabin door. He yanked the steering back, causing the plane to make a steep climb. This threw James all the way to the other end of the plane. He crashed against the backseats. The others started screaming and shouting.

June tried pushing the steering forward, trying to get the aircraft to level off again, but she couldn't. Jeff leaped out of his seat and was soon on top of his sister. Clawing at her face. He started chewing at her throat. Blood splashed onto the windows and walls of the cabin. Suddenly the plane started nose-diving to the ground as it lost altitude.

Maria got out of her seat, much to the protest of Amy and Dafydd, and made her way to the cockpit. The door flew open as Jeff rushed her. She ducked his outstretched arms and got behind him. But Jeff was on her, grabbing her by the hair, pulling her backwards, and almost to ground.

Maria fought to get out of his grip, but Jeff was much too strong. He pinned her to the floor. The slobber hanging from his mouth was in danger of getting into hers as he got his face close to hers.

Then he was off her. She was free to get up and try to make it to the cockpit. She had been saved by James, who now had Jeff in a bear hug. By the time she got to the controls, tacky with blood, the plane was hovering over a motorway. She sat down just as they ploughed into a moving 4x4.

Maria was thrown forward, and her face smashed against the dials and controls; her head bounced off the roof as she was violently flung around in her seat, and then the cabin. Seats in the back, along with Dafydd's, were ripped up and tossed about. The plane smashed, bumped and ricocheted its way along the motorway.

Amy, who held fast to Gypsy, yelped in pain with the violent movement, prayed her seat would not come unstuck. Dafydd could do nothing but watch, as he was pinned under his seat.

As the plane bounded off a jack-knifed lorry, James was thrown to the ceiling of the plane. He landed on one of the upturned seats which had been ripped free; the metal legs punctured his chest, killing him instantly.

Dafydd managed to unbuckle himself from his seat and crawl free from beneath it as the plane came to a complete halt. He got over to Amy first, who was screaming and crying uncontrollably. He shook her to try and calm her down.

"It's okay, it's okay," he told her. He could see Jeff was unmoving, and that James was dead. He tried not to look at the bloody, metal spikes poking out of James.

"Come on, Amy, let's go. Now!"

She sniffled, and choked out a reply. "What about Maria, and June?"

"I'll go and check on them," he said.

"Is James okay?"

Dafydd looked down. "No, he's dead."

He heard Amy gasp, and just as he looked up her head slumped to one side. She'd passed out.

"Amy," he said, shaking her by the shoulder. She didn't move or say anything. Dafydd sighed, and beckoned Gypsy down off Amy's lap so that he could undo her seatbelt. Before scooping her out of her seat, Dafydd checked on the cockpit.

First he caught sight of June – her throat had been torn open; one eye gouged out; her cheeks and forehead clawed to ribbons. Maria was under her seat, moaning and holding her mouth, which was spewing blood. Her face was cut all over, and she was bleeding from the ears.

Dafydd helped Maria up and over to the door of the plane. He went back to Amy and Gypsy. The youngster was still out cold. Dafydd heard Maria open the door and step outside just as a small fire burst into life behind him.

"Shit, she's going to go up," he said, and dragged Amy from her seat.

*

"I heard you shouting at Maria," Dafydd said to Scott.

"I see. And you have no idea what happened to Jeff?"

"No. But I'm guessing he was sick, like," he said. "Will we be safe out on Ronaldsay?"

They looked at each other in the rear-view mirror for a few moments, before Scott answered the teenager's question.

"Yes."

"You're not going to hurt us?"

"Why would we want to do that?"

"I was told that the army have been seen killing innocent people."

"And who told you that?" Scott said.

"Amy," he said.

"That girl with you?"

Again their eyes met in the mirror; Scott's, Dafydd thought, seemed somewhat warm – helpful. There was also fear there. But he still wasn't sure whether they could trust this man. But then again, he had just saved them.

He was confused, unsure. He was only young, and these decisions were too big for him. If he was to follow Scott, then he could get them all killed. Despite that, he knew he would have to trust this soldier.

"Yes. She's my friend, and has no reason to lie."

"Okay. Well, I can assure you that I am not going to hurt you, and neither will the soldiers at Ronaldsay. They only want to help."

"So why would my friend tell me that she's seen soldiers killing innocent people. Was she lying?"

Scott sighed. "No, she was not lying."

Dafydd gasped and stiffened in his seat.

"It's okay, calm down. I'll explain it to you," Scott said. "I'm taking it you have come from Wales?"

"Yes," Dafydd said. "The south – Cardiff."

"And your friends?"

"I'm not really sure about Maria in the front there, like, but Amy is from the Rhondda Valleys."

"I see. Well, the whole thing started in a town just outside Cardiff by the name of Twsc. There's a military and scientific research barracks there, that—"

323

"I know," Dafydd said. "I knew someone who worked there."

"You did? Who was it?"

"My mam," he said.

"She was killed at work?"

"Yes," he said, and left it at that. He didn't want this man knowing his mother may have started the whole thing off, nor did he want some stranger thinking bad of her. Because no matter what she may or may not have done, he still loved her.

"Sorry to hear that, lad."

"It's okay."

Nothing was said for a little while, then Scott spoke again:

"It started at that facility, and nobody is sure how, or what happened. The south Wales area was hit hard and fast. It caught the army and government by surprise. They panicked, and sent in execution squads to try and stamp it out – but come morning it was rife in the U.K."

"So you bastards just thought you'd kill innocent people?"

"I never killed anyone who wasn't infected. Besides, I wasn't a soldier posted in south Wales. I was sent to the English borders along with a load of other soldiers to try and stop it from getting up here."

"Well, that was a waste of time!" Dafydd said scornfully.

"Yeah, it was. It had slipped through the borders long before we arrived – we just didn't know."

They drove in silence for a few miles, leaving the motorway and joining small country-like roads. Amy came around. She asked questions about what had happened, and why Jeff, June and James were not with them. She'd been scared of Scott at first, thinking he was bad after seeing what the soldiers had done to people in her home town; Scott managed to put Amy at ease, much like he had done with Dafydd.

Then, just a couple of miles out of John O'Groats, Maria came around in a screaming fit. Scott swerved the car, almost crashing into a huge signpost. She beat her fists against him, scratched at his face, tried pulling at the steering wheel.

Amy started crying and Dafydd tried yelling at Maria to stop. Gypsy howled as Scott wrestled Maria off the wheel, pinning her in her seat.

"Stop it. For God's sake, stop it, woman!" he yelled, causing silence to fall inside the car. "Calm down. Maria. Is that your name? Maria?"

She gulped and nodded her head frantically.

"Now, please, let's all just take a deep breath and calm down," Scott said. "I'm trying to help us get out of this mess."

"My mouth," Maria said, crying. "It hurts. I think I may have broken my jaw."

"No, you wouldn't be able to talk or move your mouth if you had," Scott said, smiling. "We need to stop and get you cleaned up. I think we're only a mile off John O'Groats. Once we get there, we'll make a stop."

Maria nodded, just as they passed a sign saying – Welcome to John O'Groats.

Chapter 19

Scott drove the jeep through the main road of John O'Groats slowly, keeping his eyes peeled for any danger. The place looked like every other town he had seen in the last few days: barren, empty. Dead. Nothing appeared to be moving. Doors to some houses stood open and dead bodies were scattered here and there.

Wrecks were abandoned on the road, by curbs and in driveways. The population of the small northerly town was only three hundred, so there was not going to be much else to see, apart from a few burnt-out houses, and collapsed buildings.

"Jesus H. Christ," Scott said. "There's nothing left!"

Maria wept, she didn't know why. Amy and Dafydd huddled close to each other in the back of the car, with Gypsy between them.

Just up ahead of them the famous *Journey's End* came into sight: an old sign post tourists came to see. The man working the attraction asked where you lived, and would put up, in white blocks with numbers on them, how many miles away it was from John O'Groats so you could have your photo taken under it. Scott knew this. He had stood under the

327

white arrows before, while on a holiday to the town a few years back.

To the left of the tourist attraction was John O'Groat's House, which was once used as a hotel, but had long since fallen into disrepair; windows were boarded up, the doors sealed shut. *No longer a tourist hotspot*, Scott thought. To the right of the house was a cluster of shops to snare the out-of-towners.

"We may be able to find you a medical kit over there, somewhere," Scott said to Maria, who was still weeping and holding her mouth. She nodded.

"You two okay back there?" Scott asked.

"Yeah, we are fine," Amy answered for them both.

"Good. Not much longer and we will be in safe hands, I promise," Scott told all of them.

Dafydd made eye contact with the soldier in the rear-view mirror, and nodded.

"I might need your help down on the harbour, son," Scott said.

Again, Dafydd nodded.

"You ever handled a gun before?"

"Yes," the youngster said, his voice hoarse.

"That's good."

Scott parked the car right outside a shop that looked appropriate: a largish supermarket which looked like a glorified *Spar*. He looked for the name of the place, but along with the glass, doors and most

328

of the roof, the name had gone. Just one large letter hung over the roof. It had come undone, and dangled like a broken pendulum in the window.

"Right, you lot stay here until I get back. I won't be long."

Maria nodded.

"I could do with using the toilet," Amy said.

"Me too," Dafydd said.

Scott sighed. "Right, let me go in first, and make sure the place is safe, okay?"

They both agreed.

Scott got out of the car and drew his Browning. Just outside of the automatic slide doors, which stood apart, he stopped and listened. The whistle of the wind was sharp against his ears, and could close out any noise of footfalls close by. It was useless. He went inside.

Most of the overhead lights in the supermarket were either smashed, pulled from the ceiling, or blinking on and off, casting the shadows back. The place stank of spilt blood and rotten flesh; the air had a salty taste to it.

Flies buzzed around Scott, unseen. He spotted the cashier lying slumped over a till. Blood had trickled out of the mouth and down the front of the till they'd been using. It was dry and crusted. He averted his eyes, and moved down one of the few aisles with a flashing light over it.

He crunched broken glass underfoot and kicked loose tins. He didn't look down, just in front, unfazed by the noise he was making. Towards the back of the shop there was a pharmacy and a bakery.

Scott looked in on the bakery; he saw a few dead men and women on the floor. He spotted someone lying dead on top of a load of strewn baskets – his throat ripped apart. A baker appeared to be skewered to his ovens by a load of knives. One of which had been rammed through his throat.

The pharmacy was a different story – it was clear of dead bodies. Scott went behind the counter and looked for something they could use for Maria's wounds. Most of the shelving was bare, apart from a few useless items. He opened drawers and cupboards, finding very little.

He looked under the counter and found a large green bag with a big red cross on it.

"Bingo," he said, and smiled.

But his smile was short-lived, as he felt the iciness of a muzzle against the side of his temple.

"Don' fuckin' move, pal. Or I'll spill fuckin' brains all over the floor, right, pal?"

Scott said nothing; just waited for the bullet to come spiralling out from the barrel of the gun that was pressed tight against his head and smash through his skull.

"You got company out front, soldier boy?" he demanded, pressing the muzzle tighter still against Scott.

"Yes, a woman and two children. Don't hurt them, hurt me."

The gun was suddenly pulled from Scott's head, and the relief of pressure was soothing.

The gunman loomed over, poking his face into Scott's. He smiled. "I'm not going to kill anyone, pal." *He's no more than a kid*, Scott thought. His face was boyish, lacking any sort of stubble. His hair was cut short – skinhead-like.

"Then what do you want?" Scott felt his temper rise, and wanted to smash the kid's silly, grinning face in for scaring him like he had.

"We're just turning the place over, pal – looting, is all."

"Then get what you want, and fuck off," Scott spat.

"Aye, we will be, pal."

Scott went to get up, but the gun was back in his face.

"Just stay where yer is, pal, and you won't get a bullet in yer."

"I thought you didn't want to hurt anyone?"

"I don', just keeping you covered until the boys out back signal me."

Half a dozen minutes passed until Scott heard a new voice close by.

"Jim, if you're in here, let's get going, man."

"There you go," the gunman said to Scott. "That wasn't long to wait, was it?" He grinned nervously, looking behind him as he backed away from Scott. "Don't go following us, or we will shoot ya, pal – and the women."

Then he was gone. Slipped behind an aisle and out the back door to the rest of his buddies. Scott could hear them whooping as their car spun out of the parking area.

Maria and the children, Scott thought, springing to his feet and grabbing the first aid kit from the floor at his side as he did so. He ran down the aisle he had come up, and out the front door of the shop. He could see Maria cowered in her seat. Dafydd was out of the car, a piece of wood in his hands. There was no sign of the gunman, or his crew.

"What did they do," Scott shouted over to Dafydd.

The youngster turned to Scott, tears running down his eyes.

"They scared Maria, Amy and Gypsy, who was barking like mad at them," he said. "They went around the car kicking and punching it, before they were stopped by a man coming out of the shop with a gun. He looked no older than me."

How commendable of the little fuck, Scott thought of the gunman. *If we catch up with them again, I'll kill the bastards. Just because I'm a soldier, it doesn't mean I have to think like one all the time.*

"Here," Scott said, throwing the first aid kit over to the boy. "Give it to Maria. She can clean herself up while I get you and Amy to the toilets."

"You sure it's safe in there?" Dafydd wanted to know.

"Yes, definitely," Scott reassured. "Just try not to look at the dead bodies. It's pretty disturbing."

Dafydd handed Maria the first aid kit and she waved Scott a thanks. Amy got out of the car and joined Dafydd's side. They walked over to Scott, and all ventured into the shop.

*

Ten minutes later the three of them emerged from the shop. Scott was out in front, leading them back to the car with his gun drawn. They all got in, and found a dosed and bandaged Maria. She was weeping again.

"What's wrong," Amy wanted to know from the back.

"Jeff," she muffled out. "I can't believe he's dead."

333

"Hey, come on," Scott said, putting a hand to her shoulder. "We…"

Maria gave him a ferocious look, cutting his words dead. He faced front, started the car and said nothing, realising she was very upset.

He got the Mondeo as close to the dock as he could, not wanting them to have to walk a great distance. When they were down by the boats, Scott could see a few trawlers tied up. The first few he searched didn't have a key, but the sixth one he searched did.

"Over here," he called to Maria and the children. "Quick."

None of them had any gear with them to pack onto the boat; just themselves.

"Are you sure you know how to drive one of these things, then?" Dafydd asked.

"Yes, I did a little bit of time in the Royal Navy."

"But you are army, like."

"Yes, I know, but I started out in the Navy. Just didn't like it."

"Ahh, I see."

Amy and Gypsy went and sat down in the boat's cabin area. They were followed by Maria. Dafydd and Scott set about getting the boat ready for sail.

"Do you think we will be alright, Maria?" Amy said.

Maria looked over at the youngster, eyes streaming, and said nothing. Her silence was deafening.

"Maria, please talk to me. I…" Amy trailed off, seeing it was no good talking to her.

"Right, we're ready for the off," Scott said, starting the engine and powering the ship out of the dock. He switched on the radio, and tried getting through to someone on Ronaldson. But they were too far out just yet.

"When we get there, we will all be scanned for the virus. It'll take time, and you could get separated. But don't worry, you'll all be able to be with each other again once it has been clarified that you are healthy."

"How do you know that then?" Dafydd asked Scott.

The gentle rocking of the boat on the choppy water sent Amy to sleep. Maria watched the two men chatting.

"I've been involved in outbreak situations before. Not in this country, but in others in the world. Don't worry, you will be safe there, you all will. No matter what you have heard about the army."

Dafydd didn't bother responding to that, and instead looked over at Maria. He felt so sorry for her. She had got close to Jeff once again, much closer than himself or Amy. Of course, he knew what it was like

335

to lose someone close. The death of his family would stay with him forever.

His gaze shifted to Amy, who had her head rested against Gypsy. She was sleeping. He smiled.

He sat back in his seat and let the motion of the rocking boat soothe him as he looked out of the window. There was a storm brewing far out to sea. Storm clouds had gathered and were heading their way.

"Have you seen that over there," Dafydd said to Scott.

"What, where?"

"There." Dafydd pointed out the window.

Scott looked, saw it raging in from the west. "We should be fine. Another few minutes and we are going to be at Ronaldsay."

Scott picked up the handle to the boat's radio, and sent out an SOS signal to the military on Ronaldsay Island.

"Mayday, mayday, this is Private Scott Rhoades. I'm on a small vessel heading to the island of Ronaldsay just off the coast of John O'Groats. I have three civilians: one child, one teenage boy, a female that requires medical attention and a dog. Over."

They waited for a few moments. Nothing came back but dead static.

"Maybe it's got them too," Dafydd said, his eerie assumption setting a damp chill in Scott's bones.

"No, it can't have! They would have been well protected. Prepared. The island is deserted; they knew that before going there. No, there has to be another reason – an explanation as to why they are not picking up radio—"

"We read you, Private. Over."

"What are your instructions? Over."

"Approach the island from the east side; we will have men there awaiting your arrival, over."

"Okay, over and out," Scott said, replacing the handle.

"Did you hear that, Maria? We're going to be saved. It's all over."

She smiled at the youngster. "That's good."

Amy slowly woke up to all the excitement. "Wh…wh…what's going on?"

"Scott just had the army on the radio – we're going to be safe!" Dafydd said, and whooped. So did Amy.

Scott steered the boat to the left, and soon the island came into view. Amy got to her feet, and Gypsy jumped off her lap. "Look," she squealed, pointing out the front window.

What looked like an armada of ships and boats were slowly sailing into the makeshift dock of Ronaldsay. The navy had a few heavy battleships further out to sea and helicopters circled above. The nightmare was over, and refuge had been found; sanctuary was theirs.

Maria sank in her seat as she watched the other two celebrating. She smiled, knowing she could not join in with them. She rolled her left sleeve up, and looked at the large bites marks there. Jeff had given them to her in the struggle on the plane; a farewell gift between two friends. She sat back, sobbed, and let the sickness begin…

WWW.CROWDEDQUARANTINE.COM

Lightning Source UK Ltd.
Milton Keynes UK
UKOW03f1153070414

229525UK00002B/15/P

9 780957 648081